THE SILVER KEY

Elena Schauwecker

YOUNG
Writers
CONTEST

The BookLogix Young Writers Collection

Attack at Cyberwold

Messages from the Breathless

Rapunzel: Retold

Nothing But Your Memories

Thieves of the Flame

The Girl I Never Met

THE SILVER KEY

Elena Schauwecker

BOOKLOGIX®
Alpharetta, GA

ISBN: 978-1-61005-631-1

Library of Congress Control Number: 2016915430

10 9 8 7 6 5 4 3 2   1 1 0 3 1 6

Printed in the United States of America

∞This paper meets the requirements of ANSI/NISO Z39.48-1992 (Permanence of Paper)

In loving memory of Grandma Rock,
the greatest woman who ever lived.
You never did anything but support me.
I love you.

"We've all got both light and dark inside of us. What matters is the side we choose to act on; that's who we really are."

—Sirius Black
Harry Potter and the Order of the Phoenix
J. K. Rowling

ACKNOWLEDGMENTS

Firstly, I'd like to thank my friends and family, especially my parents. Whether it was giving me a plot idea or driving me to swim practice or coming to my shows, they were always there to cheer me on, not only in writing, but in everything.

Secondly, I'd like to thank my awesome team at BookLogix. They were the ones who gave my book a chance, and without them my book would still be a manuscript sitting on a dusty shelf. Thanks, guys. You made my dream come true.

Also J. K. Rowling and Rick Riordan, the best authors ever, who inspired me to write. I could always count on your books when I needed to get away. I now completely understand how hard writing and editing a book is, and this experience has only made me respect you more.

And finally a huge thanks to knights, castles, princes, princesses, and dragons, and all of the fairytales of my childhood that first brought the magic into my life. I owe all my imagination to them.

PART I

Chapter i

Alyssa opened her eyes in a strange, dark, cold place under a vast gray sky. She tried to turn her head, but was instantly hit by a flash of pain ripping through her body. Wincing, she placed her chin carefully back down on her chest.

The ground underneath her was hard and cold. Everything was completely silent, as if the whole world was holding its breath, watching and waiting anxiously.

Alyssa took a deep breath, unsuccessfully trying to force the gag in her mouth away from her throat with her tongue. She made an attempt to stand, only to find that she couldn't. Now that the pain didn't come as much of a shock, she realized her ankles and wrists were bound tightly together with rope, and that she was tied to a tree by a rope around her stomach. Obviously, whoever had knotted these bonds had made their message clear: *You're not going anywhere.*

Okay, she told herself. *Calm down, girl. Think. What have you learned?*

Be resourceful, her friend's voice echoed through her head. *Figure out what you have. Then make the best of it. Because when life gives us lemons, what do we do, Alyssa?*

We find something more useful. Because lemonade isn't going to solve anybody's problems.

Exactly!

Okay. She'd been stripped of all weapons: knife, staff, sword, and of course her backpack. Her T-shirt and jeans were practically shredded and half bloodstained, but at least she still had them. Her beautiful golden hair was not looking very beautiful or golden at the moment; it was now in a tangled mess on her head and full of dirt. But nothing could matter less than her appearance. She had to focus on the task at hand. *Focus, Alyssa, focus.*

Okay. *Now evaluate your surroundings.* She was in Meladyne, the darkest world in the universe. All she could see was barren wasteland: gray sky, dead grass, very few trees, all leafless and rotting.

This was looking bad. She had nothing to work with, there was no one and nothing in sight, and the silence was becoming unnerving.

Alyssa struggled against her bonds, but they'd been tied so tightly the efforts only caused the rope to dig into her skin painfully. It didn't take long to figure out there was no possible way to break free. Someone would have to show up eventually . . . right? She didn't have the Key anymore, so why did they still want her? Or maybe that was just the thing: they were angry at her for coming without it, so they were leaving her here alone to die slowly and painfully of hunger and thirst and regret.

She shuddered thinking about that, so instead she twisted to examine the wound on her side as best she could to keep her thoughts preoccupied. An unknown blade had cut her side and left calf in her desperate run, which she'd hardly felt at the time, but now the full force of them burned. Death seemed possible now. Alyssa didn't know much about cuts, but she knew these were deep and severe. They'd ceased bleeding now, but from what she could see, her clothes were very heavily stained.

Well, nothing could be done to treat them at the moment. So she just let her body slump down, her cheek pressed up against the rough tree bark, thinking. How quickly the last few weeks had passed! It was probably past New Year's Day. That was the day she had been taken captive by Meladyne in an attempt to save her friends. Alyssa shuddered, remembering that dark day. She couldn't get it out of her head—the queen's iron grip dragging her away, her sister's hopeless screams, the despair in her friends' eyes as they realized there was no chance of destroying the darkness. Forcing the image out of her head, she went back to wondering exactly where she was. She could've been out for any amount of time, dragged any number of places. For all she knew she had already died and was not in Meladyne, but some awkward phase between life and death. She tried to think back on her life. Perhaps she had done something wrong. Maybe she was being punished for her missteps in life. No, she refused to believe that. She was alive. Her friends needed her, and she'd get back to them.

But the longer she thought, the more she rethought that last one. Did her friends really need her? She'd shown up out of nowhere and sent everyone on a suicide mission. Now they were surely beaten and bruised, maybe dying or dead. And it was all her fault. The more she thought about it, the more she was touched that these kids had warmed to and trusted her, risked their lives for her, when she was a complete stranger. Alyssa was unsure if she would have done the same. No, they didn't need her. *She* needed *them*. And whether or not they would or could rescue her was entirely up to them. She owed them a whole lot more than the nothing they owed her.

What about Bella? Bella would save her. Bella was her sister. Bella would do everything she possibly could to help Alyssa because that was just what sisters did for each other. Bella would always come back for her. Alyssa knew that if her sister were trapped, she'd die before she let anything happen to Bella. If it were that important to her, her friends would surely help her.

Bella . . .

What she wouldn't give to be at home with her parents, curled up next to the warm fireplace, bickering over something completely meaningless with Bella. What she wouldn't give to wake up from this endless nightmare. She had been so happy before. Why was it that nothing ever seemed to change when she wanted it to, but when she was perfectly happy, everything just plummeted?

Alyssa snapped out of her trance as a dark figure appeared at the top of the hill. She shivered as the temperature dropped at least twenty degrees in the silhouette's dark presence. Alyssa knew exactly who the person—the *monster*—was without needing to ask questions.

Marvalonna was terrifying. Her jet-black hair was chopped short at her chin. Alyssa had thought the other Meladynians' eyes were fierce; they were nothing compared to their queen's. They were a dark, stormy gray, glaring into Alyssa's bright, beautiful blue eyes with such intensity it made her want to scream. She had the scar of a Meladynian, running from the corner of her left eye to the corner of her mouth, and she wore a skin-tight, black leather jacket and pants, accentuating her curvy figure. As Marvalonna approached, Alyssa's skin prickled with goose bumps from terror, and her heart thumped in her ears. Alyssa tried to glare fearlessly, but doubted she looked intimidating in her current condition.

"Well. Here's our little hero. The one everyone's talking about. Good morning, child."

The woman had a silky, taunting voice that made Alyssa want to smack her so badly it hurt. The girl grunted angrily, every swear she tried to spit out getting caught in the gag.

"Oh, I'm sorry! Forgive my manners, Alyssa."

With a snap of the queen's fingers the ropes and gag disappeared, freeing Alyssa. Alyssa felt an immediate release of tension as the constraints vanished, her aching arms dropping limply to the ground. She stood reluctantly, stumbling a bit, her legs trembling uncontrollably as she tried to ignore the pain. Why would Marvalonna free her? The woman saw the question in Alyssa's eyes.

"Oh, go ahead. Run. Scream. You can't escape. There's no one here to save you. It would be a terrible waste of energy."

"What do you want with me?" Alyssa asked with a hoarse voice, infuriated at how friendly and innocent her captor was acting.

"Ah, right down to business, are we?" The corners of her mouth twitched. "Just like your mother."

The fourteen-year-old reached for her knife, then remembered she didn't have it. "What do you know about my mother, demon?" she demanded through clenched teeth.

Marvalonna laughed a cold, hard, empty laugh. "Oh, your mother and I go way back, dear. But that's not important now. Plenty of time to chat later. You asked what I wanted from you. I think you know perfectly well what I desire, child."

Alyssa crossed her arms. "I don't have it," she said coldly. "Search me."

"Oh, I have, child. I know you don't."

"Then let me go, witch!"

"Oh no," Marvalonna clucked. "I couldn't do that, dear."

"And why not?" Alyssa asked. "You don't know where the Key is and you can torture me until I'm dead, but I won't tell you! And I swear if you touch my friends, I'll not stop until your blood stains this ground and you terrorize no more innocent people."

Alyssa's words came not from courage, but from anger and pure hatred. She could feel nothing but loathing coursing through her body, taking over fear and sentiment and everything but anger, which was seeping through the cracks in her hatred and filling her up.

"But that's just the thing, Alyssa. We will torture you, oh yes, we will. But why would we spill such valuable blood? You know where the Key is. You know your friends' strengths and weaknesses. You know your way around that sugar-coated little place. And they trust you completely. If you were to come knocking, they wouldn't give a second thought to letting you in. So why, then, why would I kill your friends when *you* could do it so much better for me?"

Then the woman held up her hand, palm forward as if she had a question, and clenched a fist. When she uncurled her fingers to show Alyssa, she held a cylindrical tube terminating in a frightening, thin needle. The tube, about the length from Alyssa's fingertips to the heel of her hand, was filled with a complicated system of wires, buttons, and switches, as well as a sickly green liquid. It was only about an eighth of an inch in diameter. The young girl gasped, terrified of what it might do.

"Ah, yes, dear. You see, as long as this machine resides in your body, I will have complete control over your actions whenever I choose. If it remains inside you for thirty days, the poison inside will be released into your bloodstream and you'll be dead within the hour. But don't worry. You'll have plenty of time to kill all the little sugarplum fairies and bring me the Key by then. Now, any questions before you lose control over your actions? Any last requests?"

Terror had now taken over Alyssa's emotions, paralyzing her. She only managed to croak out three words. "Don't hurt Bella." Her knees shook, and her eyes pleaded.

Marvalonna just smirked. "Oh, don't worry. *I* won't touch her. I'll save her for *you* to kill in the slowest, most painful way possible."

The thought of killing Bella fueled Alyssa just enough for her instincts to kick in, and she did the only thing she could think of, the only thing any sane human being would do: run.

So, knowing perfectly well it was pointless, she turned and bolted, running as fast as her thin, muscular legs could carry her. She was really quite agile, but she didn't get far. In an instant, she found herself being lifted above the ground. Her feet hovered about a foot from it. Though she kicked and struggled, she knew she'd never escape. Marvalonna shook her head and gave Alyssa a sad, disappointed look, as if she had failed a math test.

"Honestly dear, I thought you'd pull something better than that, clever as you are. You can run, though, I'll give you that. Now hold still and don't struggle; it won't hurt as much."

She strutted on tall, black heels around Alyssa, hips swinging rhythmically, and grabbed Alyssa's ever-flailing right arm, long, red fingernails digging into the flesh. Alyssa's heart raced. She kicked and wrestled, but her captor had an iron grip. *No, no, no . . . oh God, no . . .* Then she felt a sharp pain in her triceps, rapidly spreading through her arm. She could feel it being shoved into her arm, huge compared to a normal vaccination. She probably screamed, but her senses were so blurred she couldn't tell.

Bella! she thought desperately. Then everything went black. Her eyes rolled back in her head, and her cold, limp body dropped to the ground.

CHAPTER 2

"Have you ever thought about . . . magic?"

"Magic?" Alyssa snorted, wiping her forehead with the wet washcloth in her hand. It had been a long after-school track practice, and in the cool winter weather and light snowfall, cold sweat froze against her skin. "Not since the first grade. Why?"

"Oh . . . nothing. Just something Bella said to me the other day. About being bored all the time, wishing there was a magical world she could escape to sometimes . . . Never mind. It's stupid."

"You're going to listen to *Bella*?" Alyssa McCaw stared at her best friend incredulously. "Oh, come on. Girlfriend, we've *got* magic. I don't know what you're talking about."

Hazel Lavinski followed Alyssa's dreamy gaze across the street, then burst out laughing. "Ricky? Yeah, sure. Whatever you say, girlie."

"I'm telling you, Hazel. You will never find anything in this world more magical than those eyes."

"Why do you like him so much? I mean it's just so *weird*. You guys were friends forever," Hazel remarked, wrinkling her nose.

"Yeah, I know, I know. It's just . . . he got really hot really fast, and everything got awkward," Alyssa retorted, trying to justify her infatuation.

Just then, Ricky turned from across the street, meeting Alyssa's gaze for a moment. He gave a friendly smile, a wave, and a quick wink before turning back around to talk to his friend, who nudged him and gave him the eyebrows. Nothing out of the ordinary in the gestures, but they still made Alyssa's heart flutter as she gave him a quick wave, blushing.

Hazel rolled her eyes, but couldn't help laughing. "So how about that Snowflake Dance? Who are you going with?" she asked.

"Please, you know I don't dance. I'm not going to that."

"Oh, come on, Alyssa. You're such a stick in the mud sometimes. It's fun."

"Well, fine then. Who are you going with?"

"Ricky King."

"WHAT?"

"Ha! I knew you liked him!"

"I do NOT!"

"Of course not. Please. I was kidding. You should have seen the look on your face!"

Hazel made a high-pitched impression of Alyssa's voice. "There is nothing in this world more magical than those eyes," she mocked, batting her eyelashes.

Hazel burst out laughing. Alyssa tried to keep a straight face but found herself giggling too.

"So who are you going with then?" Alyssa asked.

"Adam Taylor."

"No way. Hey, his hair matches yours. You're perfect for each other!"

"Shut up, Alyssa. You know I hate my hair," Hazel said, tossing a fiery red braid over her shoulder. "Not everyone can be a dumb blonde with perfectly beautiful, flowing locks." She imitated Alyssa's voice again. "Look at me, everybody! I'm the most beautiful, perfect girl ever with my golden hair that *glows* in the sun and my shining blue eyes. Oh no, Ricky, I can't go to the dance with you because I'm playing hard-to-get right now because I know you're just *dying* to have me."

"Shut up!" Alyssa cried through her giggles.

They continued to stroll, joking around and laughing. They finally reached Oakland Elementary School, where Bella was waiting out front for them, immersed in breathless conversation with another little girl who appeared trapped, as if she couldn't figure out how to cut Bella off for long enough to run away. Alyssa pitied the child, understanding how easy it was to get stuck in a one-sided discussion with Bella. Upon spotting Alyssa and Hazel, Alyssa's nine-year-old sister said goodbye to her relieved-looking friend and ran to join them, a delighted sparkle in her eyes.

"Hi, Alyssa! Hi, Hazel! How was your track practice? Oh, you should have seen the dance class today. It was so hard! I learned some new moves, want to see?" Bella was supposedly a fantastic ballet dancer from what Alyssa had heard, but she would never admit it to her sister's face. She just couldn't seem to picture that kid doing anything graceful and relaxing.

By the time they reached home, having dropped Hazel off on the way, Alyssa had been educated on every minute of Bella's school day from beginning to end and had suffered through a rant about the precise shade of green that Bella preferred in shoes. Home had never been a more welcome sight.

"Hey, Mom, we're here!" Alyssa called.

"Oh, hi, kids. How was school?"

Alyssa's mother was one of the sweetest people Alyssa had ever known, but Alyssa had never resembled her even a little bit. Her dark hair and eyes made her look a little more like Bella, but not really.

"Oh, it was fine," Alyssa replied, plopping her bag down beside the dining room table and pulling out her homework.

"It was great!" Bella cried. "We . . ." Bella went on for the next three hours, babbling on to her mother, who nodded enthusiastically and feigned interest like Alyssa had never been able to manage.

Alyssa was punching equations into her calculator, muttering in frustration while shoving freezer pizza in her mouth, by the time her father strode in the door. Alyssa smiled, dropping her pencil and running to greet her favorite person in the world.

"Hey, kids!" he cried, embracing his daughters energetically. "Have a good day, Lyssie?" Alyssa nodded, beaming. Her dad was the only person in the world allowed to call her that. It just sounded dumb and immature in everyone else's mouths. Her father always knew how to make her laugh. Funny thing was, he didn't look a thing like Alyssa, either. No one ever would pick the two of them out in a crowd. Alyssa's light complexion stood out like a sore thumb. Years ago she had briefly considered the possibility that she was adopted, but quickly dismissed the suspicion, deciding her parents would have told her and it didn't really matter anyway.

He picked Bella up under her arms, twirling her around in the air. "Hey, kiddo! How's my little girl?" Bella giggled.

* * *

Several hours later, Alyssa crawled into bed, grateful for the warm covers. The icy Chicago winter air cut into her skin, the extra heat from running having long worn off. Tomorrow would start the first day of winter vacation.

What would she do? Maybe she'd go over to Hazel's or Ricky's and hang out for the day. Nothing exciting. Nothing special. Nothing exciting or special ever happened around her. That was just fine with Alyssa, though. She knew her little sister longed for adventure, but Alyssa was just fine with a normal life, normal friends, and a normal school. She didn't want anything to change, ever. But unfortunately for her, everything was about to change, and soon nothing would be normal.

CHAPTER 3

"Lyssie!" a little voice screamed. "Lyssie!"

Alyssa opened her eyes, yawning lazily. Her first thought, as was any teenager's when awakened in the morning, was, *No, I don't wanna go to school!* But as she blinked the fuzziness out of her head, she remembered with relief, *Oh yeah, I'm on vacation, it's cool.* Smiling to herself, the blonde rolled back over onto her side and closed her eyes again. But this short, blissful feeling quickly vanished at the sound of her sister's voice once again yelling at the top of her lungs.

"Lyssie!"

Alyssa moaned and rolled over, irritated. Five o'clock a.m. That was far too early for the first day of vacation. *Seriously, can't that kid ever just sleep like a normal person?*

"Lyssie!"

Ugh. Why wouldn't she stop saying that? Why did everybody have to call her "Lyssie"? Fourteen was too old to go by that dumb nickname. She wished her name was something like "Jane" or "Mary," so no one could call her anything like that.

Bella burst into Alyssa's room, panting, shoulder-length brown hair loose around her face. "Lyssie, Lyssie, get up; look outside!" she cried.

"Bella, go back to bed," Alyssa moaned. "It's five in the morning. Either sleep until ten like a normal person, or turn it down until the normal people get up." Alyssa flipped onto her stomach, pressing a pillow over her head.

Bella grabbed her older sister's arm, digging her fingernails into the skin, and yanked on it, dragging Alyssa clumsily out of bed and toward the window. Despite her size, the little girl had amazing strength.

"Okay, okay, you win."

Alyssa, finally accepting defeat, forced herself out of bed, stumbled into her jacket and slippers, and staggered into the cool front yard. The grass was concealed by a soft layer of freshly fallen snow, and icicles sparkled, hanging from the roof. The sight would've been beautiful had Alyssa not spent her whole life shivering her way through miserable northern winters.

"Okay, I give up, what am I supposed to be—" Alyssa began, taking a step forward. The second she shifted her weight, her foot slipped out from under her and she tumbled to the ground, landing ungracefully on her stomach. Alyssa muttered a curse as pain surged through her body.

"You'd think I'd know how to walk on ice by n—" Once again her speech was cut short, but this time it was a faint golden glow before her eyes that cut her off. It was a lovely color, like that of the sun, giving off a gentle light. Alyssa furrowed her eyebrows, forgetting about the pain. It seemed to originate in the ground and go upward, like a flashlight beam pointed skyward.

"What is that?" Alyssa wondered aloud, scooting forward and placing a finger into the light. Her finger instantly began blistering as if she had touched an open flame. She jumped back upon contact, popping the finger into her mouth in an attempt to soothe the burn. The girl's eyes grew wider as she watched the glow intensify until she could no longer bear the light and was forced to squeeze her eyes shut. It frightened her, as did anything out of the ordinary, and her first instinct was to run. But the ground was too icy—she'd only slip again. And while she had never been the curious type, there was definitely something intriguing about the whole situation—something that kept her rooted to the spot. So instead of running, she threw her face on the ground, covering her head with her hood and praying for the best. She lay that way for a moment, face burning in the snow, before Bella's small voice spoke from behind. "It's gone. Get up, Alyssa. Come here, this is incredible."

Trembling from the shock and the cold, Alyssa reluctantly pushed herself up into a sitting position and turned toward where the light had been. However, the light had disappeared and in its place, flat on the ground, lay a small wooden trapdoor, like one would see on a castle in a movie, only this one was tiny, probably two feet wide and two feet long. Alyssa knew it hadn't been there before— she'd walked through this yard a million times in her life and a door leading underground wasn't something you simply didn't notice. However, what Alyssa was hung up on was the fact that a door leading underground also wasn't something that simply *appeared*. She blinked a few times, trying to take it in. There had to be an explanation. No doubt it was a trick of some sort. Was Bella smart enough to come up with something like this? No. But Hazel, on the other hand . . .

"Are you just gonna sit there staring like an idiot all day or are you going to open that?" Bella demanded impatiently.

"You want to *open* it?" Alyssa cried. "Bella, it's not safe. We have to get Mom and Dad, and then we have to call the police."

"Oh, come *on*, Alyssa! It's a magic door! There could be anything in there! A genie, fairies, princesses—"

Alyssa glared up into her excited little sister's eyes. "You can't be serious. Bella, there is no such thing as magic. This is obviously a prank. Besides, you see that little keyhole there? We don't have a key. Even if we wanted to, we couldn't open it."

"*You* can, Alyssa. I saw what you did to that light. You must have some kind of magic touch!" Bella was bursting with excitement, but Alyssa was going to have none of it. She was tired and cold, and her ribs ached from the fall, and all she wanted to do was curl up under her covers and sleep. She would deal with Hazel and Bella and their games after nine o'clock. But knowing her sister, she knew the only way to win the fight was to prove herself right.

"All right, Bella," she sighed. "I'll try to open the trapdoor. If it opens, we'll go in and play with the sparkle ponies all day. But if it doesn't, we'll go inside and you won't bother me for the rest of the day. Deal?"

"Okay, deal, whatever. Now open it!"

Rolling her eyes, Alyssa bent down and gripped the small silver handle on the door. It, like the light, instantly singed the skin on her hand. Crying out, she jumped back, clenching her hand in a fist and gritting her teeth to keep from crying.

"Alyssa! Are you okay?" Bella shrieked, racing to her side.

Alyssa frowned, fist still clenched. "It's hot—like, *really* hot. Like it was baking in the sun all day. The thing is silver, and it's twenty-five degrees. Why is it hot?"

"It's *magic,* Alyssa, I *told* you. Now let me see your hand."

Carefully, afraid to see what the handle had done to her skin, Alyssa uncurled her fingers. But she found, incredibly, her skin was undamaged. And more incredible still was the miniscule silver key clenched in her palm. It was no bigger than the fingernail on her pinky and encrusted with what looked like tiny diamonds, making it glitter in the early morning sunlight. Alyssa stared, eyes wide, mouth hanging open, at a loss for words. "It's . . . but that's impossible . . . I . . ."

Alyssa could read Bella's thoughts in her eyes. She wasn't in shock; she was thrilled. Her eyes said: *I was right. This whole time I've been right. I knew it.* There was pride in her expression and pure exhilaration. "Well, go on! Open it, then! We made a deal, remember?"

Alyssa nodded numbly, grasping at straws trying to rationalize the situation. *I'm dreaming,* she told herself. *That's all it is: a dream. I'll just go along with it until I wake up. And then I'll never eat Chinese food before bed again.*

So she grasped the key between her fingers and inserted it carefully into the little slot. Taking a deep breath, she turned it and yanked the door open.

Below she could see what appeared to be grass, but not the kind of grass you would expect in December. This grass was thick and green and soft and inviting, like a cartoon. It appeared to be about three feet below—not a bad drop.

"Woohoo! A secret underground lair! Come on!" Bella cried, swinging her legs around and dropping into the hole.

"Bella, wait, no! Ugh, why do I bother?"

"Oh. My. Gosh. Lyssie, Lyssie, get your butt down here already! This is *amazing!*"

Alyssa ran her fingers through her hair, inhaling deeply. She couldn't back out now, not without Bella. "God, what did I ever do to you?" she moaned, before letting her own body slip underground.

What she'd expected was a dark, dirty tunnel leading to maybe a sewer or something. *Silly me. That would make too much sense.* Instead what she found was a picturesque meadow. The ground was alive with thick, bright-green grass and colorful wildflowers, as well as small animals like rabbits and squirrels scurrying around. Alyssa was so taken aback by this, it took a moment for her to realize she was standing upright at five foot two, even though the hole hadn't seemed anywhere near that deep. Looking up, she discovered a bright blue sky—a sky *underground.* There was no sun visible, and no explanation for the bright light, though there was a rainbow streaking across the sky in vibrant colors. Looming in the distance were massive purple mountains and a barely visible waterfall streaming down one of them. Trees sprouting lush green leaves were scattered around, housing birds singing sweet little tunes. It was like having a migraine—everything was just a little too bright, just a little too vivid, just a little too . . . well . . . *real* to exist.

The place was having a very strange effect on Alyssa's mind. An odd sort of tranquility had settled over her. Suddenly she wasn't afraid; she wasn't worried about anything. She felt almost giddy, like she could skip around in circles. A tiny, leftover bit of reason lodged in the side of her brain knew something wasn't right, but it felt so amazing not to be worried about *anything* that she couldn't listen to it. Why should she? She felt like a thousand weights had been lifted off her shoulders. *Is this what Bella feels like all the time?* she mused.

"Alyssa? Alyssa!" Bella snapped her fingers in front of her sister's face. Alyssa instantly snapped out of her daze, regaining her composure. It was unpleasant to have all of her emotions rush back so abruptly, like having an amazing dream only to be awakened by the harsh buzzing of an alarm clock.

"What, Bella?"

Her sister only pointed, so Alyssa turned, following her finger. Laid out before her was the most adorable little village she had ever seen. It was comprised of rows of little huts. They looked old-fashioned, like the kind in movies made of mud with straw roofs, except the roofs of these houses were shimmering in the sunlight, as if the straw were really made of gold. There were hundreds of rows of the little houses, all of them identical.

"Look!" Bella cried, delighted. "Little people!"

There most certainly were little people strolling throughout the tiny village. They looked as if they were carrying on everyday business: some were working in gardens, others reading in lawn chairs, and still others casually socializing. It looked very normal, very human, and very out of place in the enchanting environment. The only thing that was really abnormal was the fact that every single person was perfectly identical. They were small, only about four feet tall, and all female. Their hair was golden, similar to Alyssa's, and twisted neatly into two long braids resting on their shoulders. They all wore the same Tinker Bell-style, short, sleeveless dress and shoes with pointed toes that looked like they belonged to Christmas elves. So it wasn't surprising that the first words out of Bella's mouth were, "Alyssa, they're elves!"

The sight was a little much for Alyssa's eyes to handle. "Why's everything so golden and sparkly? Seriously, like, *everything* is the same color."

"Come on, we have to go meet them!" Bella squealed, ignoring Alyssa's comment. Before the older girl could speak, Bella was halfway down the hill, skipping as if she'd won the lottery.

Alyssa had abandoned her fruitless efforts to explain anything. What was the point? Figuring she might as well throw caution and common sense to the wind along with reason and physics, she stopped thinking and took off after her sister. "Bella, wait for me!"

Bella had already approached the first elf she saw, who happened to be sitting in the grass playing a bright melody on a flute. Up close, Alyssa could see freckles scattered across the elf's nose. Her eyes were beautiful, so bright Alyssa could only describe the color as liquid gold, very nearly giving off light of their own. The young human girl had begun running her mouth a million miles an hour by the time Alyssa got there.

"Hi! My name's Bella and this is my sister Alyssa. Could you tell us where we are? We're from Earth, up there on the surface. Did you know you were living under our entire world? Isn't that crazy? Oh, don't be afraid, we don't want to hurt you. It's just that this morning, I was looking out my window, and I saw this weird kind of glow, so me and my sister went outside to check it out, and Alyssa touched it, and it was like *bang*! And everything got all bright. Then there was this door and a little tiny key, and—"

The little elf just sat staring blankly at her, eyes wide, looking startled.

Bella finally seemed to realize this, and quickly swapped her energetic tone for a gentler one, but still refused to pause for breath. "Oh no, don't be afraid, we come in peace, we don't want to hurt you, we just—"

"Bella, you're scaring her!" Alyssa cried, empathizing with the little thing, having suffered through many of these rants herself. Then, in a softer voice, "Can you understand us? Do you speak English?"

The creature spoke quietly. "Any language is understood in Sunolia, even mortal languages. They are all translated by the magic in the air, so we can communicate with any species. We are all equals here."

Alyssa nodded, pretending she understood. "Forgive my sister for getting so excited. This has been sort of a strange day for us. Could you tell us your name and where we are?"

The elf's horrified expression changed to one of a pleasant, welcoming nature. She gestured toward the ground in front of her, placing the flute in her lap. "Please, sit down. My name is Fallianaka, but I am known to most as Falla. I apologize, what were your names again?"

"My name is Alyssa McCaw, and this is my sister—" Falla's eyes grew wide once again, and she covered her mouth with her hand in complete shock, her face not so different from Alyssa's when she had first discovered the land. "And . . . and this is Bella. I'm sorry, did I say something . . .?"

"McCaw," Falla repeated. "McCaw." She muttered it several times to herself, shaking her head slowly in disbelief. "McCaw."

"Yes, I know it's a kind of bird. Hazel likes to remind me of that. But it's just my last name. It just tells you what family I'm in. It's not a big deal."

"What are your parents' names?" Falla asked.

"Martha and Lukas. Why?" Alyssa was beginning to feel uncomfortable.

"Well, of course, you would've been raised by other mortals, it would only make sense. You would've had to forget, you were only children . . ." she was muttering to herself now, clearly in deep thought, not even paying attention to the girls.

"Hey!" Alyssa snapped her fingers in Falla's face. "We're still here! What are you talking about? You can't know anything about my parents." She jumped to her feet, thoroughly nervous now. "Bella, get up, we're going home."

"What? But why? We just got here! Falla was about to tell us about this place!" Bella protested, refusing to stand up.

"Bella, we don't know anything about this kid. For all we know she could be dangerous. Mom would kill me if anything ever happened to you!" Alyssa was yanking on her sister's arm, but Bella wouldn't budge.

"Oh, is that all you're worried about? I hope Bella doesn't *die* because I might get in trouble! Shut up, Alyssa! All you care about is yourself. You just can't accept the fact that maybe I was right and you were wrong. That maybe magic *does* exist. So you can leave. Do whatever you want. But I'm staying, and you can't make me go."

Alyssa was caught off guard by the outburst. Bella was always teasing her for something, and they argued on an hourly basis, but very rarely did one of them actually explode like that. It triggered something in Alyssa's brain, and she finally grasped exactly how serious her sister was. So without speaking another word, the blonde sat down, lowering her gaze so as not to look Bella in the eye.

Heavy silence filled the air for what felt like an eternity until Falla finally cleared her throat. "I imagine you must be very confused. You must have so many questions. I think I'd better start at the beginning, and by that, I mean the beginning of time. In the beginning there was absolutely nothing, just darkness. Slowly, over long periods of time, the sun and the moon came into existence—that's just science. But what they leave out of your mortal textbooks is that they were alive, like people. The moon was called Luntai, and the sun was called Solaris, back before the people named them differently. And the love they shared was greater than anyone could possibly comprehend. Never have two people loved each other the way they did. Luntai did not have enough strength to create light of his own, so Solaris would lend her own to him. It is said the sun loved the moon so much she died every night just to let him breathe. They lived in peace together for thousands of years. And this is where the debate starts.

"Some say the moon and the sun had a child—Earth—that was neither light nor dark, but a mixture of both. Others say Earth came from pure science, the Big Bang Theory. Still others believe it was God, or some other powerful being. But it doesn't matter where it came from; it was there. Luntai and Solaris loved Earth (thus the child theory) and protected it with their lives. They took turns controlling it—half of the earth would be dark and half would be light, and then they would switch—so both sides of the earth could experience both things. All the normal stuff happened on the planet, the stuff you already know: dinosaurs, evolution, and people and all that. But Luntai and Solaris both decided they wanted claims of their own on the earth.

"Solaris created a land on Earth, which she called Sunolia, and people to live there, as well as a king, Perseus, and a queen, Cressidalaina, to rule it. Luntai also constructed a kind of kingdom of his own; he called it Meladyne. Three of his people were left in charge: Marvalonna, Karvokono, and Rebeccina. For a while they coexisted peacefully. But then the dark days came. Luntai began to realize that while all the mortals depended on, loved, and even worshipped Solaris, they hardly paid him a second glance. This angered him, and he pleaded for more power, but Solaris refused to give it to him. Enraged, he ordered his Meladynians to attack Solaris's Sunolians, and everything fell into chaos. To protect her people, Solaris divided Sunolia into four sections, closing each one off to Meladyne, the Mortal World, and each other. She created four Keys of great power to access the different regions of Sunolia, resolving to present them to mortals who proved worthy.

"Years later, the first Key was presented to a little French boy, very brave. This was the Key to Pyrocladia, one of the divisions of Sunolia, where fire was first born. Now the boy—his name was Chase—was a good friend of the fire spirits and the Sunolians. Such a good one he was. Taught us to speak French, told us stories about his world. Oh, how we loved him. But when Luntai, who had been biding his time patiently for just such an opportunity as this, learned of this Key, he sent Meladynians to capture Chase's family because they knew there was power in his Key. Chase tried to save his family, but he failed, losing his Key to Meladyne in the process."

"That's terrible!" Bella cried, eyes wide, listening more intently than Alyssa had ever seen her, as if there were going to be a test.

"Yes, it is," Falla agreed. "And it happened again to a young girl two hundred years later. Her name was Aolani. It's Hawaiian, meaning 'heavenly cloud,' and that suited her perfectly. She was the sweetest, most beautiful thing you'd ever seen. The second magical Key was presented to her. This was the Key to Whisperia, Sunolia's second division, and birthplace of all winds. But, like Chase, Meladyne took something very important from her—her baby sister—and captured Aolani, stealing her and her Key away, never to be seen again."

Horrified, unbelieving gasps came from the girls, but Falla continued.

"It was nearly a millennium before the next Key was given away. But this Key wasn't given to a worthy child this time, oh no, it wasn't. This time Solaris chose Rebeccina, one of Luntai's own creations made to kill, and the third ruler of Meladyne. She found it one day in a dead field. It was the third Key, the Key to Terralith, the land of the earth—to the soil and what lies beneath. She should have turned it in to Marvalonna and Karvokono to contribute it to the dark power. But she didn't. Rebeccina was different, and though she was fabricated from pure darkness, sculpted from the very depths of chaos and darkness, for whatever reason, there was something light in her heart, and Solaris could see that. Rebeccina decided to keep the Key, but she was terrified she'd be found out and punished, so she fled to the Mortal World.

"She lived there for a long time, doing her best to blend in with the mortals, and met a man named Percy. After several years, she married Percy and started going by the name of Rebecca. They had three children—a boy and two girls—before Meladyne discovered them. They fled to Sunolia for refuge, but before they could reach it, they were attacked. Karvokono stole the Key, and though he couldn't kill his sister, he turned her mortal and threw her and her husband into Terralith, where they'd remain trapped without the Key. Marvalonna demanded to have all of their children. The oldest, Nicholas, insisted he was the only child, leaving his sisters, only five and one, with a trusted family to keep them safe. Karvokono took Nicholas into Meladyne. He hasn't been seen since."

"So you're saying this place is Sunolia? And you're a Sunolian?" Bella reasoned.

"That is correct. But now, this place has become a sort of haven. Marvalonna and Karvokono have become reckless and impatient. They capture mortals all around the world at random, taking them in and torturing them for information. Once they are convinced they don't have the Key, they enslave them, forcing innocent people to work for them. We have been able to rescue a few children before Meladyne got to them. We take them in, we train them, and we prepare them for the war that will surely come soon."

"But then . . . how do you find the children if they are all over the world? And how do they get here if no one has had the Key before us?" Bella asked, fascination in her eyes as she clung to every word.

"Ah yes. You see, our queen, Cressidalaina, is a very wise ruler. She can sense when bad things have happened, particularly dark, magical things. She can track down a person in need in seconds. And as for how the children get here, there exists something known as a Haven Portal. These portals, suggested to Solaris by Cressidalaina, are rare, and only accept people whose families have been broken by Meladyne. They are naturally drawn to children; magic tends to linger around people who believe in it. The portals provide a gateway between Sunolia and the Mortal World, but only the person they were created for can pass through. It's a very delicate process."

"Okay . . . but back to the key thing. You're saying I have the fourth Key?" Alyssa asked. She didn't believe any of the story, of course; it was ridiculous. But what could she do at the moment other than play along?

Falla took a shaky breath. "Yes. The fourth and final. The Key to Aquamarinia, land of the rivers and the seas. That is where you are now."

"And you think that this woman . . . this Rebecca . . . was my *mother*?"

"I'm almost certain of it. The things the Key must see in you, the daughter of this heroine . . . you have to be."

"Whoa, whoa, hang on. So this Rebeccina ran off into the Mortal World and married a guy named Percy, yeah? But that was the king of Sunolia's name," Bella noticed.

"You pay attention," Falla complimented. "Around that same time, the king of Sunolia—Perseus—was becoming unhappy with his life in Sunolia. He was restless, tired of doing the same thing all the time. He wanted a normal life, a mortal life, so he, like Rebeccina, ran away and blended in with the Mortal World. This is where he met Rebeccina and had kids and all. You could say they were drawn together because neither of them fit in with mortals. Legend refers to their children as the children of light and dark because only once has light blood and dark blood mixed, save the first time Solaris and Luntai were together."

Alyssa's head was spinning so badly it took her a moment to pick out a single question. "Wait, *legend* refers to them? You think we're some kind of fairy tale characters out of a story?"

"As I said before, Meladyne believed Nicholas was the only child of Rebeccina and Perseus. But Cressidalaina kept a close eye on the two of them using Haven Portals during the time they lived in the Mortal World. She knew about the births of the two of you and was able to watch over you, make sure you were safe. She knew you were something special right from the start and did her best to protect you. But she wanted to keep your existence quiet in order to stop Meladyne from discovering you. So whispers were passed around, rumors about other children of light and dark. But no one ever knew what to believe."

"But . . . but we don't have a brother," Bella insisted. "It's just Alyssa and me."

"Not one that you've heard of. But you were so small, you wouldn't remember him."

"What about me?" Alyssa protested. "You remember things that happened when you were five."

"Not when you've had your memory wiped."

The older girl wasn't ready to accept this insanity yet. "But . . . but we have parents! Martha and Lukas, remember?"

"I told you, Nicholas left his sisters with family friends. These people, Martha and Lukas, they are not your parents. They have just been kind enough to pose as parents to you in your real family's absence."

"Do they know? What happened to our real parents?" Bella inquired.

Falla shook her head. "Nicholas altered their memories along with yours before he left. He gave them false memories of having children and raising you. Martha and Lukas honestly believe they are your biological parents."

Alyssa just sat in silence, thinking on that. But it wasn't really her parents that were occupying her mind. She wasn't sure she was buying into all of that. How could her parents not be her parents? But there was one question she couldn't seem to let go. "If those bad guys—Meladyne—if they have this Key, they will . . . ?"

"Unlock the greatest power in all the universe and enslave every man, woman, and child on this planet, destroying the earth and all life as you know it. There will be nowhere to go but Meladyne. Then they'll leave the Sunolians, the spirits, and all the magical creatures here to die."

Alyssa pulled the Key out of her pocket and held it up. "Unless I protect this little thing?"

"Yes."

Alyssa's mind was spinning. How could she possibly do that? How could she possibly save the world? This was too much. If it was true, of course. And after all she'd seen and heard, she was starting to run out of ways to deny it.

"What am I supposed to do, then?" she asked, a desperate edge in her voice.

"Come back tomorrow," Falla replied. "We'll train you. We'll protect you. Keeping you safe has to be top priority, at least for now, because once they find out the Key has been presented to you, Meladyne will stop at nothing to have you dead."

"Why dead?" Alyssa asked. "Why can't they just take it and let me go?"

"Because," Falla replied, "it belongs to you. No one else can use its power but the owner. And the only way to become the owner of a Key is to be willingly and consciously given the Key by the chosen owner, or to kill the owner."

"And what about my friends? What about my parents in the Mortal World? Will they be captured too? And what about my . . . my *brother*? We can't just leave them!"

"I'll discuss it with the other Sunolians, but for now you must be very, very careful. Keep an eye on Martha and Lukas and on each other, all right? Now, I want you to go home and rest. Come back tomorrow and we will begin your training. For now, please, Alyssa, please do *not* let that Key out of your sight, do you understand? Good. Now go home. Good night."

Alyssa was utterly speechless. But Bella managed to find the voice to ask, "How exactly do we get home?"

"Oh, yes, of course, I'm sorry. Travel back to the portal, where you came in. Hold the Key up, so it shines in the sunlight and recite these words exactly: *Sic crestaes aloma.* You should shoot right back up there."

The girls did as the Sunolian had instructed and soon found themselves back in their front yard. The cold felt strange; it had been so warm in Sunolia. The sun was already setting, though the trip had felt like an hour at most.

"Let's hurry and get back inside before Mom sees—"

Suddenly their mother (*Well, I think she's my mother,* Alyssa thought) came storming out of the house, looking half furious, half relieved. Her hair was in a tangled mess atop her head, her eyes red-rimmed with tears. *Oh God.* They had both completely forgotten about Mom in all the excitement.

"Where have you two been?" she screamed.

Alyssa began to stutter, but Bella could always come up with a story on the spur of the moment. Not only that, but she could play it out really well too. She ran into her mother's arms, crying pathetically. "Oh, Mommy, we were on our way to Hazel's house to play in the snow. I slipped and twisted my ankle. Lyssie tried to help, but she slipped in the same spot and hurt her leg. We went to Hazel's house anyway, because it was closer, but it took a long time to get there since we were limping. Hazel's dad told us to stay and rest for a few hours, and when we felt better we could go home. I wanted to call you, but their phone service wasn't working. I'm sorry, Mommy, we didn't mean to scare you."

Bella was full-on sobbing into her mother's arms. Alyssa didn't think it was the most believable story but couldn't help being impressed. Bella's reaction could've convinced a cop. Alyssa wanted desperately to rant about the insanity of her day to her mother, to know she wasn't going crazy, but how could she? No, this had to stay between Bella and herself. If she denied it enough, maybe that would make it go away. Mom embraced them both, blubbering about the safety of her daughters and how anxious she had been, but as they followed their mother inside, the girls shared a glance that said their adventures were far from over.

CHAPTER 4

Knock knock.

Alyssa was awakened by a knock on the front door. She rolled over and checked her clock. 7:30 a.m. *It was all a dream*, she told herself.

Moaning about the fact she wouldn't get to sleep in for the second day in a row, she stumbled her way out of bed, threw on her slippers, and walked to the door. She figured it was just the paper boy. He was always chucking the newspapers a million miles an hour. He'd busted a window once.

But when she opened the door, she let out a little whimper. Standing there, fully dressed, his white teeth sparkling as if he were a cartoon, clutching a bouquet of flowers, was Ricky King. Now Ricky King, in Alyssa's opinion, was the most attractive person in tenth grade, Illinois, and possibly the world. Black hair hung in his eyes. His eyes were gray, soft, and comforting, but when you looked deeply enough into them, there was something stormy and fierce about them. Even the way he stood was confident and tall.

"I, um, I, uh, wasn't expecting you, Ricky," Alyssa stammered, very aware that she was still wearing her pajamas, hadn't brushed her teeth, and her hair was piled in a tangled bun atop her head. Her eyes darted around the room in an attempt not to linger on him for an extended amount of time. "What are you doing out so early? Oh, I'm being so rude. C-come in."

He stepped inside, smiling his brilliant smile. "Your house looks great. I haven't been here in a while," he said. "I heard you and your sister slipped on the ice yesterday. I hope you're all right. Oh, these are for you." He held out the sunflowers.

Alyssa took them, furiously trying to comb out her tangled golden hair with her fingers. She stopped abruptly as the realization dawned on her. Yesterday hadn't been a dream. It had really happened. But how had he heard about the ice story? Had Hazel overheard them? Had she been eavesdropping? Either way, Alyssa was furious with whoever had made her sound clumsy and stupid in front of her crush.

"Oh, uh, yeah, thanks. We're fine," she replied.

All of a sudden, Bella burst into the room, her short, chocolate-brown ponytail swinging behind her, closely followed by their father.

"What's going on?" her dad asked groggily. "Alyssa, why are you up so early?"

"Alyssa's got a *boyfriend*!" Bella sang in her obnoxious, teasing voice.

"I do *not*! Dad, you remember Ricky King. He used to come over in elementary school. He just came by to make sure we were okay after what happened yesterday," Alyssa explained, going red in the face.

Bella nudged her sister. "I know you like him. Don't try to say you don't." Alyssa fought the urge to smack Bella. It was too early and she had been through too much to listen to her sister's relentless taunting.

"Hello, Ricky," said Dad politely. "It's nice to see you again. I hope you're doing well. My daughters are both all right. They're just a bit worked up. We appreciate your concern."

There was an awkward silence. Ricky and Alyssa had been best friends in elementary school; he used to come over every day. But in the past few years, they had kind of drifted apart, and now they hardly ever spoke. Standing so close to him was weird. Ricky finally cleared his throat and said, "So, I guess I should get going. Alyssa, maybe we can, uh, do the science fair together or something?"

Alyssa couldn't help giggling. "Ricky, science fair is halfway over and you know I'm already working with Hazel. *And* you're not even in my grade."

"Oh. Yeah. Right. So, uh, later."

"Later."

Alyssa smiled. She liked that the awkwardness between them was going both ways. That meant they were getting somewhere, didn't it? Though she had to admit, she missed the days when they were just carefree little kids playing with action figures.

Lost in her memories, Alyssa followed her friend out onto the porch to see him off, Bella trailing nosily behind. But right as he was walking down the steps, he whipped around and stared at Alyssa. His smile was gone. His eyes didn't look beautiful anymore. They were like steel, burning a hole through Alyssa.

"Ricky?" she asked, startled. "Ricky, are you all right?" She took a few steps backward, her hand reaching for the doorknob, but froze as he slowly reached a hand into his pocket. *Why are you freaking out?* Alyssa chided herself. *It's just a—* Her body and her mind froze solid as his hand emerged gripping a sleek knife. It was gleaming silver, and engraved neatly in the handle, Alyssa could make out the word *Meladyne*. Alyssa's stomach felt as if it had been flipped upside down. *What? No, this can't be happening. He can't be a part of this too. I've known him my whole life.*

No, please, I need him to be normal. I need him to be on my side.
He grabbed the girls by their shirt collars in one swift motion.
Alyssa lifted her head, trying to make eye contact with
her father, but he was already back in bed, oblivious.

Ricky clenched a ball of Bella's shirt in one hand, pinning
her shoulder up against the wall with his elbow, and held
the knife to Alyssa's throat with the other. The sisters
didn't dare speak. They didn't dare run. They stood,
frozen in terror, ready to give him whatever he desired.

He leaned in toward Alyssa, his face barely two inches
from hers. She could feel the cold metal of the knife digging
into her throat. Her heart was racing a million miles an
hour, and her stomach felt sick. She was horrified, and
yet some sick, irrational part of her was thrilled he was so
close to her. So close she could kiss him . . . What was she
thinking? He had a knife! He was one of those crazy, evil,
magic people! She didn't want to kiss him; she wanted to
curl up in a ball and squeeze her eyes and cover her ears
and wait for the bizarre fantasy to go away.

But unfortunately, that wasn't going to happen, and
Alyssa knew it when Ricky began to speak in a thick, evil
whisper that made every hair on the back of her neck
stand up straight. It was nothing like the warm, comforting
voice he'd spoken in earlier.

"I know where you were yesterday, child of light and
dark," he hissed. "Don't deny it. Run along and tell your
parents—your *real* parents—to rest in peace tonight
because soon they won't rest at all. Tell them Marvalonna
and Karvokono are back and revenge-hungry."

Then he let go of Bella, taking the knife from Alyssa's
throat and placing it back into his pocket, and she gasped
with the release, bending over with her hands on her
knees. After a minute of recovery, she glanced back up,

still panting, to see him loping toward the sidewalk. His eyes were cheerful, and he was smiling again. Ricky waved from his bike, ignoring the looks of pure terror on Alyssa and Bella's faces.

Alyssa stood for a moment, blinking, completely stunned. How could Ricky be mixed up in all this? He was a real person, not a fantasy character. Not Ricky, anyone but him. That wasn't possible. It couldn't be. Bella slapped her in the face, hard, bringing her abruptly back to her senses. "Ow, what was that for?"

"Alyssa, were you even paying attention? We have to do something!"

"Are you crazy? We can't call the police, they won't believe us!" Alyssa cried. She didn't want to be labeled as a lunatic; she had enough to deal with as it was. Getting the police involved would only make things more complicated. But then again, she couldn't simply let someone run around town with a knife. No, this wasn't someone, this was Ricky, he wouldn't . . .

"Alyssa!" Bella cried, smacking her once again, even more forcefully this time. She had run back inside and retrieved the phone, and was now shoving it into Alyssa's hands vehemently. "Call 9-1-1!"

"But—"

"Now!"

Alyssa finally gave in due to the urgency in her sister's voice. Bella might not have had the best judgment, but when she had made her mind up about something, there was no changing it.

"Nine-one-one, what is your emergency?" came a man's voice from the receiving end. Alyssa quickly explained about Ricky and the knife, fully aware of how absolutely insane she sounded. Then, upon request, she provided her name, phone number, and address. Finally, he asked, "Are your parents home, Alyssa?"

"Yes," she replied.

"Is it possible you and your parents could come down to the station and talk about it? Or do you need us to send some people over?"

"Um, yeah, sure we can come over. We'll be there in about half an hour."

* * *

The second Alyssa hung up, she tore upstairs to her room, locked the door, cranked up the music in her earbuds, and ignored everyone completely. Her parents had banged on the door insistently for about ten minutes, then had finally given up and left her alone. When twenty minutes had passed, she tromped back downstairs, out the front door, and into the car, keeping her eyes on the floor, never saying a word.

Alyssa knew her parents should be angry, and she knew what was holding them back from completely freaking out. They were confused; everyone in the neighborhood was used to crazy stories spilling out of Bella, but Alyssa? She had never participated in any of her little sister's games. This, Alyssa knew, was the reason her parents hadn't become angry yet—they were puzzled. Their oldest daughter loved the truth more than anything. So why would she suddenly lie? Alyssa watched them discussing quietly from the back seat, occasionally glancing back at her and shaking their heads. She really hoped they were her birth parents. How was she expected to believe they weren't, after all these years? *I don't care if I'm adopted,* she decided. *I don't care if my real parents are trapped in Terralith. They haven't been here for me, and I've been just fine without them.*

Neither of the girls had ever been inside a police station before; the interior was different than they had expected. Alyssa had been imagining a terrible, cold, dungeon-like place filled with crazed criminals in orange jumpsuits. But instead, the interior was like any other building— boring, cream-colored walls, brown wooden floor, several small desks spread around the large room, behind which sat friendly-looking people in uniforms typing away on their laptops.

"Can I help you?" asked a young Latina officer seated at a desk toward the front of the room.

Alyssa's father cleared his throat. "Yes, my name is Lukas McCaw. We were told to come here half an hour ago."

"If you will follow me, Officer Wilson has been expecting you."

The four of them followed her back through a long hallway and into a small, cozy-looking office where an obese cop sporting a moustache sat questioning Ricky King, taking notes on a small pad of paper. Alyssa glanced around the room, her eyes searching for Ricky's parents, but they were nowhere to be found. Come to think of it, Alyssa had never seen his parents anywhere. He had always claimed they worked a lot and that had been the end of the discussion. But how would he even manage to get to the station without them?

"Oh, hello," the cop greeted upon their arrival. "You must be the McCaws. I was just talking to Ricky here. I assume you are the one who expressed concerns earlier today?" he asked, looking at Alyssa.

She nodded. "Alyssa."

"Alyssa, if you could please take a seat and explain what happened this morning?"

She nodded, inhaling shakily and taking a seat in the chair next to Ricky. He looked at her, conveying no emotion in his expression, and she could suddenly feel her cheeks turning pink. *There goes any chance I ever had with him.*

She began to tell her story, fixing her gaze on a picture of the policeman's family she spotted on his desk in order to avoid making eye contact with anyone. Bella squirmed with impatience, making a face like she had been holding her breath for five minutes and was about to explode. It was clearly painful for her, going so long without talking. Normally the only times she wasn't chattering her face off was when she was chewing or sleeping, and sometimes even then. Alyssa was convinced it had to be a record for her.

When she had finished, the officer questioned Ricky for a while. He answered the questions robotically, saying no more or less than was required. He admitted he had been to their home earlier that day, but denied ever having seen a knife like the one Alyssa had described.

Finally, the question was asked that Alyssa had been waiting for. "Ricky, your story seems perfectly plausible, but what incentive could these girls possibly have to make up a story like this?"

"The two of them slipped on the ice yesterday and hurt themselves. I'm guessing they're just a little worked up from that and can't really think straight. I know they would never do anything like this on purpose; I have been friends with Alyssa for a long time."

Finally, Bella's bubble of patience popped. "Oh, come on, people! Open your eyes! He's a criminal! You want proof? I'm not worked up. I saw him clear as day, and so did my sister!"

And with that, she charged forward, jammed her hand into Ricky's left jacket pocket, and withdrew the ten-inch knife. How he had managed to keep a ten-inch knife in his pocket without it bulging, Alyssa didn't know, but given all that had happened in the past two days, it really wasn't surprising to her.

Bella waved the knife dangerously in the officer's face. "Look! There's your proof!" she cried triumphantly.

The man just stared at her, blinked a few times, then frowned. "There's nothing there." Then, more sternly, "If this is your idea of a joke, you need to fix your sense of humor. I'm letting you off the hook this time. Calling the police and accusing an innocent boy of a serious crime is not a joke. Ricky, of course you understand we cannot simply ignore something like this; we will have to call your parents later today. But for now, you may go home. Mrs. McCaw, Mr. McCaw, thank you for your time, and please talk to your daughters. If it is true they slipped on the ice, there very well may be trauma to their heads."

Head trauma? Alyssa was enraged. Talk about jokes that weren't funny! But somehow she held her tongue.

Bella, however, did not.

"Are you telling me you don't see this? Here, hold it!"

She seized her mother's hand, who was looking extremely bewildered and not quite sure who to believe. Bella tried to force the knife into her mom's hand, but to the girls' horror, it went straight through it as if she were a ghost. There was definitely something abnormal going on. As much as Alyssa tried to deny that magic existed, even she had to admit that this wasn't right.

But it didn't really matter what Alyssa did or didn't believe. Before she knew it, she was being dragged home by her ear and yelled at for nearly half an hour. Alyssa wasn't used to being yelled at. Of course she and her parents had the occasional argument—curfews, punishments for Bella, wanting her own cell phone. But never had her parents looked at her with such utter disappointment. It made her want to melt into the couch and disappear.

"So," Mom finished, "instead of enjoying your time with Hazel, you will both spend the day in your rooms. I don't want to hear a peep out of either of you or you will be grounded for the next month, and that includes Christmas and New Year's Eve. You may come down at seven for dinner, and then it's straight to bed with both of you. Understood?" Groaning, the girls began to stomp up the stairs, when their mother stopped them. "Wait, Alyssa. I want to talk to you. Bella, go on." Alyssa took a deep breath. *This* couldn't be good.

"Yes, Mom?"

"Alyssa, I am going to be completely honest with you. When Bella was six, she punched someone in the face at school for saying the Tooth Fairy didn't exist. When she was seven, she poured pink glitter glue all over your father's work papers and clothes. When she was eight, she got a toy unicorn horn stuck in her nose and we had to go to the hospital to get it removed. I love her to death, but she's a crazy kid. I expect her to do crazy things that don't make sense. But you? I have never had a single problem with you other than arguing with your sister. You go to school, you get good grades, you do your chores, and you always tell the truth. So what I can't understand is why you would suddenly team up with Bella and make up some story to try to get Ricky arrested! I thought you two were friends! And as for yesterday, you slipped on ice and twisted your ankle, but couldn't find a single phone anywhere you could call me with? Alyssa, please, I'm your mother. You know you can tell me anything, don't be afraid. Is there something you want to talk about?"

Alyssa looked up into her mother's eyes. She wanted to tell her the truth. She wanted to tell her everything. It would be so much easier to cope if she had her mother to understand. She owed it to her mother to tell her the truth. But how would she ever believe her? She could show her, of course. But how could Alyssa drag her innocent mother into all of that magic? If the story Falla had told was to be believed, darkness was coming soon. If she told her mother, she too would have a target on her back. Nicholas had altered her memory for a reason. The less she knew, the safer she was. But with Martha's dark eyes begging, *Let me help you. Please, don't shut me out. I love you, and I can't watch you suffer,* it was almost impossible to keep that secret. But what could she possibly say? *Okay, Mom, here's the thing. You know all those memories you have, like my first steps and my first day of school and reading me bedtime stories? Those are all lies. None of them actually happened because you're not really my mom, you just had your memory changed by my older brother, who is trapped in this evil world that may or may not be real. So I think I'll be on my way now, but thanks for taking care of me, and try not to get kidnapped by the evil monarchs that live in Meladyne. Bye!* Not a chance.

"Mom, I . . ." she looked down at the ground, shaking her head. "I can't." Unable to look her mother in the eye, Alyssa turned and raced up the stairs to her bedroom before her mother could say another word.

Slamming the door behind her, Alyssa ran to her jewelry box. Shaking, she pulled the lid open. The first thing she laid eyes on was that stupid little Key, hanging on the end of a necklace chain, right where she had put it the night before. Loathing filled her body as she glared at the thing. "You," she growled at it. "You are destroying my life. I don't want you. Get away from me!" Turning around, she hurled the object as hard as she could out the window.

"Alyssa!" Bella cried, and Alyssa jumped, not having realized her younger sister was sitting on her bed. "You're going to lose it! You have to save the world with that thing. Solaris is counting on you!"

"Yeah, well Solaris can find herself another hero, but it's not gonna be me!" The blonde girl stuck her head out the window. "You hear that, sun? You've got the wrong person! Your little sun people don't concern me, I don't care how cute they are! So you can just go—"

"Alyssa, would you look at yourself? You're going crazier than me! You honestly think Solaris can hear you? You're talking to yourself," Bella cried, pulling her back inside. "Now listen. I don't care what you do. You don't have to be a part of this. Just stay here and be grounded. Whatever. But I'm a child of light and dark too. I have just as much right to make that decision as you do, and this is my chance to make a difference, to do something important. So you can do what you want. But I'm going back there, and I'm going to save those people." And with that, she swung her legs over the windowsill and slipped down into the front yard to look for the Key.

"Bella!" Alyssa cried, looking down at her sister. But Bella had landed safely on her bottom in the grass. Alyssa sighed. Of course Bella was right. She would end up down that stupid rabbit hole somehow or other today. Might as well get it over with. So, after a moment's hesitation, she slipped out the window herself, first landing on her feet, then stumbling to her knees.

Bella was already searching for the door. "Here it is," she called. "Hey, how come nobody saw this? It's in plain sight."

Alyssa shrugged. "Same reason they couldn't see the knife, I guess. And by the way, what did you do with that knife? I was already in the car when you came out."

"Returned it," Bella said casually.

"You *gave it back*?"

"Well, maybe I kind of threw it at his head and narrowly missed his face and made a gaping hole in the wall and screamed something I'm not going to repeat," she confessed. "But yeah, I gave it back."

Alyssa shook her head and muttered something that sounded a lot like, "I am *never* going to have a boyfriend."

Bella recovered the Key in the middle of the street, and used it to unlock the door. She held it out to Alyssa, a solemn look in her young eyes. "This is yours if you want it." Alyssa took a deep breath before holding out a trembling hand. Bella cupped one hand underneath Alyssa's to steady it, placed the Key in her palm, and closed her fingers over it. Bella smiled up at her sister, and Alyssa managed to smile back.

The girls dropped down those couple of feet and hit the soft ground.

"Coming?" Bella asked.

"No, maybe later," the older girl replied. "I need some time to think. You can go play."

"You *always* need time to think, you stick in the mud," muttered Bella. "Come on."

She followed Bella to the village at a walk. By the time she reached the bottom of the hill, Bella was already playing with a group of little Sunolians. They beckoned Alyssa over, and as hard as she tried, she couldn't resist a little fun. As Alyssa soon discovered, the Sunolians absolutely adored music. They played flutes and clarinets and the prettiest little instrument called a *hinra* that made a sound like tinkling bells. They would stand in circles and hold hands and dance graceful little steps on their toes, lighter on their feet than any ballerina Alyssa had ever seen. There was something amazing about the dance, something so fun and lighthearted that Alyssa laughed and twirled and sang along, not worried about Ricky or her parents or anything else. When the dancing was finally over, she joined the Sunolians for dinner, where they had a great feast in celebration of the final Key and the return of the McCaws. The food was incredible, and Alyssa couldn't stop smiling. *Maybe magic isn't such a bad thing after all,* she thought, glad Bella had convinced her to return.

When the festivities had ended, at what she thought was nearly sunset based on the colorful streaks in the sky, Alyssa found herself near a sparkling, beautiful lake. When she looked at the water, she was startled to not see her reflection, but three moving pictures of herself. The first was her when she was little: she had pigtails and was blowing out six birthday candles on a cake as her family cheered.

In the second one, she saw nothing but her reflection.

In the third image, she was a much older version of herself. She was standing with an attractive, tall man with sandy hair and dark eyes. A girl and a boy were standing in front of them, both of them with bright blue, smiling eyes.

"You found the Lake of Time," said Falla, who had come up quietly behind her. "It shows past, present, and future. The water has incredible power that will heal the light and pure, and destroy the dark and evil. Beautiful, isn't it?"

"Incredible," Alyssa breathed.

They sat together quietly for a moment. Alyssa ran a finger through the cool water.

"How is this possible? This can't be magic. Magic isn't real. It doesn't exist. It doesn't cooperate with science."

"'Magic's just science that we don't understand yet,'" Falla replied.

"Arthur C. Clarke?" Alyssa guessed, a smile tugging at the corner of her mouth.

"Yes. A very smart man. He was one of my students, you know. I have taught many scientists, authors, philosophers, teachers, soldiers, leaders, and poets. I've always loved humans. They come here through Haven Portals as children, and when they grow older, if they choose, they may leave through these same portals, though it is dangerous, especially these days. Unfortunately though, your Haven Portal must be created before you come to Sunolia, when you are still a child. That is why your parents cannot leave Terralith."

"Hold on, you're telling me Arthur C. Clarke's teacher was a seven-year-old girl?" Alyssa frowned, trying to push aside the lecture about her parents.

Falla laughed. "Absolutely. Though I wouldn't call her seven years old."

"Oh, forgive me," Alyssa joked, happy she had changed the subject. "I forgot you just turned seven and a half."

The Sunolian smiled. "I also taught Socrates, Robert Frost, George Washington, Albert Einstein, Amelia Earhart, and Nicholas Capricorn, to name a few."

Alyssa laughed. Though she didn't believe a word of what she was saying, Alyssa enjoyed Falla's crazy stories. "Falla, can I ask you something?"

"Of course."

"How is it so easy for Bella to believe in all this? Why can't I look around at something I never believed was real and just think, 'Oh yeah, it's magic, of course'? Why does my brain want to hold onto logical things so hard I can't accept this?"

"You remember when I told you your brother Nicholas wiped your memories?" Alyssa nodded. "When he did that, he removed everything magical from your memory. He forced your mind to believe that magic cannot ever be possible so, should a small memory from your past happen to come back to you, you would dismiss it as a foolish dream. The love of science and logic you possess comes from magic being forced out of your mind," the Sunolian explained. "So it will be much harder for you to accept that which cannot be explained. But it is possible if you are willing to try."

Alyssa nodded. Suddenly everything made a lot more sense. Then she frowned. "Wait. I might have been a whole different person back then. I might have had an entirely different personality if Nicholas hadn't made me forget who I was."

"That is true, but it was necessary. If you don't know anything, no one can force information out of you. Besides, you were only five years old. You have built your personality through your actions in the Mortal World. And don't beat yourself up. Love of reason and logic is not a bad thing. It is what the Mortal World is built on. It is what makes your doctors and scientists and inventors able to do what they can. Logic, like magic, could be the best or the worst thing in the world. It just depends on what you decide to do with it."

Alyssa smiled. "Okay. I'll do my best. Well, we'd better be going," she said, standing up. "I'm late for my appointment at the crazy doctor. They're checking my head today. C'mon, Bella. I had fun today, Falla. Thank you."

Falla grinned back. "In the words of Walt Disney, 'It's kind of fun to do the impossible.'"

As they headed back toward the portal, grinning with satisfaction, Bella commented, "You know what, Lyssie? That was the best punishment ever."

Even Alyssa couldn't argue with that.

CHAPTER 5

It was around nine on Monday morning when Alyssa and Bella sat at the breakfast table. Alyssa swirled the milk in her cereal around with her spoon, lost in thought. Bella glanced up at her mother, who was standing at the counter spreading peanut butter on her toast. "Alyssa," she hissed, "let's go back today."

"Back to where? The police station? No," Alyssa replied loudly, knowing full well that Bella was talking about Sunolia but refusing to acknowledge it. "I'm going to Hazel's. I need to clear my mind. I want to have fun like a normal person, with a normal person. Go wherever you want."

"You want to have fun? You've had loads of fun the past two days, and you know it!" Bella exploded.

"Fun?" Mom asked. "You nearly broke your ankle on the ice, and you were threatened by the police. What was fun? And Bella, you know perfectly well you can't go anywhere alone. You can stay here or go with your sister."

"Fine, I'll go with Alyssa," Bella grumbled. "And I was being sar-kiss-tatic about the fun."

"Sarcastic," Alyssa corrected. "If you're going to try to sound smart, you have to pronounce your words right."

"Shut up, Alyssa," Bella replied.

"Bella, don't tell your sister to shut up," Dad ordered, hoisting his work bag over his shoulder and grabbing his keys off the counter.

"Whatever," she muttered, which earned a glare from her mother.

"It's like I have a teenager and a baby teenager," Mom remarked. "Get out of here, you two. Go have a good time, and stop acting weird."

"No promises!"

"And be home by nine!" she called as they dashed to the front door, both shoving each other in an attempt to get out first. "And be careful, Alyssa! And—"

"Martha!" their father interjected. "Relax. They can take care of themselves. Right, Lyssie?"

"Uh, yeah, sure. Can we go now?"

"Yes, go. And don't—"

"Mom!"

"Sorry."

They made the three-block journey to Hazel Lavinski's house, careful not to slip on the ice for real, all the way waving at neighbors and wishing them a merry Christmas. It was a nice little neighborhood, right on the outskirts of the city. Almost everyone was friendly, and sometimes old Mrs. Azalea would let you stop at her house to eat cookies and drink milk. Alyssa knocked on Hazel's door three times and imitated Adam Taylor's voice, making him sound like a prince.

"Hazel? My beautiful Juliet? My goddess of beauty? The eternal love of my life? Do come to the door, so that I might sweep you off thy feet and we may be together. Oh, do not make me beg, darling. Have I done something? Wherefore art thou, darling? You simply must join me in a romantic candlelit breakfast together before our romantic walk in the park. Please open the door, for I am just a poor man in love."

"You are so weird," muttered Bella.

She waited a few minutes, leaning against the wall. Their car was in the driveway. It was strange; Hazel never ignored her. Wondering if she might be sick, Alyssa pushed the door open, which was surprisingly unlocked, and walked cautiously inside.

The first thing she noticed was the family picture. On the mantel there was a picture of the Lavinskis, one that had been there for nearly two years. In the back were Hazel's parents: a woman with jet-black hair and brown eyes, and a man with fiery red, curly hair and bright, merry green eyes. They each had one arm around the other. In front of them was Hazel: a girl of fourteen with red braids, her father's green eyes, and freckles scattered across her face. She had her arms around her little twin brothers, Logan and Aiden. They had their mother's raven hair and dark eyes. With the mischievous grins on their faces, much like Hazel's feisty one, they looked so identical you'd think the same person was in the picture twice.

Alyssa had always thought the picture was cute and portrayed their family perfectly. But today, there was something *very* wrong with the photo, and it didn't take but three seconds to realize. There was a knife protruding from the middle of it, as if it had been thrown from the other side of the room with seamless accuracy. It was just like Ricky's—silver with *Meladyne* engraved on the handle. There was a note rolled up around the blade.

Alyssa stood on her toes to retrieve it, her hands trembling furiously, her breath shaking. She forced herself to read it aloud:

We have taken your friends where they will meet their bitter ends. Those loyal to us will thrive, but those who aren't will fight to stay alive. If you wish to put us to the test, come and we'll show you who is best.

Fight or die trying, McCaws.

Karvokono, Marvalonna.

"I can't take it anymore," Bella decided, a hysterical note in her voice, and dropped to the ground in a faint.

Alyssa collapsed too, but she didn't faint. She wept. It just wasn't fair. Sunolia was an amazing place. In spite of her greatest efforts, she was growing to love it. But Ricky had acted so strange, and who knew what was happening to Hazel? It seemed as if everyone in her life was somehow tied up in this. She was going to go back to Sunolia. She was going to strangle Falla if she had to in order to get the information she needed.

Alyssa forced herself to her feet. She had to get a grip on herself. She had to be strong for Bella's sake. She hooked her arms under her sister's and half carried, half dragged her into the cool morning air.

CHAPTER 6

It felt like miles trudging three blocks under Bella's weight. When Alyssa finally got home, she felt like passing out. Then she had to prop Bella up behind a tree so she wasn't visible from the street, and so Mom wouldn't ask questions. Even so, as Alyssa dashed into the house, her mother called, "Alyssa, where's your sister?"

"Outside," she panted. "Waiting for me. Forgot . . . something."

Without waiting for a response, she sprinted to her room, yanked open her jewelry box, grabbed the Key, and bolted back outside. Alyssa unlocked the little portal in the ground, her fingers fumbling with the Key. She held her sister under her arms and slowly lowered her into Sunolia before hopping down herself.

"Falla!" she screamed at the top of her lungs. "Falla! Falla, it's Alyssa, come here, I need you!"

Faster than she could blink, the Sunolian was at her side, eyes shining with excitement.

"Whoa!" Alyssa jumped, alarmed. "How did you get there so fast? Never mind—"

"Alyssa!" Falla cried, disregarding what the older girl was saying. "You came back! I have so much to show you!"

"Yeah, whatever, but Bella—"

Falla began to rant, still ignoring Alyssa. It made Alyssa think of Hazel, the way she did that. "I have to tell you . . . Oh goodness, what happened to the child?" She looked down, suddenly noticing Bella lying in the grass.

She knelt, placing Bella's head in her lap.

"She just fainted," Alyssa assured her. "Just from shock or maybe exhaustion. She hit her head pretty hard, though. Might be out for a while."

"Stay here with her. I'll be right back," Falla instructed.

She turned on her heel, took a few running steps, and disappeared. Barely seconds later, their new little friend returned, carrying a small bowl full of water. It had a pretty glow to it that made the liquid sparkle like a lake glittering in the light of day.

"Prop her head up on your leg. There you go . . ." Falla poured the liquid down Bella's throat. "Water from the Lake of Time," she said, answering Alyssa's question before she could even ask it. "It can heal her future, as she is a light soul, and her future includes the unbearable pain she'd suffer in a few hours from the fall."

"Oh. Sorry I . . . er . . . should have caught her," said Alyssa, turning bright red.

It was barely five seconds before Bella sat bolt upright like someone had poked her with a needle. "What was that?" she said. "It was the best thing I've ever tasted. Thick, creamy, and sweet. Like a milkshake, but better."

"Well—" Falla began to explain, but Alyssa interrupted her.

"Falla, I've had enough. You are going to tell me what's happening right now and you're not leaving anything out!"

Falla sighed with exasperation, much like Alyssa's mother did when trying to explain something to Bella. "I've told you everything I know. There is nothing more I could say."

"Yeah, actually, there is." Alyssa gave a full account of the morning with Ricky, and by the end, the Sunolian had a look in her eyes that told Alyssa things were worse than she'd imagined.

"What is your relationship to that child, Alyssa?"

"Who? Ricky? Uh, we're friends. I've known him since we were little. Why does that matter?"

Falla buried her face in her hands, muttering, "Oh no, they know. We need more time than this. How do they know already? We can't afford to lose this one . . ."

"Falla, tell me!" Alyssa cried. "What does Ricky have to do with this?"

Falla bit her lip. "Well, um . . ."

"Tell me!"

"Okay, okay! You remember Marvalonna and Karvakono, the remaining king and queen of Meladyne? I'm sorry, there's no way to sugarcoat this; he's their son. My guess would be he's been suspicious of you and your sister ever since you were kids, so he pretended to be a high school kid to keep an eye on you. And it paid off for him now; he's got you figured out. Which means he's already told them about the Key, which means they'll be looking for you. As I said, you must be very, very careful."

"Hang on . . . I thought Marvalonna and Karvokono and Rebeccina were all Luntai's kids? How can Marvalonna and Karvokono have a kid, then?" Bella asked, wrinkling her nose.

"It's not a bloodline, Bella. They aren't his kids; they're his *minions*. He created them to rule Meladyne. It's not like a mortal relationship," Falla explained. "But that doesn't matter. Remember when you asked about your parents? I figured out what they're trying to do by keeping your parents in the Mortal World. They want to lure you into the Mortal World. Without the protection of Sunolia, you are much more vulnerable. If you are concerned about your parents, you will be tempted to protect them. But you must not leave Sunolia again after tonight. You'll have to stay here. If he knows where you live, he'll be able to track you down and steal the Key; then we're done for. This is the only safe place in the world for you now. I'm going to need you to make a clean break from your parents. I don't care how you do it, but tomorrow morning I need you here to stay. Bring anything you need, but after tomorrow, you can't go home again for a while."

Alyssa opened her mouth to speak; there were so many questions she wanted to ask! How could she just be expected to drop her parents, her friends, her school, her *entire life* just like that? But she had already made her choice the morning before when she had taken the Key back from Bella. She couldn't dispose of the Key. She couldn't get rid of the burden. This was her responsibility now. She had chosen to believe, chosen to accept the challenge. Now everyone was counting on her to save them. Hazel needed her. Closing her eyes, she inhaled slowly, held her breath a moment, then let the air out. And in a more confident voice than had ever escaped her mouth before, "I'm ready."

CHAPTER 7

Of course Alyssa and Bella had been up all night wondering what they were going to say to their parents, how they were going to leave their lives behind. However, the following morning, due to her mom's insistence and despite Alyssa, Bella, and their father's pleas, all the McCaws found themselves wandering aimlessly around the mall Christmas shopping, bored out of their minds.

"This is torture," Alyssa murmured.

"You can say that again," Bella replied.

Alyssa sighed, glancing around at the stores around her. So many adorable shops full of cute clothes. And here she was, standing with her little sister, looking at mugs for their mother.

"Do you have any ideas for Dad? Because I'm fresh out," Bella called from the opposite side of the shelf.

"Yeah, I was thinking maybe—"

"Alyssa, stop talking," Bella interrupted, her voice suddenly sharp.

"Bella, what is it?" Alyssa cried, dropping the mug in her hand and wincing as it shattered on the ground.

"I said be quiet!" Bella hissed, creeping around to Alyssa's side of the shelf. Her eyes were wide, her chest heaving up and down rapidly in a panic. Alyssa had never seen her so frightened. "Where are Mom and Dad?"

"Um, I don't know, food court, I think. They were going to get dinner," Alyssa stuttered, panicking. "But what's going on?"

"Okay, turn around, but go slowly and *keep your head down*. Put your hood over your hair and your face."

Alyssa did as she was told, hands quavering in fear. She could hear her heart pounding in her ears. What could be so petrifying Bella would make a face like that?

Trying to go unnoticed and still not appear suspicious, Alyssa turned and glanced up through her eyelashes. At first, she didn't understand what she was looking at. Everything appeared normal—little kids' train, stand with chocolate samples, group of teenagers giggling, fat mall cop looking bored . . . She was almost ready to turn back and ask Bella what she was supposed to be afraid of when her eyes landed on a boy with black hair and gray eyes. *Ricky,* she thought, nearly knocking over the whole shelf of cups behind her. He was dressed in silver armor, grasping a silver knife with a wickedly sharp blade— exactly like the one she had been threatened with the previous day. She was ready to bolt when another movement caught her eye. Another boy had stepped out from behind Ricky, and it took a moment for Alyssa's brain to process the fact that this person was a perfect duplicate of Ricky. Like the Sunolians, it wasn't as if there was a little family resemblance. He had the same sharp features, the same fierce gray eyes, the same black hair, the same silver armor, the same knife—all of it. He was a perfect clone of Ricky King.

"There are two of them," she breathed.

"Four," Bella corrected, and Alyssa caught sight of two more, one to the right, the other to the left of the others. It was peculiar—they should have been drawing the attention of everyone in the mall, but the shoppers just seemed to stroll past them, not even paying attention. The mall cop sat in his chair, lazily glancing at his watch, and the lady at the stand didn't even offer them chocolate. Alyssa thought she saw one little boy, about four years old, point and say something, but his mother just dragged him along, oblivious. It seemed the boys, like the knife and the portal, were invisible to all the world with the exception of Alyssa and Bella.

Alyssa cast her eyes down, afraid of making eye contact with Ricky. "What are they, like clones?" she asked.

"I think they're the Meladynians Falla was talking about," her sister replied. "They're identical, like the Sunolians, because they're all made out of the same stuff."

That would make sense. They didn't exactly have DNA—they were all exactly the same thing, like living robots. But knowing that didn't solve the problem at hand. "Bella, we need to act natural. Nobody else can see them. Don't make eye contact or they'll know we can see them. We need to get away without getting spotted."

"That plan's all fine and dandy, but they have the store surrounded. They probably already know where we are. And I don't know which one of them is Ricky, *if* one of them is Ricky, but he knows what we look like. We can't get out of here without being seen."

"What about Mom and Dad?" the little girl worried.

Alyssa shook her head. "They're on the other side of the mall; they'll be fine. It's not them the Meladynians are looking for—it's me." It was at that moment that Alyssa made the mistake of glancing at Ricky's face. She didn't know what made her do it. Most likely just the temptation that results from trying not to look at something. But for whatever reason, she looked at him, and for a split second they locked eyes. Alyssa instantly realized what she had done and tried to look away, but it was too late. They had located her now. There was nothing to do. "Run!" she screamed.

Alyssa and Bella tore out of the store, Alyssa running to the right and Bella to the left, but that was a good thing. If Alyssa could lead them away from Bella, they wouldn't hurt her. All four Meladynians on her tail, she bolted down the hallway, darting in and out of people. The people were aware that something was going on now, but to them, it was just a crazy kid running through the mall like her life depended on it.

Years of track paying off, Alyssa didn't stop running, no matter how many people yelled at her to watch where she was going. Her legs began to burn with the strain, but she had never run so fast before and wasn't ready to stop yet. *This is all I need to win a race,* she thought. *Motivation.* Unfortunately for her, the mall she was currently in wasn't by any means a small place, and happened to be stacked on top of a movie theater, which made her seven stories off the ground. Getting to the front door, or any exit, would not be as easy as it sounded.

She was coming up on the elevator, but there was no time to wait for that—they were gaining on her by the second. To the left was a dead end, so she had no choice but to go right. On her right was nothing but a little clothing store—she was cornered. But, not ready to give up quite yet, she took off into the shop, gasping for breath. She had been running for nearly ten minutes at a sprinting pace, and it was taking a toll on her body, fit as it may be. The cashier, of course, looked at her like she was crazy and began to shout, "Hey, what are you doing—" but Alyssa was already at the back of the store, yanking open the door, praying for a fire escape.

Unfortunately, rather than a fire escape, Alyssa found herself on a balcony, looking down on the bustling city. Her heart leapt in her chest, as heights had never been her strong suit. She whipped around, clutching the Key hanging on her neck, to be met by all four Meladynians, knives drawn. Panting, she grasped the railing behind her, trying to keep her balance.

"Don't be afraid, sweetheart. All we want is that pretty little Key of yours. Be a good girl and hand it over now," the one in the front snarled.

Alyssa tried to shove the fear out of her head enough to think clearly. There had to be something she could do. If this were a movie, she would be in a higher position because she had what they wanted. Of course they had weapons, but . . . she had a bargaining chip.

Fumbling with the clasp on her necklace, she managed to unhook the chain, nearly dropping it over the side.

"That's a good girl, just hand it over now," the Meladynian prompted impatiently. This couldn't be Ricky. Everything about him radiated power and intimidation— his stance, his eyes, his voice. Alyssa wanted so badly just to hand him the Key and escape with her life, and his cold eyes boring into her made it even more difficult to resist. *At least Bella is getting away*, she reminded herself. *If nothing else, I can buy her some time. I'm holding the ace. I have nothing to be afraid of.* Hand shaking like a leaf, rather than hand the Key over, she dangled it over the edge of the balcony, leaving it dangerously swinging back and forth. All four Meladynians tensed and froze in place.

Taking a deep, shaky breath, she forced some words out, trying and failing to sound strong. "Make—make one more move and I'll—I'll d-d-drop it," she threatened. "Kill me and it falls into the street. It'll get run over by a car and carried away and you'll never find it." She grew increasingly more confident as she spoke. *They can't kill me without destroying their entire mission. I'm winning.* But this rather positive attitude very suddenly vanished as all four Meladynians began to laugh hysterically. The laugh was harsh and icy cold. Alyssa felt goose bumps prickle her arms. Clearly she had done something wrong.

"Do you honestly think we will be unable to relocate the Key with nothing but a few flights of stairs and some vehicles between us?" the leader laughed. "If you drop that Key, we will first kill you and then the rest of your family. And then we will recover the Key and take over the earth, destroying all the pathetic cities you humans refer to as *progress* one by one. Solaris will bow before us, and the humans will worship our master Luntai. We are going to get the Key one way or another. If you hand it to me now, I will spare the lives of those closest to you. Otherwise, your dear sister Isabelle will suffer more than anyone else on this planet. Is that what you want?"

Forehead in a cold sweat, Alyssa turned and looked down at the streets, feeling dizzy from the height. Seven stories. She could drop the Key and die. She could give the Meladynians the Key and die. Or . . . she glanced down. On each story, directly below her, was a balcony like the one she was standing on. If she could land this . . . no, that was insane. But it was the best option she had. It was death by magic or death by sheer drop. Before she could talk herself out of it, she swung her legs over the side of the railing.

"Wait, what are you—?" the Meladynian panicked, but before he could grab her, Alyssa muttered a quick apology for all she'd ever done wrong, and let her sweaty palms slip from the railing, shrieking as her body plummeted toward the bustling streets of Chicago.

* * *

Her first thought was, *I'm dead.* Her second thought was, *I've got to land this.* Her third thought was, *Aaaaaaaahhh!*

She screamed louder than she ever had, knowing perfectly well it couldn't do a single thing for her. There were six balconies below she could land on, but they were directly below the one she had jumped from, so she was too far in front of them. Desperately reaching out a flailing arm, Alyssa missed the first balcony, but her fingers scraped against it and started bleeding.

Alyssa's tears fell into the streets as she gave up hope, and all she could think was *I don't want to die.* But just as she was ready to give up, she caught a glimpse of something on the second balcony. No, some*one.* A tiny figure; a silhouette in the city night. All this happened in about half a second, and Alyssa reached out a hand, trying desperately to reach for it. The silhouette reached over the edge and caught her hand. Alyssa's shoulder snapped from the abrupt stop, sending pain shooting through her body. For a split second, she thought she was saved. But her momentum was too strong for the figure to hold on, and it toppled off the balcony after her. Alyssa hadn't stopped screaming, squeezing the figure's hand like he was her lifeline.

As they approached the third balcony, the figure reached a hand out and grabbed hold of it. His shoulder made a sick cracking noise, and Alyssa heard him groan, but he said nothing. With incredible strength he pulled the two of them up, swinging her onto the platform. For a moment, Alyssa blacked out. When she opened her eyes she was alone.

The mysterious figure that had saved her life was gone. Vanished into the night.

She tried to stand, but was blasted by pain. She was bleeding badly. In only a few minutes, her parents would arrive with the police, but the Meladynians would be on her too. Then the blood, the pain, the mystery of her savior would all be a waste. It would all mean nothing.

As soon as Alyssa thought nothing could get worse, it started raining—that cold, frozen, sleety December-in-Chicago kind of rain. She peered into the store, a cute little candy shop, and saw a little body. It was walking around, its head concealed by the hood of its sweater, whispering Alyssa's name.

Alyssa tried to scream out her sister's name, but all she could force out was a weak, barely audible "El. El. El."

It was scarcely more than a whisper. Fortunately, she was heard.

Bella dashed over to Alyssa's side.

"Oh my God, oh my God, what happened? Wait, there's no time to talk now, just come on."

Bella put her arms under Alyssa's. She was heavy for a nine-year-old to carry, being somewhere around a hundred pounds, but Bella didn't care.

By the time the girls made it out to the street, darkness was falling rapidly. Bella flagged down a taxi.

The driver gaped at Alyssa as he helped Bella hoist her into the cab.

"What happened to her?" he asked, shutting the door behind Bella and getting in himself.

Bella proceeded to tell a bizarre story about Alyssa getting beaten up by some kid from school. Alyssa was in so much pain. She wished her sister would just shut up so they could go.

"Okay," said the driver, making a strange face. "Where do you two want to go?"

"Hazel's," Alyssa muttered.

"What? We have to go home, Alyssa. And then to a hospital," Bella insisted.

Alyssa lowered her voice, cradling her undoubtedly dislocated shoulder. "No way. You heard what Falla said. If we go home, we'll be leading the Meladynians straight to Mom and Dad. And if we go to a hospital, the first thing they'll do is call Mom and Dad. I'll be fine."

"But—"

"Bella! I am not risking our parents' lives over this. There's no one at Hazel's anymore. We can stay there until morning to make sure they're not tracking us. Then we can go to Sunolia. Okay?"

"8342 Summer Breeze," Bella replied.

Alyssa started to feel dizzy and nauseous. It was likely she had at least a few broken bones, if not a few cracked ribs. At least she hadn't hit her head.

As they started down the road, the cab driver asked, "So, where are your parents?"

"Oh, we were separated when my sister was beaten up. We were told to meet them at home."

None of them spoke until they reached Hazel's. Alyssa tipped the driver with her Christmas money and he helped Bella drag her into the house.

Alyssa felt a bit bad about using the driver as an accomplice, but what were they supposed to do? Walk?

"Mom, we're home!" Bella shouted.

She thanked the driver and he left.

As soon as he was out the door, Alyssa collapsed on the couch. Bella hurried to the bathroom and emerged a minute later with towels and bandages. Alyssa thanked her and let her wrap the wounds, talking her through it using her knowledge from first-aid training.

Alyssa knew she needed medical attention, but somehow she felt like she'd be okay, at least for the night. Her head was throbbing, and she'd definitely broken some bones, but most important body parts felt okay. The bleeding had been stifled by the cloth. She was so exhausted, and she knew there was no way to get to the hospital. So the two girls passed out on the couch, exhausted, overwhelmed, hurt, cold, hungry, thirsty, and most of all, feeling like traitors. They had left the people who had taken them in and loved them and treated them like their own children for almost ten years alone to be killed.

CHAPTER 8

Alyssa opened her eyes the next morning to be greeted by a whirlwind of pain. She attempted to push her body up into a sitting position with her hands but failed miserably, crying out in pain and falling back onto the couch. She placed a hand on her chest, pushing gently on her ribs. She winced and clenched a fist; they were definitely broken.

There was so much pain everywhere she couldn't isolate one place that hurt the most. She wished she had never woken up. Sleeping had been blissfully painless.

"Bella," she moaned, kicking her sister. "Bella, wake up."

"What?" the little girl mumbled, stirring.

"Bella, I'm bleeding through all these bandages, and I'm light-headed. I've lost too much blood."

Bella was instantly awake.

"We have to get you to Sunolia, Alyssa. You'll die here. I may be only nine, but I know most of that blood is supposed to be in your body."

"What, are you going to carry me? Our house is three blocks away, and I can't even sit up."

"Well . . . we can . . . ummm . . ." It must've been driving Bella crazy, not having the solution to a problem, and it showed in waves of frustration and deep thought on her face. Finally, she came up with something, but it wasn't Alyssa's favorite plan. "I'll just drag you."

"What?"

"Come here." Bella hooked her arms underneath Alyssa's and dragged her off the couch. The sudden movement made Alyssa vomit, and Bella dropped her, shrieking, "Ew, don't throw up on me!"

"Sorry," Alyssa moaned, rubbing the back of her already-sore head. Bella tried again, and this time they made it outside. Dawn was just breaking, the sidewalk covered in a disgusting slush. Alyssa didn't have a comfortable ride either. Her feet dragged through the snow, soaking her sneakers and socks, and it took all the strength in her abs to keep her butt from dragging the ground as well. On a good day, she could sprint to Hazel's house in a minute and a half. But that day, the trek was endless. The only good thing was that no one was crazy enough to be outside in the cold. They spent the time exchanging accounts of the previous night.

"The minute I got outside, I knew something had gone wrong. You should've been right on my tail. I came back up, expecting you to come running down the stairs at any second."

Alyssa forced the story out, panting and groaning and sweating all the way.

"Lyssie, you're absolutely *insane*! What on the planet did you think you were doing? If it hadn't been for this mysterious guy, I'd be downtown scraping little bits of you off the street to bury with a gravestone that says 'Alyssa Claudia McCaw, died from *stupidly* jumping off a *freaking seven-story-high balcony*'! I can't have a sister who committed suicide; I have a rensumation to think about!"

"A what?"

"You know, what everybody thinks of you . . ."

"A *reputation*, Bella. Not rensumation."

"Yeah, whatever. But still, why did you jump?"

"It wasn't suicide; I had nowhere else to run and nothing to fight with. It was my best chance. And I'm still alive now, aren't I? Hallucinating about magical solar worlds and evil bad boys, sure, but alive."

"Barely," Bella groaned, dragging her sister over a bump in the concrete.

"I wonder who this guy really was," thought Alyssa. Bella shrugged. "He felt male. He was strong and sturdy and, somehow, calm. He saved my life." Alyssa couldn't help feeling a little excited by it. It was so romantic, after all, and romantic fantasies were one of the few kinds of fantasies Alyssa allowed herself. She could just imagine his strong arms wrapped around her, his silhouette against the city lights, the mysterious way he had disappeared into the night . . . *Oh, shut up,* she told herself. *I can't believe you're seriously thinking about that right now.*

By then they'd reached their front yard. They flattened on their stomachs so as not to be seen from the front window. The girls crawled over to the little door, and Alyssa unlocked it. Bella lowered Alyssa in with some difficulty, Alyssa crying out and smacking her several times, and then followed.

Falla was waiting for them. She obviously had been for a while. She was pacing feverishly, muttering things under her breath, looking anxious. The second the Sunolian spotted them, she jumped, placing a hand on her chest like she was having a heart attack.

"Where in the . . . Where were you two yesterday?" she screamed, startling Alyssa. A strong wind began to blow suddenly, whipping their hair around their faces. Alyssa and Bella looked around, startled, and watched as dark, stormy clouds appeared out of nowhere. Thunder shook the ground, and rain poured from the sky in buckets.

It reminded Alyssa of what hurricanes looked like on the news just before they started. She looked to Falla, who had to be the one controlling it. The ribbons tore out of her hair, golden locks unraveling and flying in the wind behind her like a banner. Her eyes had gone hard and cold. Alyssa couldn't understand how she was causing the storm until she glimpsed her hand. The Sunolian's small hand was slowly clenching into a fist, and the more her fingers curled, the more intense the storm became.

Alyssa lay on the ground, powerless to stop it, and watched as tiny Sunolians creeped out of their houses to see what was going on. She didn't understand what Falla was doing. Had she been wrong to trust her? Bella, luckily, was able to move, and sprang into action after getting over the initial shock that maybe their little elf wasn't what she appeared to be. She grabbed Falla and threw her on the ground, but the storm continued.

"Her fingers, Bella!" Alyssa cried.

Bella quickly understood and pried the Sunolian's fingers apart, wrestling her the whole time. Finally, Bella managed to flatten Falla's hand and press it on the ground under her own. The swirling wind died down into its soft breeze, the clouds cleared to reveal the blue sky, and the rain stopped. Panting, Bella reluctantly stood, releasing Falla. Alyssa winced, expecting to be attacked, but was startled to see the Sunolian grinning. Not just grinning. *Beaming.* Beaming with pride and admiration. Then she began to laugh out loud, as if she had won the lottery and just couldn't believe it.

"I'm sorry, am I missing something here?" Alyssa cried, confused. "Did you just attack us?"

"Congratulations," Falla laughed. "You two have passed your first test."

"Test?" Bella cried. "I thought you were going to kill us!"

Falla shook her head. "It was only a storm-conjuring spell. But let that be a lesson to you. That barely scratched the surface of what I am capable of, and that is just alone. Magical creatures are very, very powerful, especially when they work together. We are strong, but the Meladynians are even stronger. Do not underestimate them. And with all four Keys? They could drain the oceans creating a hurricane to wipe out all of humanity in an instant. There would be nothing they were unable to do. This is why your mission is so important."

"My mission?" Alyssa asked. She hadn't thought of it that way.

"Yes. For now, you must stay here and protect the Silver Key, but eventually we must recover the other three Keys to ensure Meladyne cannot harm us. You are the children of light and dark, which means the two of you can be more powerful than all of Sunolia and Meladyne combined if you are willing to let me train you."

"Wait, wait, wait!" Alyssa cried. "You never said I have to save the world. I just want to get Hazel back."

"Do not worry, my child. We will rescue your friend and the world, but all in good time. For now, you must be patient, and you must train. Can you do that? It will not do any good to walk into Meladyne untrained."

Alyssa sighed, a painful motion. "Okay, then yeah, I'll train. I'll do whatever it takes to get Hazel back. But can you heal me first? I'm kind of in a lot of pain right now."

Falla brought Alyssa some of the water she had given Bella before, and she discovered Bella hadn't been lying about the taste. It wasn't water. It was like a smoothie. Thick and creamy, it tasted like oranges and strawberries and everything sweet. She watched in awe as her cuts and bruises faded away until they were nothing but small scratches. And it didn't just make her feel okay; it made her feel better than she had in months. Like she could leap up and touch the clouds (if there were any clouds). She found herself grinning for no reason.

The girls had to roll into an explanation of the day before. After listening to Falla tell them how brave, stupid, and clever they were, and some side comments on how much they were like their father, it was time to begin training.

"Now as you both know, there is an enemy out there that needs to be defeated. They go by the name of . . .?"

"Meladyne," Bella piped up.

"Yes. So I am here to teach you how to fight. First I will take you to see where you will be staying. Tomorrow we will begin our training."

Alyssa felt a pang, remembering that she wouldn't be able to see her family for a while. They must be so worried! But there was no turning back now. With a deep breath, she replied simply, "Okay."

* * *

"But . . . but how could people survive there? Without food, I mean. You just said you needed the sun for everything." The walk from Sunolia to the living quarters was long, nearly three hours. The conversation at first had been stimulated by Bella, so the topic varied from chicken nuggets to pillow fluffiness levels to grass length to other weird things. However, when Bella finally ran out of random things to say, Alyssa ended up asking more questions about the only thing she could think about—Meladyne— so the lighthearted talk turned once more into a serious conversation that made Alyssa nervous about more things.

"Oh, they have food. Just not food you'd want to eat. They feed their prisoners old bread and water. The first thing they would do when they take over the world is steal all the food, plants, and animals from everywhere in the world. Then they'd clone the animals the way they cloned the Meladynians so they could keep reproducing. But food is not something you want to clone. It becomes less nutritional and less flavorful each time. Eventually it would be like eating a pile of stones." Falla seemed to have an answer for everything, which made Alyssa even more nervous.

Alyssa imagined a dark, depressing world with no sun where all her food tasted like rocks and she was forced to be a servant just to live—a world where death sounded inviting. It wasn't a pretty picture.

They walked for another half hour in silence before coming upon a lovely grassy meadow. Before her were the misty, purple mountains Alyssa had seen upon her arrival in Sunolia, now looming massive and intimidating over her. A gorgeous river flowed downhill and poured into a pond. There were waterfalls rushing out from cliffs overlooking the river. There was green grass and palm and evergreen trees, along with dozens of other plants and flowers the sisters had never seen before. A rainbow stretched through the sky, which had turned a light, pleasant shade of purple. Drinking serenely from the pond were two golden horses.

Words were hardly great enough to describe it, so Alyssa didn't speak.

Without saying a word, Falla led the two girls through the mountains. Alyssa suddenly felt very small and insignificant walking in the shadows of the great peaks. Keeping her balance on the uneven, rocky ground was difficult, and she nearly wiped out several times.

Half an hour later, they came into a clearing, the mountains sloping downward and halting. Alyssa could just barely make out snowy caps against the blue sky in the distance where the range picked up and continued. Spread out before her was a huge, grassy valley, not unlike the meadow they'd previously been through. There were rabbits, squirrels, chipmunks, and many other little creatures scurrying around playing in the soft greenery. In the center of the valley, just a little ways from where the trio stood, sat a little circle of about ten tents surrounding a large fire pit, like a campsite. Milling about outside the tents were simple human teenagers, carrying on everyday activities—some sat in lawn chairs reading books, others chatted casually, and still others stretched their arms and legs as if warming up for a workout. Alyssa was taken aback by how utterly *normal* the whole scene looked. Anyone could have mistaken it for an ordinary group of kids hanging out on a camping trip. There was nothing incredible or mystical about any of it. It was certainly not what Alyssa had been expecting, but it made her feel much better. Perhaps life in Sunolia would not be so different from life in Chicago. Maybe the teenagers here were not so different from her own friends. It filled the older girl with hope for the future. Bella, on the other hand, appeared bitterly disappointed—she had no doubt been looking forward to another picturesque scene like that of the Sunolian village. Still though, she seemed determined not to show it as she forced a smile onto her face and looked around, as if desperately telling herself, "It's not so bad. The . . . the daisies are very nice."

"Heroes!" Falla called in a commanding, authoritative voice Alyssa had not heard come from the Sunolian's mouth before. "Warriors! Gather around, my children! I have a surprise for you, and I do not believe you will be disappointed."

The kids, clearly having a great deal of respect for Falla, instantly dropped what they were doing and hurried to form a circle around Alyssa, Bella, and Falla, looking expectantly at the Sunolian. Alyssa suddenly felt uncomfortable with everyone's eyes boring into her, like an interesting object at an auction the others were considering bidding on.

"This," Falla introduced, "is Alyssa and Bella McCaw. They are the children of none other than our own King Perseus and Meladyne's Queen Rebeccina."

"Good Lord," Alyssa turned and laid eyes on a tall, muscular boy a few years older than herself. He stood, fingers entwined with a petite girl, a look of complete disbelief on his face as if he had just caught the Tooth Fairy in action. "The stories are true, then. The children of light and dark. They're real." He moved forward as if to touch them in order to prove that they were real, but at the last minute seemed to think better of it and moved back, clearing his throat and shooting a confused Alyssa an apologetic look.

"Yes, they are true. And that is not even the best part. These young girls were not rescued by Cressidalaina and sent through Haven Portals. These girls came strutting straight through the front door."

A blonde girl to Alyssa's left gasped as the realization set in. Her thick British accent was full of hope and awe, not unlike Bella's. "You don't mean—"

Falla nodded. "The portal. These girls have been entrusted with the fourth and final Key to Sunolia."

For a moment, nearly tangible stunned silence hung in the air. No one seemed to be able to breathe. Alyssa recognized the look on their faces. It was the too-good-to-be-true expression. *These kids have almost lost all hope of seeing their families again,* she realized. *I am that distant hope they've been clinging to, that thing that helps them sleep at night. I can't fail them. I am what they have been waiting for, and they are counting on me to save them.* It terrified Alyssa to think about what they expected her to do. How was she supposed to live up to their expectations? They looked up to her like she was a goddess. That would terrify anyone. But it also gave her an odd sensation, one she couldn't quite place at first. It was a feeling of being needed. And it was then that it finally dawned on Alyssa: she had never really been needed before. Sure, she had a family and friends that loved her to death. But they didn't *need* her. Had she never come into their lives, they could have functioned just fine. No one had ever depended on her for anything. Until now. And suddenly, everyone in the universe was depending on her. It was frightening, yes. But some twisted part of her brain also loved it. *They need me,* she thought with pride. It also made her feel a bit less guilty about leaving her parents back in the Mortal World. *My parents will be fine without me. These people are depending on me, though. I can't let them down.*

"Hi, my name is Violet Rosa." Lost in thought, it took Alyssa a moment to realize people were talking to her. She snapped back into focus to find a girl of about seventeen standing before her. Long, dark hair tumbled in curls to her waist, and her skin was olive colored, vaguely Middle Eastern. Muscle-toned arms and bags under her eyes showed hard work and dedication. She had an intimidating stance—not mean, but tough. "Sorry, Alyssa, are you listening?"

"Oh yeah, sorry, what was your name?"

"I'm Violet Rosa. I am, for all practical purposes, the leader here. I'll be teaching you most of the essential skills in your training. I've been here since I was five—longer than anyone else—so I know my way around this place. If you ever need anything, I want you to feel welcome here."

"Thanks," Alyssa replied, a little uneasy.

Next in the circle was the tall, muscular boy who had spoken briefly earlier. His body language was much more relaxed than Violet's. His eyes smiled, giving off an aura of calm welcome. He was obviously the kind of person people just liked in general. Alyssa found herself tempted to go stand next to him. "Hi, my name is Caleb West and this is my girlfriend, Maegan Williams." He gestured to the girl beside him, who was short and pretty and covered in head-to-toe freckles. Maegan also had a friendly smile, and looked more like a cheerleader than a warrior.

There was also Malcolm, an attractive boy with dirty-blonde hair tied in a ponytail on his head and a strange foreign accent Alyssa couldn't quite place. It was a unique sort of look, but one he pulled off rather well. And then there was Sylvie, a peppy girl with hair so blonde it was nearly white and eyes so blue they were almost transparent. She had a thick British accent, and her overly optimistic nature reminded Alyssa very much of Bella.

The final member of the group was so quiet Alyssa almost didn't notice her—she almost blended into the shadows. Probably around twenty years old, her hair was long and raven, her eyes slightly slanted like those of a Pacific Islander. However, this girl was not the friendly, smiling hula dancer in the tropical colors you saw on your postcards. Everything about her was intimidating—

her firm posture, her sharp features, her unsmiling, unblinking face. Alyssa locked eyes with her for a split second and instantly got chills. She felt strangely violated, like the young woman was staring straight through her soul.

"We call her Silent Selena," Violet explained in a low voice. "She just showed up one day about five years ago, so we trained her. She doesn't talk, she doesn't smile, she doesn't communicate with anyone in any way. But don't underestimate her. She's by far the best fighter we've got, and don't you get on her bad side when she's got a bow in her hand. Her arrow never misses its target."

A little mystified by this young woman, Alyssa couldn't help staring for a second before turning back to Violet.

"Okay, so you've met the whole crew. This is base camp. There's a tent for each of you over there with a sleeping bag in it. If you go right up that hill over there, there's a little bathhouse at the top. There are showers and bathrooms and extra clothes and toiletries up there, so take whatever you need. We eat at seven a.m., noon, and six p.m. around that fire pit. The Sunolians make us food; it always tastes amazing. So you have an hour or so to get cleaned up, then you can meet us back out here. All right?"

After showering, changing, and brushing her hair, Alyssa found herself sitting cross-legged in the smooth grass around a campfire with Malcolm and Caleb, eating a strange but amazing meal of all kinds of Sunolian sandwiches, pastries, and beverages. The guys bombarded Alyssa with questions about her life in Chicago: what she liked to do, her friends, what she was good at. The conversation was lighthearted and simple, no different than that of an ordinary discussion. No one mentioned their families or Meladyne or the Keys or the impending war or magic or any of it. It was too painful. So they simply didn't talk about it. *These kids have been through more than most adults ever have,* Alyssa thought. *Everything was taken from them—their lives, their homes, their families, their friends, all of it. And yet they're coping. They cling to each other because that's all they have and pretend nothing is wrong.* Alyssa couldn't help feeling a sense of admiration. She wished it were that simple for her. She wished she could just leave everything behind and laugh like it was all okay. *But why can't I?* she realized. *It's not like sitting here moping is going to do any good. Maybe, just maybe, this won't be so bad after all.*

"So then the first guy said—Alyssa, are you all right?" Caleb interrupted himself, suddenly concerned by the look on Alyssa's face.

"Yes," Alyssa replied with a smile and a sigh. "Caleb, I am just fine." And for once, she was being completely honest with herself.

Chapter 9

Clang! Clang! Clang! Clang! Clang!

It was to the harsh sound of someone banging a piece of metal with another piece of metal that Alyssa was suddenly aroused the following morning. *Clang! Clang! Clang!*

Ugh! I am not getting up like this every day! Clumsily untangling herself from her sleeping bag, tripping and falling on her face in the process, the blonde stumbled out of her tent to find Malcolm whacking a giant, old bell with a large metal spoon. "All righty, kiddos, get up, get up, get up! Time to start the day, don't wanna miss breakfast, hustle, hustle, hustle! Good *morning,* Sylvie, looking beautiful today, as usual. Alyssa, my dear, lovely to see—*Owww!* Hey, what was that for?"

Alyssa stood gripping the silver spoon, smirking with satisfaction as Malcolm rubbed the back of his head, where there would surely be a bruise.

"It's bad enough living with Bella all the time. If I wake up to you banging on this thing one more time, this spoon is going down your throat. Understood?" Alyssa had given up everything she had for these people. The least they could do was let her sleep.

The emotion she was going for was intimidation, a sense of control. However, the reaction she received from Malcolm was laughter, pure amusement. "What's so funny?" she demanded, her temper inflamed by his merry eyes. "I just whacked you in the head with a spoon."

"You're feisty," he laughed. "I like feisty. Makes for a good leader. You're not willing to lie down and take it."

"Don't worry, we won't usually wake you up this way," Violet promised, pouring a bowl of Mini-Wheats. "It's just a personality test we do on the first day to see how you react. You'll have to get used to that. For the first few weeks you're here, we'll be watching every single thing you do, every reaction you have to everything. And we expect you to do the same. That's how we roll. We're a team. We have to know each other's strengths and weaknesses inside and out. You can take any secret that you have and just throw it on the table right now. Secrets are weakness. If we know each other as well as we know ourselves, Meladyne can't use us against each other. So like I said, we'll be testing you. Don't try to manipulate anything because that won't do you any good. Just be yourself. Like Malcolm said, just from your reaction to the wake-up call, we can tell you're a good leader. An obedient soldier would've just woken up and done as they were told, a rebellious teenager would have refused to even get out of bed, and a good sport would have kindly proposed an alternative way to wake up. On Sylvie's first day, she took the spoon out of my hand and ate breakfast with it. That's resourcefulness."

Alyssa understood the logic behind this system, but did not entirely trust its accuracy. "But I'm not a leader. I'm a follower. I blend into the crowd and do what I'm told. That's who I am."

Violet snapped her fingers as if Alyssa had made an excellent point. "That right there is the reason we do this. You don't know yourself as well as you think you do. Even if you sat down and spilled your deepest, darkest secrets, we wouldn't know everything about you. I can tell things just from the fact that you admitted you go with the flow and do as you're told. Not many people would say that about themselves, even if it was true."

"What are you, a psychologist?" Alyssa asked.

"My dad was," Violet replied. "He taught me a lot about people when I was little. But that's not important. Go get cleaned up; you look like a witch. Grab some food and I'll take you out to our training center. You won't be disappointed, I promise."

* * *

The arena, a large field a few miles from base camp, was most certainly not disappointing. The field was a perfect circle, about a mile in diameter, surrounded completely by a thick, dense, foreboding forest, broken only by a single narrow path. "Don't go off the path," Violet insisted. "Ever. These woods are teeming with monsters of all shapes and sizes. If you're on the path, they can't get you; there's a force field. But once you're in the woods, you're fair game."

In the center of the field sat a pile of weapons, at least eight feet high. It contained swords, throwing knives, spears, staffs, bows, and arrows—everything in the movies. There were also many different foreign weapons with sickly sharp blades Alyssa had never seen before. It was quite a frightening sight.

"All right," Violet announced, putting herself in front of the group.

"Remember what she was talking about this morning?" Caleb whispered to Alyssa and Bella. "Look at her. Look at her stance, her eyes, the way she stands in front of everyone. You can hear the confidence in her voice, and she projects it across the field. What does that say about her?"

"Well, she's a natural-born leader," Alyssa replied, relieved she finally knew the answer to a question, even if it was an easy one. "Anyone could tell you that."

"See?" Caleb winked. "You're already picking up. You'll be fine."

Alyssa seriously doubted that, but it did boost her confidence just a little bit. A compliment of the simplest kind can go a long way for a person, and Alyssa was not an exception to that rule.

"There are seven basic components of our training. They are magic, flexibility, physical strength, endurance, agility, survival skills, and weaponry. Master all seven of these skills and your training is complete. Then, and only then, will you have the strength to face Meladyne."

"How do we know we've mastered them?" Bella asked.

"When I believe you have, I will take you to Her Majesty the Queen, Cressidalaina. You will perform all of your skills for her, and only when she gives you her approval will you have completed your training. But I must warn you now—it will not be easy. The average time for most of us was two to three years. You cannot simply know how to do these things. You must be able to work together or alone. You must be able to fight in the middle of the day or the middle of the night. You must be able to control these skills in your finest moments and in the face of certain death. You must be willing to sacrifice yourself for the greater good. Mastery means you could do all these things in your sleep. It's not just a physical thing. Physically, mentally, socially, and emotionally, you must commit yourself to this. If you cannot do that, you cannot master these skills and you cannot defeat

Meladyne's armies. You can back out now if you want. Are you with us?"

Alyssa had made her choice. It wasn't a choice anymore—it was the only way. "Yes," she replied, with barely a moment's hesitation. "We're in."

* * *

Alyssa quickly discovered a particular dislike for weaponry. She had expected to pick up the sword, ride majestically into battle, and kick Meladyne's butt, all before dinner. That wasn't quite how it played out.

"This is so *heavy*! How am I supposed to swing this around?"

"Alyssa, listen to me," Violet sighed. "Left foot forward; you're unbalanced. It's like playing catch with a baseball. Grip it here. Don't hold it so tight, you won't be able to swing it like that. All that will do is hurt your wrist. There you go."

Alyssa was becoming increasingly frustrated. "I can't do this, Violet!" she cried, dropping her sword on the ground.

"Did you just miss the whole 'this is going to be really hard' speech? This is what you signed up for, sweetheart. Now pick that thing back up right now. I will not tolerate the whining and complaining. Let's go again. Lunge, parry, lunge, feint! Very good! Again. Lunge, parry, extend, you should've blocked that!"

Alyssa didn't find it quite fair that she was fighting Violet, the best swordsman of all of them, on her first day, but she had learned quickly that fairness was not a part of war. You could cheat and lie and beg and steal and anything else you want. The only rule was to survive. So she continued to prance around on her feet, even as her arm ached, lasting a little longer against Violet each time, though coming nowhere near winning.

Alyssa didn't complain for nearly an hour, simply doing as she was told. The outcome was always the same—Violet holding Alyssa's own sword to Alyssa's throat—but considering she had never touched a sword before, she figured she was doing all right. Finally, Alyssa could no longer take it and begged Violet to let her take a break for water.

"Get up. One more time."

"But Violet, I physically—"

"Get up! That wasn't a request. You're not in charge yet! You follow orders. Get up. I know you're tired, but that's how you get better. I've hit your breaking point. Every day, in everything you do, you are to push yourself exactly one step past your limits. If you do that, your limit will get higher. Meladyne will not stop when you ask them to. They have no mercy. The second you show weakness, they will kill you. Get back up."

Every muscle in Alyssa's body felt like Jell-O. Her head was spinning from dehydration, and she could see little black spots dance on the edges of her vision. She knew this feeling—it was the one she got after running too hard in a race. It wouldn't be the first time she had fainted from exhaustion. But she didn't want to disappoint Violet. She knew Violet saw her as a whining, weak little brat at the moment, and she wanted to earn the respect of the superior girl. So, muscles aching in protest, she pushed herself back off the ground and picked up the sword with shaky hands.

"Thank you. *En garde!*"

Staying light on her toes as she had been taught, Alyssa lunged forward but was blocked by her opponent.

As Violet went for her, she quickly countered the attack and managed to slice a cut on Violet's cheek. The older girl stopped, a bit surprised, and touched the wound on her cheek, examining the blood on her fingers.

"I'm so sorry!" Alyssa cried. "I didn't mean to hurt you! Are you okay?"

Violet turned her gaze back on Alyssa, and for a moment the blonde thought the fight was over. But quicker than Alyssa could react, Violet sliced Alyssa's arm, giving her a cut almost identical to the one on Violet's cheek. It stung terribly, a whole lot worse than Alyssa had imagined it would. She cried out in pain, and Violet took that moment of shock to her advantage, using it to twist her student's arm around and take her sword. Alyssa held her hands up as Violet pressed the cold blade into her neck. She had lost the fight, but she had struck the first blow. And by the looks on the faces of the crowd that had silently gathered around them, that meant something.

"We're done," Violet muttered coldly. "Go get your water."

* * *

"I don't understand what I did wrong," Alyssa said, releasing her arrow and missing the target by a mile for the thousandth time.

"You did nothing wrong. That is exactly what you did wrong," Sylvie explained as if it made perfect sense, picking up another arrow and loading her bow. "You struck the first blow. You were the first one to actually pierce her skin. People never do that on their first day. She's good, even when she's going easy. But you are amazing."

"Don't mock me. I suck."

"Alyssa, I know you think that, but you do not suck. Most people can't even hold a sword on their first day. You have potential. You have a *lot* of potential."

"I still don't see why that makes her mad at me." Alyssa released another arrow, hitting the lower right corner of the target.

"Aim higher, you always undershoot. Gravity, remember? She's not mad at you. She's being hard on you for a reason. She intimidates people, I know. But that's what makes her a good leader. She's gonna push you to your limits so she knows where your limits are. If you're already this good, and she makes you work harder, you'll be the best we've ever had. Also, just between you and me, I think she might be a little jealous of how good you are. You might take over her leader position. Don't tell her I said that, because she'd never admit to it, but I can tell. I'm her best friend. One more arrow, go on then."

Alyssa took a deep breath, squeezed one eye shut, and released her final arrow. She watched it sail through the air and lodge itself in the very edge of the outer ring. "Woohoo, you did it!" Sylvie cried, squeezing Alyssa with pride. "You're a natural."

* * *

"Whoa, Bella, look out! You're gonna kill somebody with that thing!"

"Isn't that kinda the point?" Bella chucked another knife at the target, her third near bull's-eye.

"No, it's not," Maegan replied sternly. "We save lives. The only time we take them is when it's absolutely necessary. Don't ever kill unless you absolutely have to."

"I don't think that will be a problem for me," Alyssa mumbled, making yet another weak throw land on the ground two feet in front of her.

"It has to spin, Alyssa. It's all in the wrist. You have to flick—"

"I know, I know. I'm trying, Maegan, I really am."

"I know you are. It's only your first day. You're doing fine. You should've seen me on my first day."

"Why don't you try this?" a voice asked from behind, and Alyssa spun around to find Malcolm behind her holding a long, wooden pole, at least six feet tall. It reminded Alyssa of when Hazel used to take karate classes and Alyssa would watch.

"What am I supposed to do with that?" she asked, taking it from him and moving away from the others so as not to hit them.

"You hit people with it," he said simply in an obvious tone.

"Well, yeah, I got that, but am I just supposed to whack you and run, or is there, like, some complex skill?"

Malcolm grinned. "There's always a complex skill. But I think you'll like this one. It's my favorite. It just makes the most sense to me. Do you like to dance?"

"Excuse me?" Alyssa inquired, taken aback by the random question.

"Do. You. Like. To. Dance?" he repeated slowly, as if talking to a preschooler.

"Well, not . . . not in public," she stammered. How was she supposed to answer that question? "Does dancing with a broom while you're sweeping the floor home alone count?"

Malcolm smiled. "That's the best kind."

"But what does that have to do with anything?"

"Fighting with a staff is just like dancing. There's a rhythm to it, an exact choreography. Let me show you." The boy moved behind Alyssa and wrapped his arms around her, as if he were teaching her to hold a golf club. "You put your right hand here . . . and your left hand here. Swing it around this way and flip your left hand . . . there you go. Now when you do that, take a step forward with your left foot. It's like sword fighting—you need to stay on your toes the whole time. Sweep at the feet like this. Don't just use your arms—put your whole body into it."

Alyssa was already liking the staff much more than any other weapon she had used that day. Malcolm was right—it felt natural, like dancing. It reminded her of the girls on the color guard at her school, spinning their flags around at the football games. Alyssa, quite honestly, had never known she could dance, but it came easily to her. It was simple: forward, backward, swing, swing, twist . . .

"And then grab it with your other hand at the bottom, and yank and twist at the same time. Flip your hands quickly so he's thrown off balance and not you . . . and then you grab his staff with your left hand. Now you're holding both and he doesn't have a weapon. Very good! I want you to show me all of that again, and then we'll go to lunch, okay? Awesome."

Alyssa performed the routine a second time, experiencing only slight difficulty remembering a few motions. When she had finished she was sweating, but also beaming with pride.

"Excellent," Malcolm smiled. "Perfecto. I told you, it makes more sense than other weapons. Tomorrow I'll bring some music to show you the rhythm, but I think you could probably already feel it a little, couldn't you?

Yeah, I knew it. You'll still need to learn to handle other weapons, but if you walk into a fight with one of these, I think you'll do great. In the event that your staff should be taken, of course you should still have a sword in your belt and a knife in your pocket and a spear in your hair, but if you ever have to pick a weapon of choice, pick this one. Okay?"

Alyssa nodded, and they began to make their way toward the fire pit for lunch. "Why do you use all this old-fashioned fancy stuff? Why not just use guns?" she wondered.

"Oh, both we and the Meladynians developed bulletproof technology years ago. We have to constantly come up with new kinds of metals they can't defend themselves against."

"They always seem to use silver."

"Oh, yeah, they love silver. Awful cliché if you ask me, using silver for the moon and all, but it's not real silver, just looks like it. It's titanium."

"Titanium swords?"

"That's right. Most of our stuff is a mixture of different metals, I think. I'm not really sure about all that. Caleb is a better person to ask. Yes! *Mirachinos!*"

"Um, bless you?"

Malcolm laughed. "No, the little sandwiches. They're called *mirachinos*. They're my favorite. Come here, you have to try them."

* * *

"Speed is one of the most important things to learn. It hooks right in with agility and endurance. The next lesson is simple. Run as fast as possible down to that tree.

It's about one hundred meters. Think you can do that?" asked Violet, pulling her hair into a ponytail like Alyssa's and Bella's.

"Absolutely," replied Alyssa. "I'm on a track team, you know. I hold the fifty-meter sprinting record for the school."

"Excellent," said Violet. "That may increase your chances of not dying."

"That's reassuring," Bella mumbled.

"Ready, go!"

Alyssa was incredibly fast, coming in with a time of eleven seconds. Bella's was twenty seconds.

"Well done, Alyssa!" Violet cried. "Bella, you need to pick it up a little, but not bad at all!"

The girls beamed with pride.

"Now, I want you to run halfway to where we were standing before and come back as fast as possible. Ready, go!"

Alyssa got a time of thirteen seconds and Bella a time of thirty seconds.

"But I don't understand. It's the same distance. How were we slower?" Bella asked.

"Agility," replied Violet.

"Agility is how quickly you can change directions while running," Alyssa explained. "The split second you had to stop to turn around and the second it took you to rebuild your momentum affected your time."

"I couldn't have said it better myself," Violet said proudly. "Now let's test your endurance. The arena is one mile around. Don't go in the forest, just around the perimeter of the arena. Ready, go!"

Alyssa, amazingly, only took six minutes, fifteen seconds. Bella took eighteen.

"Where've you been? I took a nap while you were gone," Alyssa joked when her sister got back.

"Laugh all you want now, but this could be a matter of life or death someday in the near future. Remember, always fight to the best of your ability, but sometimes, your best survival chances are running."

After that was strength. Push-ups, pull-ups, bar hangs (on a tree branch, and it really hurt when it broke and everybody fell), sit-ups, curl-ups, wall sits, six-inches, leg lifts, and burpees.

"Well done, both of you," Violet complimented, and Alyssa noticed she was in a considerably better mood than she had been that morning.

After physical training, Maegan taught flexibility. They were simple stretches, and Maegan stretched muscles Alyssa didn't even know she had. Bella, being a ballerina dancer, looked beautiful and graceful. Alyssa's looked kind of clumsy and awkward, but she could do something kind of related to a back handspring.

"There may come a time when you must survive on your own for days or weeks on end. You need to be able to do that. I will teach you basic survival skills now," Caleb said. "This isn't really my strong suit. My favorite thing, really, is weapon forging. But you two don't get to see my secret lair yet, so this is what we're doing, and it's important, so pay attention.

"The number-one most important skill is making fire. If you have a fire, you have clean water, cooked food, and warmth—in other words, you can live. Without fire, it isn't likely you'll last more than three days. There are two ways to make it. First, if you have glass nearby, there is a certain way to position the glass. If you can get the sunlight to reflect off the glass and hit a dry leaf, it will start a fire."

He retrieved a shard of glass from his backpack. Holding a hand up in the air and muttering a few Sunolian words, sunlight streamed down out of nowhere, reflecting off the glass. In a few minutes, a small flame had formed. Caleb immediately dropped the glass and held his hands out in front of the flame.

"Aqualan," he cried.

Water shot from his hands, extinguishing the flame.

"Niquan!" he yelled, and the flow stopped.

"That's cheating," muttered Alyssa.

"Sometimes cheating is the best way to stay alive."

"Are you sure you're a teacher?"

He handed the glass to Alyssa, grinning. "I don't teach ethics, I teach survival."

Alyssa's turn didn't go nearly as well as Caleb's, and Bella wasn't having any more luck. After about half an hour, the blonde just dropped the glass resignedly and sighed, "All right, what's the second way to make fire?"

"I think you know," Caleb replied with a grin, gathering two sticks from the ground.

"This is Campfire Girls all over again," Bella moaned, glancing at Alyssa.

A couple years before, they had been sent to a really lame summer camp. Long story short, they'd spent a week doing nothing but sitting in tents and staring at each other. No activities, no swimming pool, no cabins. Just a couple of sticks, a tent, and a bunch of really bored girls.

So there they were for another thirty minutes, rubbing sticks together and waiting for something to happen. At one point, Alyssa got really excited when she saw a spark for half a second, but then it died with her enthusiasm.

"Come on! There has to be another way to do this," Bella cried.

"What about, like, a match or something?" asked Alyssa, exasperated. "Or a lighter? Ever heard of those?"

Caleb glared at her. "Alyssa, how many times in your life are you going to happen to have a match in your pocket? Be resourceful. Find out what you have, and figure out how to make the best of it. Because when life gives us lemons, what do we do, Alyssa?"

"We find something more useful," Alyssa grumbled. "Because lemonade isn't going to solve anybody's problems."

"Exactly! Well, Bella, there is one more way," Caleb said, hesitantly. "But it's incredibly difficult, not to mention dangerous."

"How?" Alyssa asked, an edge of desperation in her voice.

"You'll . . . you'll have to call on the power of Pyrocladia. And if the flame spirits don't like you . . . forget it. It's magic too complicated for beginners."

At that moment, Bella fell down on her knees in tears. Alyssa rolled her eyes, sighing. Poor Caleb had not yet fallen for the Bella Trap.

"Bella! Bella, are you all right? What's wrong?" Caleb cried, kneeling down beside her.

"It's just that," the little girl sniffed, "my parents, my friends, they're going to die, all of them, unless we help. And we're running out of time and . . ." She lay down flat on the ground and sobbed, her pathetic, fake tears spilling dramatically over the ground.

"All right, come on, get up," their teacher said. "I know what you're playing at. I'm not that easy to break."

He folded his arms. Alyssa kicked Bella. She stood up, face disappointed and tearless. At the glares that met her, she shrugged. "What? It works with plenty of people."

Alyssa sighed. "You're a handful."

"I can't teach anyone magic without Her Highness's permission. And as I'm underage and not qualified, I probably won't be granted that permission."

"Come on, Caleb," Bella persisted, giving him the best we-need-your-help-so-darn-bad-we're-gonna-die-if-we-don't-get-it look.

"Hey, it's not my decision. I can't just teach you a spell out of nowhere. Magic is difficult stuff. You have to start with the basics."

"Can we please start with the basics *now*?" Bella begged.

Poor girl, Alyssa thought. *We have the ability to learn magic, and all we've been doing is running and stuff. She's probably about to explode.*

Caleb sighed. "You two, I swear. I have never seen anyone so eager to learn anything."

"Even Alyssa looks excited," Bella commented.

Alyssa blushed, having really hoped the eagerness inside wasn't showing on her face. Sure, she liked reality, she valued truth. Magic scared her because it didn't make any sense. But there was something just incredible about it all, something so thrilling about the idea of being able to control things. She had never had a desire to be in control of anything before, but now that it was possible . . . maybe it wouldn't be so bad. Fun, even.

"Well, it's just . . ." She was grasping at straws, trying to find a way to defend herself. "I mean, come on. Who wouldn't want to be able to get a Pepsi out of the fridge without getting off the couch? That's every American's dream."

Caleb smiled. "Miss McCaw, while I can't say that I disagree with you, it's okay to just admit magic excites you. Magic excites *everyone*—it's human nature to be excited about something you've never seen before."

"It does not excite me," Alyssa replied firmly. "Magic is the reason my best friend is gone. And I'm dealing with it, and I know you guys are dealing with a lot too, but how can you sit there and be *excited* by magic when it has taken everything you have?" Alyssa hadn't meant to get worked up, but it had just slipped out. Thinking about magic just made her remember Hazel and Ricky and her parents, and she just couldn't handle it.

Caleb closed his eyes, taking a deep breath. "Alyssa." He talked slowly, like he was afraid she might explode. "Magic is the same as everything else in the world. There are good and bad people, there are good and bad cities, there are good and bad foods, and there is good and bad magic. Magic is not a good or a bad thing. It just exists. That is what separates us from Meladyne. We use magic to help and to heal, and they use it to destroy and conquer. Just like a weapon. You could use a weapon to rescue your friend or you could use it to murder people. It's how you use it. You're powerful, Alyssa. You've been powerful since you were born. Let us teach you how to control it."

"Okay," Alyssa nodded. She couldn't argue. Everything he had said made perfect sense. And she would do whatever it took to rescue Hazel. "How do we start?"

"Well," the boy replied, glancing down at his watch. "We start by eating dinner and sleeping on it. We'll spend all of tomorrow doing magic, and I'll let Sylvie and Violet teach you that—they'd be better at it. But for now, get some rest. You've both done amazing."

CHAPTER 10

"The most important part of magic is focus," began Sylvie as she paced back and forth, hands clasped behind her back. Everyone sat cross-legged in a circle around her. Of course, the others already knew how to do magic, but as Violet had said, "There's no such thing as too much practice." Sylvie was the best with spells, so she had been elected to teach the lesson.

"Focus is much more difficult than it sounds. It is the act of clearing your mind of all thoughts except that of the spell you are currently performing. The average human uses ten percent of their brain. To do magic, you use one hundred percent of it. You need to access parts of your brain that most people never can. The levels of concentration that it requires are almost impossible. Do not take this lightly. You must dedicate yourself to it. Does everyone understand that? Good." Alyssa could tell this was serious just by the tone in Sylvie's voice. In the two days she had known her, Sylvie had taken *everything* lightly. She skipped around and giggled and squealed and talked a million miles an hour in her cute little British accent. Sylvie sounding dead serious was like Bella sounding that way. It made Alyssa pay attention. "Now close your eyes. Imagine darkness. An empty, dark space. This space is the world. You are alone. You see nothing. You feel nothing. You are nothing."

Alyssa thought of that like outer space. She sat on the moon, looking at the stars. But then the stars vanished, sucked away by an invisible force. The planets around her disappeared along with the moon underneath her. She was floating in empty darkness. *I am not afraid,* she told herself. *I feel nothing. I see nothing. I am nothing.* She blocked out the song stuck in her head by humming quietly. It was difficult not to think about things because thinking about not thinking about things was another way of thinking about them. But she finally calmed herself down and began to understand how people meditate. Then she heard Sylvie's voice again, cutting through her concentration.

"All right. Has everyone reached their dark room? This area is called *the Nahia Zorta,* the Neutral Zone. You will eventually be able to reach this stage momentarily, in action, but for now we are just learning to find it. There is no incorrect way to reach it, as everyone finds it differently.

Like The Twilight Zone, Alyssa thought, remembering the old shows she used to watch with Bella. But then she quickly pushed that thought aside. *Neutral. Dark. Alone.*

"Now we will attempt to perform simple magic. Everyone imagine now that in the darkness you see a little white light. Only a light hovering in front of your face. Now hold your hands out, palms up. Imagine this light coming toward you until it is right above your hands. I want you to say the word *clain*; it means *come* in Sunolian."

Alyssa attempted it as Sylvie spoke. She pictured a little ball of white light and did as her teacher told her. In her mind she had it, but she had no way of knowing what was going on in real life. She guessed that was good; it meant she was completely in the Twilight Zone—or whatever.

"All right. Now everyone recite the words *clain sinta*; come, light. I want you to say it out loud, but don't come out of the Neutral Zone."

Alyssa whispered the words, careful not to break her focus.

"Loud and firm. Command it."

"*Clain sinta!*"

Alyssa felt a surge of warmth spread over her hands, as if she'd put them in front of a heater. It wasn't the feeling of power and adrenaline and pure exhilaration she had expected. It was simply a bit of heat. It was a bit relieving, yet a bit disappointing. If this was what magic was, it certainly wasn't all Disney cracked it up to be. She winced at the thought of Disney and did her best to shove it out of her head before the magic disappeared. It was amazing how the slightest stray thought could completely throw all her concentration off. *Alone. Darkness. Nothing.*

"Very good, very good! Everyone has it now. Now here is the hardest part. Open your eyes, but keep your mind in the Neutral Zone. Find a fixated point—a tree or blade of grass maybe—and look only at it. But don't think about anything. Only think about that light in the darkness. One of the most difficult things to learn is how to remain in the Neutral Zone in action. You must train yourselves until you can reach it momentarily in battle. Alyssa, Bella, this is not the magic you see on television. You cannot wave a wand and say some funny words to perform spells. You cannot break your focus."

Slowly, Alyssa opened her eyes. She glanced down and saw a little, white, glowing ball, exactly the one she'd pictured. Carefully looking up, her eyes found a tree. Its leaves shifted a bit in the gentle breeze, but it was mostly still. *The tree,* she thought. *The tree is with me in my Twilight Zone. Just me and the tree.* She mentally tuned everything else around her out into darkness. Her head began to ache from the strain, but she dismissed it with her teeth gritted. *Just the tree.*

"Now, if you haven't lost your light, stand up slowly. Walk a few steps, then extinguish your light by saying the word *hana*: dark."

Alyssa stood up very, very slowly, never leaving the Neutral Zone. She took a shaky step toward the tree. God, her head was hurting now. It felt like it was about to explode. *I am walking through the empty air toward the tree. The tree is the only thing here.*

Soon, taking it one step at a time, she found herself directly under that same tree, staring up at its branches. Alyssa took a deep breath and cautiously turned around. But losing her fixated point made her catch sight of Malcolm, standing completely steady with his light. His lips were pressed tightly together, his brow furrowed. She realized she'd never seen him do magic before. He was clearly much better at fighting physically, as he appeared to be struggling. Only when her light flickered and went out did she realize she was examining every perfect little detail of his face: full lips, deep brown eyes, tanned skin. Blinking hard, she looked away quickly. She couldn't make him lose focus too.

Her head hurt even worse now, so she sat down and pressed her palms to her eyes. It was a terrible feeling, like a migraine.

Several moments later, when Alyssa thought she could handle looking up, she glanced up to see Silent Selena with her little orb of light. She was rolling it around in her hands, twirling it about in the air. It lit up her beautiful face, and Alyssa smiled, watching her. Selena, however, didn't smile—in fact, Alyssa hadn't seen her make a single expression in the past two days.

She just stared off into the distance, like she was waiting for something. It was sad to watch. Why did she look so sorrowful? Sure, she was mute, but that didn't mean she couldn't smile and have a good time. Was there a history there worse than that of the others? Alyssa watched as Selena released the orb into the sky and it exploded in an enormous firework, lighting up the heavens and making everyone turn their heads up. Then the hundreds of pieces began to glide back down to earth. As they neared, Alyssa recognized the little crystals—they were snowflakes, glittering like little diamonds.

"It's beautiful magic," Caleb whispered, breaking Alyssa out of her daze and startling her. "Have you seen her shoot? Perfect bull's-eye, every time. It's amazing. She's so good at everything. It's poetic, isn't it? Dark, beautiful, silent, mysterious. I could write a poem about her. That is, Maegan could write a poem about her. Look at me, Maegan's got me sounding like her now. I'd better watch it or I'll be composing love songs soon."

"Excuse you, sir, you certainly had better watch it," Alyssa teased, smacking him lightly. "I don't think Maegan would be too happy about you writing poems about other girls."

Caleb grinned. "You're right. Seriously, though, ask Maegan to read one of her poems some time. They're amazing."

As the snow ceased, Sylvie began to speak again. "Very well done, all of you. Some of you lost focus, but we'll work on it more tomorrow. I understand this is very basic for those of you who can already do this, but the practice won't kill you. This was a simple illumination spell; it does no more than light up a dark room. But once you get a grip on focus, you'll be able to do many more spells much more easily, and even do more with simple charms, the way Selena just did."

There was an awkward sort of silence for a moment, and Sylvie took a deep breath. "Right then, okay. Fantabulous job everybody. Class dismissed."

CHAPTER II

"Hey, we have a little while before training today. You want to learn some water magic?" Malcolm asked.

"Um, yeah, sure. I'm not too good at magic, though," Alyssa replied hesitantly.

"Don't worry, they were starting you out on the hard stuff. Everything that involves controlling the sun is incredibly difficult. Once you can do that, everything else is a piece of cake. Come on, have you seen the little pond by the mountains?"

Alyssa followed the boy through the woods, glancing at the breathtaking sights all around her. "It's so odd, the way the sky is blue twenty-four seven," she commented. "And the way it's this bright but there's not, like, a real sun anywhere."

"Yeah, it takes some time to get used to. It would be weird to actually look up and see the sun."

Despite these feeble attempts at small talk, most of the trip was uncomfortably quiet, so Alyssa was relieved when finally they came upon the little pool. It lay at the base of one of the massive mountains and was fed by a waterfall rushing down the slope. Alyssa could feel tiny water droplets spraying her bare skin as she neared, cooling her face and neck. The water was unrealistically blue, the way it would be in a cartoon, and it sparkled in the light, as if a thousand tiny diamonds had been spilled across it. It was a fair-sized pool, with a diameter of about twenty feet, but Alyssa couldn't manage to see the bottom.

"Why is it sparkling if—" she began out of habit, but was quickly interrupted by Malcolm.

"You ask too many questions. Stop trying to make everything make sense. That's the great thing about magic. It doesn't *have* to make sense. It's a beautiful pool, okay? Leave it at that."

"But—" Alyssa started to protest again, but stopped when she spotted the cheeky grin on the boy's face. "Enjoying this, are you?"

"Oh, Alyssa," he smiled. "I do envy the man you are going to marry. You will make a fantastic wife. And an even better mother-in-law."

"You little . . . you have no idea what wives are like!"

"I had parents, remember? I had a life before all this chaos. I used to go outside and talk to people and watch TV and everything." Malcolm replied, all out cracking up at this point.

Alyssa crossed her arms over her chest, pressing her lips together in an attempt to hide her smile. "What are we out here for, anyway?"

"Come here, I want to teach you something," Malcolm squeaked, trying to get his laughter under control. "Close your eyes and concentrate like you did yesterday. You remember the Neutral Zone? I need you to forget everything we just talked about, drop everything, and just focus. Like I said, this is not nearly as intense as solar magic, so if you slip and think about something else, you'll probably be okay. The balance isn't as delicate with water magic. Just do your best to clear your mind."

Alyssa took a deep breath, trying to push away everything on her mind. *Outer space, no stars, no planets. I'm alone, I feel nothing, I am nothing.*

Malcolm spoke softly now, doing his best not to break her concentration. Alyssa felt him slide his hand over hers, guiding it. "Now hold your hand over the water like this. Palm down. Good. Imagine a little bubble of water. Hold it, play with it, get used to it. You're in charge of it. Imagine commanding it to go up, down, sideways, go away, come back. You control it. Okay?" Alyssa did as she was told, rolling the bubble around on her hands, blowing it up in the air, and commanding it to come back. She began to feel odd and light-headed—a giddy kind of happy, the way one does when given laughing gas at the dentist's office. It was nice not feeling emotions, not worrying about things. She could just float around and let her little bubble tickle her nose . . . "Alyssa!" Something struck her face very suddenly and painfully. The bubble popped and she had the awful sensation of free-falling . . .

"Alyssa, Alyssa, shh, it's okay! Come here, come back to me, you're okay. Alyssa, look at me, sweetheart, I need you to say something."

Alyssa found herself not falling but curled up on the ground, rocking back and forth on her heels, hands pressed over her ears. She was screaming hysterically, and tears streamed down her face. She was just so afraid, of what she did not know. She felt someone strong pull her into his arms. He stroked her hair, whispered soothingly, "It's okay, it's okay, I've got you." Slowly at first, Alyssa began to find her bearings. She wasn't falling but sitting in soft grass. Malcolm was protecting her, and everything was all right. There was nothing to be afraid of.

"Open your eyes, Alyssa. Look at me."

Alyssa obeyed, cautiously exposing her eyes to the nearly blinding light. "I was falling . . ." she moaned, voice trembling. "It was so dark, so cold. I couldn't feel anything."

"I'm sorry, it's my fault. We've pushed you too hard— you're exhausted. It's a side effect of magic. If you try to do it too often at first, it will overwhelm you. Your brain isn't used to focusing that hard for that long. People have gone insane trying to perform too much magic."

"I was so scared. It was like nothing I've ever felt before. It was like it was clinging to me and wouldn't let go. Like I would never be free. There was nowhere to run, no one to save me. I didn't know who I was or where I was or what I was doing. All I know is I was falling, and I was terrified." The girl shuddered just thinking of it.

"Alyssa, how long do you think you were out?" Malcolm asked, concerned lines deepening in his forehead.

"I don't know. It felt like days, maybe even weeks. I didn't have a concept of time."

"It was only two minutes. You weren't responding, so I slapped you, and you fell down and started screaming. Hysterical screaming. You scared me."

"I'm sorry," Alyssa replied. "I'm not strong enough."

Malcolm shook his head. "It's only been two days. You'll get stronger, I promise. Just be careful."

Alyssa nodded, staring up at the mountains, trying to shake the feeling, to forget the traumatizing experience. She embraced the peaceful silence, so very different from that cold, dark, empty silence.

Malcolm finally broke it, nudging the girl with his elbow. "Alyssa, look," he muttered, pointing straight ahead at the water. Alyssa's eyes shifted downward, and she jumped back in shock. There was a girl standing on the surface of the glossy water—standing barefoot on it, like it was ice. She was young, maybe eighteen years old, and had an angelic figure—pale blue skin, long white dress, thick silvery hair brushing her skin. Her hair and dress appeared to be flowing around her, as if she were underwater.

"I've read about those before in mythology!" Alyssa cried, thrilled to actually know the answer to something. "They're called naiads. They live in the water and drag people underwater . . ." she faltered, recalling suddenly what the creatures were famous for, "and they drown you."

"Good guess, but no, she's not a naiad. You have nothing to be afraid of. She's a water spirit. See, once you complete your training, you have the option of becoming a spirit. Remember when Falla told you about the four divisions of Sunolia? We live in Aquamarinia, land of the waters; you know that. So when you complete your training, you can become a water spirit. Water spirits protect the waters of Sunolia. They keep the water fresh and clean for us to drink, they keep the rivers flowing, that sort of thing. There are also fire, earth, and wind spirits, depending on which division you were trained in. They're immortal creatures, and they always appear young and beautiful. She could be hundreds of years old."

"That doesn't sound like a bad life. Live in the water forever, controlling it and watching people. You would never have to worry about anything." Alyssa thought it sounded like a much better life than what she was going through.

"Yeah, it's a great life. And because they completed their training, if ever Sunolia was to be attacked by Meladyne, their magic is unbelievably powerful. The only bad thing about it is once you become a water spirit, you can't ever leave Aquamarinia. Same goes for the spirits in the other divisions. That spirit has bound her life to Sunolia's waters—it's the only thing keeping her alive. She can leave the water, yes, but if she left Sunolia, she would die," Malcolm explained.

Alyssa was confused. "But why would you want that? Why would you want to never see your family again?"

"She's just like the rest of us. Meladyne took her family. They are probably already dead. There is nothing for her in the Mortal World. There is no reason to leave."

Alyssa looked sympathetically at her, but the spirit looked perfectly happy. She smiled, wiggling her fingers in a little wave, and Alyssa waved back.

"Watch, she'll do some magic for you if you're quiet," Malcolm whispered, and Alyssa obeyed.

Letting her eyes linger on Alyssa as if to judge her reaction, the spirit bent forward with otherworldly grace, placing her hand on the water's surface for a moment. As she lifted it, a little bubble about the size of a baseball hovered six inches beneath her hand. She then flipped her hand over, and the bubble followed her palm. Bringing her small hand to her face, she put her lips together and blew gently on the bubble. The bubble began to morph oddly, and at first Alyssa could not figure out what was happening. But when she looked again, she discovered the bubble had morphed into the shape of a little, blue butterfly. Its wings still flowed and shimmered in the light, like they were made of water, but they made a solid shape. Alyssa watched, now smiling, as the butterfly left the spirit's palm and flew around the pond on its own.

"Hold out your hand," Malcolm whispered, and Alyssa did. The butterfly flew its way to her until it hovered right in front of the blonde's face. The spirit waved her hand and the butterfly's wings stopped beating. Its whole body froze in place, and a little ice statue of a butterfly dropped into Alyssa's hand. Alyssa smiled up at the water spirit, and the girl smiled back. With a graceful leap into the air, the spirit put her hands above her head in a diving position and slid gracefully back into the water.

"Wow," Alyssa breathed, examining the statue in her hand. The craftsmanship was flawless.

"It's the best kind of magic," Malcolm agreed. "When all this craziness is over, that's the kind of thing we'll hold on to. I love it." He sighed contentedly. "But unfortunately, all this craziness is not over. They'll be missing us. Let's get back to training."

CHAPTER 12

The following two weeks were a blur. Alyssa worked harder than she ever had and collapsed into bed every night feeling half dead. Her body no longer hurt from sleeping on the ground but embraced the soft sleeping bag, it being the most comfortable thing in her life. Each morning started bright and early with a healthy breakfast—fruits, oatmeal, fiber bars. Immediately following was an intense workout, complete with push-ups, sit-ups, running, jumping jacks, wall sits, stretching—the whole package. Then they did weapons. Alyssa still dueled Violet with swords every day, improving a bit each time. She had all but given up on throwing knives, but Bella was almost scary to watch when she started chucking the things at the targets, hitting near her mark almost every time, eyes almost glazed over. Neither of the girls did well with a bow and arrow, but they would still go out and watch Silent Selena release arrow after arrow after arrow, scoring perfect bull's-eyes every single time. Alyssa continued to train on her staff with Malcolm, making unbelievable progress. By the end of the week, she felt confident enough to challenge the others, and Malcolm was beaming with pride.

After weapons was lunch, again, everything nutritious and hydrating. Alyssa longed for a cheeseburger or a chocolate bar, but never brought it up, knowing the only thing that would happen would be Violet jumping into a rant about the way unhealthy food impacted your performance in battle, and that would hardly help anyone.

After lunch they practiced magic. They always did that same spell, over and over, trying to capture sunlight and control it. "Focus, Alyssa, *focus!*" Violet would scream, but as hard as Alyssa tried, she just couldn't do it. She managed to capture it and hold it, using it as a light, but if she tried to throw it, use it against someone, or make it brighter, it would just fall down and die.

Violet was a pleasant, friendly person when Alyssa spoke to her at mealtimes, but when it came to training she was not messing around. She would push Alyssa past her limits, scream in her face, smack her with her own staff, and tell her to get up. Some nights Alyssa would end up on the ground sobbing and bleeding, barely able to move because she was so sore. "Thrust your hands forward, Alyssa! Hit me! I stole your friend, I killed all these people's families, *I am the reason your family is in danger!* What are you going to do about it? Come on, Alyssa, you're weak! Do it!"

"You're angry now, aren't you?" Sylvie whispered from beside her, her lips inches from Alyssa's ear, her voice an intense hiss. Sylvie wasn't nearly as hardcore as Violet, but she was certainly serious about training too. "Use that anger, feel it! Let it course through your blood. You hate her, don't you? You want to tear her to shreds for what she did to your family. So do it! Channel all of that anger into your light, let it fill you up. Now throw it!"

Alyssa thrust her arms forward and watched as the orb of light shot forward and grazed Violet's skin for a split second before falling and burning out. Violet cried out in pain, shocked at the impact. Alyssa felt instantly guilty, watching the angry burn mark grow on Violet's arm. The angrier she had become, the hotter the light had grown until she could hardly contain it anymore. The skin on Violet's forearm had been singed off and Alyssa watched the blood trickle down her arm.

"Violet! I'm sorry, I didn't mean to hit you. Are you okay?"

But when Alyssa reached the older girl, she found her beaming from ear to ear like an idiot, a slight wince in her eyes from the pain. "Alyssa! What was that?"

"I . . . I don't know, you just made me angry—"

"Girl, that *hurt*! Look at this! That was insane! Do you know how difficult that spell is? Yeah, you only hurt my arm, it could've been a lot bigger and more powerful, but oh my God!" Violet threw her arms around Alyssa, startling the blonde. "You are exactly what we have been looking for! The rumors are true! You are going to save us!" Violet was jumping up and down on her toes giddily, apparently completely forgetting her tough act. "Haha, I knew it! You're dismissed until survival skills, Alyssa. Go get some food. You deserve it!"

Violet practically skipped off, dancing around with glee. Alyssa just glanced at Sylvie, eyebrows raised. Sylvie shrugged. "Hey, don't ask me. I will never understand that girl. She's the perfect example of mood swings at their worst." Alyssa grinned and followed Sylvie to dinner.

After dinner they practiced survival skills. This became Alyssa's favorite lesson, as every night it was something different. They learned to perform fire spells, as Caleb had promised they would. These charms seemed incredibly simple after the difficulty of the solar magic, and Alyssa made sure to be careful so as not to have an attack like she had before. Once they had mastered fire building, they learned to build shelters, track people through the woods, find water, dress wounds, send SOS signals—all of the classic Boy Scout tricks.

"Remember, we have no idea what the geography of Meladyne is like. We have to be prepared for anything," Maegan lectured, wrapping a bandage around Violet's arm and concluding her demonstration. "Okay, good job, you two. That's enough for today. I'll see you in the morning."

"Wait, Maegan," Alyssa called before she could depart. "Can you ask everybody to gather around the fire pit before bed? I want to talk to you guys."

"Sure thing, kiddo. I'll get everybody and we can meet up in, say, twenty minutes?"

"That would be awesome. Thanks, Maegan."

"No problem."

* * *

"All right, McCaw, let's get this over with. I'm tired," Violet ordered, leaning against her tent, eyes half-closed.

It annoyed Alyssa how bored and careless the girl appeared. Clearly all the previous excitement about the magic had worn off, and everyone just wanted to go to bed. *I've listened to all of you go on and on about training and magic and psychology and battle and everything for two weeks and pretended like I cared. But now it's my turn. I'm your dang savior so you'd better pay me a little respect if you know what's good for you.*

"Okay, um, hello, everybody," Alyssa began awkwardly, suddenly dropping all of her irritation. While she didn't exactly have stage fright, she had never been one to stand out in a crowd and make a speech. She liked to blend in, watch the show. It gave her a whole new perspective, actually *being* the show. "So, here's the deal. I don't like being the center of attention, and I want to go to bed as much as you, so I'm going to make this as simple and straightforward as possible." She had rehearsed what she wanted to say hundreds of times in her head but still had trouble finding the words. "I want to go rescue my friend from Meladyne. First thing in the morning. I've been training with you for two weeks now and no one can deny the progress I've made. I'm not talking about a huge rebellion and a battle to the death and a war. I'm talking about sneaking in, freeing Hazel and her family, and coming back. I've agreed to be the savior. So now I want to save someone."

Alyssa glanced around hopefully. For a moment everyone remained quiet. Then, all at once, the entire gathering erupted into an anarchic clamor of protests and arguing and yelling. Alyssa stood shocked at the level of excitement she had caused. She hadn't really known what to expect, but it certainly wasn't this. She took a few steps back, unsuccessfully attempting to disappear. It took Violet nearly five minutes to calm everyone down, and even after the noise had subsided, it was clear no one was finished speaking.

"Shut up, all of you!" Violet cried. "What is this? Since when do you have the right to explode when someone proposes a suggestion? This is an open community, and Alyssa has every right to voice her opinions. Does anyone have a problem with that? I didn't think so. We are going to do this like civilized people and not a pack of wild animals. I will talk first. If anyone has an objection to anything I say, you can state your opinion calmly, *one at a time*. Okay?"

She turned to address Alyssa. "Now, Alyssa. I know you want to rescue your friend. Believe me, there is not a soul here that doesn't understand what you're going through because we are all in the same situation. But the thing is, you don't realize what you're up against. You cannot simply sneak into Meladyne and expect to make it out alive. Yes, you have been excelling at your training and we have been able to move at a much faster pace with you than we ever have with anyone. But Alyssa, you have only been training for two weeks. You are the only hope we have left. If you die, Meladyne will destroy everything we have. Sending you to Meladyne with so little experience is too risky. You are simply too important. Can you at least try to understand that?"

Alyssa took a deep breath. Violet hadn't said anything even remotely unreasonable. Alyssa's eagerness to rush through her training and into battle surprised herself more than anyone else. But she couldn't give up. She wanted Hazel back. Once she had Hazel, she could go back to her parents and get on with her life and forget about Sunolia and Meladyne and magic completely. And there was Bella to think of. Bella wasn't safe in the midst of all the darkness, she didn't belong on a battlefield. She had to get her home safely. So Alyssa stood her ground and argued back. "I want to take the test," she decided.

"What test?"

"On my first day, you said once I pass the queen's test, I can become a Jedi master and take on Meladyne. Right? I want to take her test."

"Alyssa, be real. You can't possibly—" Maegan started, but Violet cut her off.

"Anyone can take the test when they feel they are ready. If Alyssa feels she is ready, we must take her to the queen. But Alyssa, I must warn you. This will not be an easy evaluation. It takes even the best—"

"I *know*, Violet, you keep telling me this. 'It takes years for even the strongest and brightest of warriors to unravel the deepest secrets of Sunolia's magic.' I don't care. I'm the savior. I'm a magical little princess and I have power and I'm going to prove it to you." Her tone was final, and she crossed her arms, glaring challengingly at Violet. Much to Alyssa's surprise, the older girl cracked a tiny smile.

"You're stubborn. Stubborn's good. I knew you were a good leader. We leave for the Garden of the Dawn first thing in the morning. Now for crying out loud, go to sleep. You're giving me a headache."

CHAPTER 13

The trip to the Garden of the Dawn was a long one, as were most of the trips to anywhere in Sunolia. It was maybe a three-hour walk, and that was without stopping to eat or drink water or get the rocks out of your shoes. The scenery was pretty but repetitive, primarily containing lush, green grasses and vibrant flowers in every direction as far as the eye could see. Alyssa and Violet were happy to make their way in silence, but Bella quickly grew bored and started into one of her rants. "So I've been thinking lately, what's with the color orange? I mean, it doesn't match, like, anything. They don't make orange pens. What is the point of it even? There are, like, two things in the world that are actually orange. There are pumpkins, the sun . . . that's about it. When was the last time you walked into a room wearing an orange shirt and somebody was like 'whoa, that's a beautiful orange shirt'? And pants? No one has ever worn orange pants. Why—"

"Bella!" Alyssa and Violet cried out in perfect unison.

"Sorry," the little girl muttered, casting her eyes down at her shoes.

"Look, we're almost there," Violet stated, gesturing in front of her. They were approaching a thick forest. The foliage was rust colored and dense—a picturesque image of autumn. Out of the corner of her eye, Alyssa caught a glimpse of a dark, humanoid figure leaping stealthily and soundlessly through the wood, and though it was only a glance, she could have sworn his clothing was woven with leaves.

"This is called the Crimson Forest. It completely surrounds the Garden of the Dawn. Don't worry, it's not too thick—only about a ten-minute walk. Watch out for dryads, though. They're tree spirits. They're cute, but they'll pickpocket you in an instant," Violet warned.

The rest of the walk was indeed only ten minutes with no trouble from the dryads. The trio soon came upon an immense weeping willow tree, the branches sweeping elegantly to the ground, green leaves so thick whatever was behind was completely concealed. Violet shot a threatening look at Bella with a finger to her lips, then called out in a projected voice, "Permission to enter, Your Majesty?"

The response was immediate. "Please come in, my children. I have been expecting you."

Alyssa reached down for Bella's hand and squeezed it. As they passed through the boughs, Alyssa's jaw dropped. Colorful, beautiful, and peaceful weren't even capable of describing the place. All around were flowers and bushes in every shade of every color. As Violet had promised, a tree trunk too big in diameter for three people to stand around holding hands stood proudly in the center, towering over their heads so high Alyssa could not even see the top. The branches extended outward and drooped down so that the greenery formed an opaque curtain all around the garden. Even though the sky just outside had been bright and blue, a beautiful sunrise of pinks and purples and oranges peeked through the branches above. Leaning against this tree was a Sunolian, though she didn't look like the others. Her long, golden hair wasn't braided, but fell down her shoulders gracefully and perfectly to her waist. Her dress was sleeveless, and it came several inches past her knees, glittering in the light. She wore simple golden flats for shoes, and her hazel eyes were warm and welcoming with golden flecks in them. She also looked older than the other Sunolians—maybe twenty. But the most breathtaking thing about her was the pair of shimmering golden wings sprouting from her back, like a fairy's.

Violet curtsied with a smile, never taking her eyes off the beautiful queen, so Alyssa and Bella followed suit. "Welcome," Cressidalaina said, "to the Garden of the Dawn."

"Thank you," Alyssa replied, awestruck. "We're—"

"I know what brings you here," the queen interrupted. "Please sit. I understand you want to use magic."

"Yes."

"So you can rescue your friend; she was taken by Meladyne."

"Yes."

"You want to get your parents back from Terralith."

"Yes."

"Well, I can tell you one thing. You have time. The Lavinskis are not dead," Cressidalaina said.

"How do you know?" Bella asked, a ray of hope sparking in her eyes.

"Hazel is the reason you are going to Meladyne. She's the bait. If you were a fish and there was a hook in the water without food on it, you wouldn't bite it. If they kill her, you'll have no reason to go, and they can't get what they want."

Alyssa had read enough war stories and listened to Falla enough to know this already. "Okay, that makes sense. But I've been training for two weeks now, and I believe I am ready to face Meladyne and recover my friend. So I would like your permission to show you what I can do."

"Very well. You are a stubborn child, I can tell that much, and arguing will do no good. So much like your father." Alyssa saw a brief spark of emotion in the queen's eyes, and remembered the queen had once been in love with her father. *It must be hard for her,* Alyssa thought, *seeing us, the children of the man who left her and the woman he left for.* A rush of sympathy ran through her, and she thought about saying something, but Cressidalaina had already moved on like nothing had happened. *Maybe I just imagined it.* "First you will demonstrate your abilities, and then your sister will take her turn."

"Wait, no. Bella's not coming."

"What?" Bella cried.

"It's too dangerous. You'll get hurt. I'm doing this myself."

"I've been working just as hard as you have! What makes you think I'm just going to stay behind while you save Hazel? If I didn't want to help, I would be at home now with Mom and Dad, because I know you don't notice, but I cry myself to sleep every night because I miss them so bad!"

Alyssa took a step back, stunned. She had been so wrapped up in the training and Hazel and keeping Bella safe, she hadn't actually thought about how her sister felt. It wasn't easy for Alyssa to be away from her parents so long, but Bella was only nine. She had barely been away for a weekend. "Bella, I'm sorry, I—"

The little girl shook her head, wiping a tear from her cheek, blinking rapidly in an attempt to force the tears away. "No, it's okay. There's a lot of pressure on you. I get it. You go first."

Alyssa took a shaky breath. She had never seen Bella so serious and emotional before. She missed her fun little goofy, obnoxious Bella. This place was doing something to her personality. This was the perfect example of why Alyssa needed to get her sister home and away from all the madness and darkness as soon as possible.

With this to motivate her, Alyssa demonstrated her skill with a staff and a sword. She made a little bubble and a whirlpool in her water bottle, then showed off her impressive speed. When asked to perform the solar magic, Alyssa was able to capture the light and hold it, but failed to launch it at the tree when asked to. Bella did fairly well, throwing a knife so close to Alyssa's head it nicked her ear. She was also able to throw a rock twice her weight using wind magic, an ability Alyssa hadn't known she possessed, and was flexible enough to put her foot over her head. She managed to make a little spark that almost became a fire, but her solar magic was nonexistent. By the end of the demonstration, Alyssa knew exactly how well they'd done. It was an awful feeling in the pit of her stomach, the way she remembered feeling when she was failing a math test miserably and knew she could do nothing about it. Her heart sank at the apologetic look on the queen's face.

"I am very sorry, girls, truly I am. But aside from being the most important people in the world and the only ones who can save the world, you are also mere children. And I care about you, I really do. We have lost too many of our people to Meladyne. I could not bear it if we lost you. As I said, Hazel will remain safe for the time being because she is their leverage. I am very impressed with your progression, and given a year or so, the two of you may be the strongest soldiers we have ever raised.

You simply have to be patient. Can you please try to understand that?"

Alyssa sighed. Perhaps Cressidalaina was right. Perhaps she was rushing things along. After all, she didn't really want to die. Hazel would be all right. They were a strong family, glass-half-full kind of people. "All right," she agreed.

"Thank you. I do hate what this awful war is doing to us. I do not like to think of children as soldiers or warriors. It is not how they should grow up. That is why you must be very, very careful. You can bring an end to that. With your help, children can grow up with their parents. They won't have to be afraid anymore."

"Yes ma'am, I know," Alyssa replied. "I'm doing my best."

Cressidalaina smiled. "I know you are. You are braver than even you know, my child. Now I want you to journey back to your camp. Rest well tonight. Continue your training and work hard, but please try to have a good time too. Make friends with the other children. I don't want your life stolen away from you."

"Thank you very much, Your Majesty. I'll try." Standing up from her spot on the ground, Alyssa did an awkward sort of curtsy and left without another word.

* * *

Three more hours of sauntering across Sunolia, a quick, lonely dinner, and Alyssa found herself standing outside Malcolm's tent. She could not explain why, exactly, she was standing there. The others had just retired to their tents to calm down and relax a bit before bed, but Alyssa just couldn't seem to make herself go to sleep. She didn't want to talk to Bella, or Violet, or anyone else. But for some reason she felt like Malcolm would listen to her, like he would understand.

She tapped lightly on the pole of his tent. "Malcolm?"

She heard him stirring for a moment, then the flap opened and his head poked out. His hair had been released from its ponytail and was disheveled around his face. He wore sweatpants and a muscle shirt that displayed his strong, sturdy body. "Hey, Alyssa. Is something wrong?"

Alyssa shook her head. "I don't know, I just . . . what is that music?" A soft, gentle melody had begun to play, seemingly from all around her. She turned, trying to locate the source of the music, but couldn't seem to find it.

"Sprites," Malcolm replied. "They're little tiny creatures, almost like fairies. They're hard to see, but at night they play music—little tiny flutes and violins and Sunolian instruments. They sing sometimes, too."

"I never noticed that," Alyssa furrowed her brow.

"You'll only hear them if you really listen." Malcolm stepped out of his tent. "What's the matter, Alyssa?" he asked, taking her hands and pulling her in close. Placing his hands on her hips, he began to sway from side to side, and before Alyssa knew what was happening, they were dancing.

Alyssa leaned her head against his chest. "I have to go after Hazel," she whispered. "I know you're going to protest. I know they won't kill her, but Malcolm, she has these little brothers . . . they have to be torturing her. I can't get it out of my head. I can't just sit here and do nothing."

"I know," he said. "And I also know you're planning on going after her tonight. And there's nothing I can do to stop you short of chaining you to something, which I'm not planning on doing."

"You're . . . you're not going to stop me?"

"No, I'm not. And I'm not going to try to come with you either because I know that you'll whack me in the head with that staff and run if I do."

"Sounds like you've got it all figured out," Alyssa moaned.

"I certainly do. Alyssa, look at me. I just want you to promise me you'll be careful. You're not a stupid person. Don't do anything stupid. If you think you're going to die, you get out of there. Do not be afraid to run. Sneak in there, take your friends, and sneak out. If you get caught, don't try to fight them. Just run. Okay? We can always go back. I can't have you dying on me. I can't lose another person. You got that?"

Alyssa nodded, tears brimming in her eyes.

"You're braver than you believe, stronger than you seem, and smarter than you think. Don't forget that."

Against her will, Alyssa's face broke into a small, teary smile. "You think you can sneak Winnie the Pooh quotes in on me and I won't notice?"

Malcolm grinned sheepishly. "Sorry. I guess I'm out of lines."

The slight laughter only managed to linger for a moment before molding back into paralyzing fear. "I'm so scared, Malcolm," she whispered. The dread was building up in her, threatening to break down.

"You don't have to do this."

"Yes, I do." Alyssa reached her quivering hands behind her head and unhooked the chain around her neck. She pressed the Key into Malcolm's hand and closed his fingers around it. She clasped his fist with both of her hands and looked up into his eyes. "I'll be back. I promise." She planted a kiss on his cheek and turned around quickly, knowing she wouldn't be able to bear the look on his face. Slinging her bag over her shoulder and strapping her staff to her back, she began her journey to the portal, taking shaky breaths in a fruitless attempt to calm herself down. It was only about ten minutes into her expedition when she felt a tiny hand slip into hers. "There's no stopping you, is there?"

"Nope," was all Bella said, and together the girls made their way toward the portal.

A thought occurred to Bella about halfway there. "Don't we need the Key to open the portal?"

"I snuck out and opened it last night, just in case this might happen. It stays open for twenty-four hours, remember?"

Bella grinned. "And you say you don't know what you're doing."

"Bella, you realize we're probably going to die."

"I know."

"*Sic crestaes aloma!*"

Eyes wide, hearts racing a million miles an hour, the girls shot up the portal to what promised to be their deaths.

CHAPTER 14

 It was nearly midnight when Alyssa and Bella found themselves once again in their front yard. Alyssa's eyes had difficulty adjusting to the darkness; everything in Sunolia was always so bright and vivid and colorful. It was strange how ordinary, realistic colors could appear so dull in comparison.

"Alyssa?" Bella asked. "It's pretty late, isn't it? Why is everyone so awake?"

Alyssa, so caught up in her current mission, hadn't previously noticed, but the street was much more lively than usual. Lights were on in nearly every house, cars were parked all over the street, and flamboyant laughter echoed from every house. The only explanation was . . .

"It's New Year's Eve," she realized.

Bella glanced up at Alyssa, a mischievous light in her eyes. "Then let's make this a real good year for Hazel."

"Agreed." Alyssa smiled a bit despite the knot of fear in her stomach and took a step forward. Then a thought occurred to her.

"Um, Alyssa?" Bella said, as she had clearly discovered the problem as well. "Where is Meladyne, and how do we get there?"

All the intense, terrified feelings inside Alyssa melted away. How could she have been so stupid? Why hadn't she asked someone? Shivering in her light sweatshirt, she looked around for any sign of the way. Who was to say Meladyne wasn't on the other side of the earth? Who was to say it wasn't on the moon? Alyssa was almost ready to give up and go back to Sunolia when at that moment, most definitely not by coincidence, a bright light shone in front of them, light so bright they had to squint to see it. It began to take form until standing before them was an absolutely albino young woman. Her hair, her dress, her skin, everything was pale white, and she was glowing softly. Not pale like Sylvie. *White* like a ghost, with absolutely no color anywhere.

The strangest thing about her were her eyes. They might have been blue, but they were so shockingly pale, they were almost white. They stared into Alyssa's own blue eyes, mesmerizing her. It was obvious they were expected by Meladyne.

Reality became hazy, and all Alyssa could see were the apparition's eyes. All the sounds and shapes and colors around her blurred together. *I know I should be doing something now, but what?* Alyssa thought. *I want something desperately, something I can't live without. I need it . . . but what is it? No, that's stupid. I don't want anything . . . I don't need anything. Nothing really matters as long as I can stare into those eyes forever . . . those eyes, those eyes, those eyes . . . There is a little girl behind me, pulling me back, screaming but her words are muffled. What's her name? Do I know her? What's my name? Where am I? I don't care. All I want is to look in those eyes . . . such beautiful eyes . . .*

Entranced, she began walking forward, arms outstretched, trying to reach the woman, but she remained a few feet away no matter how many steps she took. She followed the apparition down the street and into Ricky's house. Bella was dragging her backward, screaming, but Alyssa ignored her. She was led downstairs, into the basement. At the bottom was a door covered in a complicated series of foreign letters and keyholes. The apparition outstretched her hand, and on contact, the door swung open. Alyssa followed the ghost, entirely entranced, inside the room. As suddenly as it appeared, the ghost vanished, and Alyssa's whole world went dark.

* * *

The next time she could focus, she was on the cold, hard ground. When she opened her eyes, Bella was slapping her face.

"Alyssa! Alyssa, wake up! Oh, come on, Alyssa, I need you. Why'd you have to pick now to pass out?"

She sat up dizzily and Bella squealed and threw her arms around her.

"Whoa, whoa, space," Alyssa mumbled.

"Oh, right, sorry." Bella let go and Alyssa rolled her body over. The motion caused her stomach to lurch, and she vomited violently, all the contents of her stomach burning her throat.

"I'm so dizzy," she moaned.

"I know, but you have to try to get up. We can't just lie here."

Bella helped her sister to her feet and the older girl, holding one hand to her stomach, the other to her head, took in their surroundings. What little grass there was was dead and brown. There wasn't a single leaf on a single tree. The place looked like a barren wasteland, a dark desert that stretched endlessly into the gloom.

"Where are we?" Alyssa breathed.

"In Ricky King's basement," Bella replied.

"You're kidding."

Bella gave a brief summary of what had happened, and Alyssa's mouth was hanging open by the time she was finished.

Suddenly, Alyssa vaguely remembered a birthday party from when she was younger, only six or seven years old.

"Ricky, why can't we go downstairs? It's too loud up here."

"No, Alyssa! Don't go down there! Um, I mean, we have . . . rats."

"Rats? Ew! Hazel, wait, there are rats down there!"

"I want to go home. Where are your mommy and daddy? Why aren't they ever around?"

"They're not here right now, Alyssa. Just stay upstairs. Don't ever, ever go down those stairs for any reason, okay? There are bad things down there, and I don't want you to get hurt. Do you hear me? Don't ever go downstairs . . ."

His voice rang through her head, and her eyes widened with the memory. He had been *warning* her. The day had faded from her memory; it had been almost eight years ago. But now she could hear it, clear as day in her mind. *I don't want you to get hurt . . . Don't ever go downstairs . . .* He had told her not to go there because he knew. He knew Meladyne was in his basement, and if he hadn't stopped her from turning the doorknob, she would've spent her life there, a captive. So why had he stopped her then?

"Alyssa? Earth to Alyssa?" Bella waved a hand in front of her face. "What are we gonna do?"

"Uh, where's the door we came in from?" Alyssa asked.

The little one shrugged. "Heck if I know."

"Well then, I guess there's only one way to go."

"Forward," Bella sighed.

"Forward," Alyssa agreed.

They wandered aimlessly for a while over the hard, cold ground. An inexplicable feeling of depression and misery began to spread over Alyssa, and she could tell her sister felt it too by the uneasy look on her face. She wanted to curl up in a ball and cry, she wanted to go home and let her mother hold her. She was so cold, so alone, so afraid . . . When the emotion had reached its peak and she was on the verge of sobbing, another thought occurred to her. It wasn't fair that her parents couldn't hug her and make her feel better. It wasn't her fault Hazel was in trouble. But it was most definitely *someone's* fault. The depression slowly molded into a deep loathing, an anger coursing through her blood and filling up her soul. She wanted to hurt someone. She wanted to *kill* someone. Someone had made her suffer, and now they deserved to pay. They should suffer too. The whole world should suffer and be tortured in the most brutal ways because she didn't have her family, because her sister was in danger, and because her best friend had been captured. *They should feel how I feel, they should know the pain I'm in. Then they would understand, then they would help me . . .*

On a sudden, unexplainable impulse, she yanked out her staff and started running, dashing, bounding, chasing, sprinting forward. The world was a blur and she didn't know where she was going, she didn't care what she was doing.

There would be blood, death, tears, suffering . . . and that would satisfy her.

Then she was being shoved to the ground, smacked in the face, shaken.

"Come on, Alyssa, come on, girl," Bella hissed. "You can't keep doing this. We gotta go!"

Alyssa sat up groggily, the feelings of hatred replaced by fear.

"Get up." Bella helped her sister to her feet. "Why do you keep losing control?"

"I don't know. I think it's this place. It's having some kind of effect on me. Like it's sucking all the light out. You don't feel that?"

"A little. But it's not that bad. I can fight it."

Alyssa took in her location. They stood in a village. All the houses looked like they could've once been mansions, beautiful ones, but now they were old and crumbling like haunted houses straight out of a horror movie—broken windows, collapsing porches, and all. Looming in the distance was a huge, dark palace so old and depressing it looked as if no one had lived in it in hundreds of years.

Roaming the streets were hundreds of boys, perfect replicas of Ricky King, like the ones they'd seen in the mall. Like the Sunolians, they were all completely identical. They all had dark, murderous looks on their faces, and were riding on the backs of pitch-black horses with glowing red eyes. They wore only black and gray with swords sheathed at their sides and knives in their belts. Each bore a scar running from the corner of his eye to the corner of his mouth.

They glared at the girls as they passed timidly, but none attacked. Alyssa saw one fingering his knife; it looked just like Ricky's, with the word *Meladyne* on the end. He glared at her and coldness swept over her, so she quickly looked away.

Alyssa had never been so afraid in her life. She wondered why they would not attack, but neither she nor Bella dared to speak as they made their way through the town. Fear spread from the tips of their fingers to the ends of every strand of hair, straight through their hearts and souls to their toes, but they were both thinking one thing: Meladynians.

Bella gripped Alyssa's hand tighter, walking closer to her.

"It's all right," Alyssa said in barely a whisper as they neared the castle. "They're not hurting us." But as she said it, she knew she was trying to calm herself more than her sister.

They found themselves standing directly before the castle, which stood even taller, darker, and more foreboding close up. Alyssa was wondering whether they should try and find a way inside when a piercing scream broke the silence.

The girls dashed down to the end of the castle wall. As they approached the corner, Alyssa's arm shot out across her little sister's chest and shoved her back to keep her from tearing out into unknown territory. They stood with their backs to the cold castle wall, breathing hard for a minute. The shriek came again, louder and clearer this time. The girls peered around the side of the castle at the grounds. Alyssa clapped her hand over her mouth to keep from screaming at what she saw.

"Stop, no, please, AAAHHH!!! Don't make me do it again, please, no, OOOWW!!! Okay, okay, okay . . ."

It was Hazel.

She was dressed like a slave. Her piles of red hair were pulled back off her face in a high ponytail. She wore a loose piece of fabric that came to just above her belly button and a black, torn skirt in rags.

She was being beaten by a man who resembled the Meladynians but older, taller, more handsome, with silver hair instead of black that was about shoulder length and a very short beard. But he had the same stormy, gray, foreboding eyes, sharp features, and scar.

Hazel's little brother, Logan, was standing before her, in rags himself.

"Hit him!" the man yelled, and gave her a hard blow in the stomach.

Hazel screamed and doubled over, coughing.

"Hit him!" he repeated.

She stood up, tears brimming in her eyes, and slapped the boy in the face, who cried out in agony.

"Now, *properly* finish polishing and sharpening my sword." And the man undid the belt his sheath was on that contained his sword and dropped it in Logan's tiny arms. The little boy stumbled under its weight and took off toward the castle, too afraid to look back or slow down.

"Now, as for you . . . Ricky!" the cruel man shouted.

Hurrying out of the palace was none other than Ricky King himself. Alyssa felt her fists clenching.

"Yes, Father?"

Father? Alyssa thought. *That's Karvokono!*

Karvokono reached into empty space, curled his fingers, and yanked his hand back. His fingers now curled around a few yards of rope.

"Ricky, tie the girl to the tree."

Alyssa didn't know why; it was a simple enough order, and the rope looked just like ordinary rope, but Ricky's face paled, and he began to tremble.

"But . . . but Father, I . . ."

"DO IT, RICKY!" the man bellowed.

Shakily, Ricky forced Hazel onto her knees and tied her wrists together behind her back. Then he bound her hands to the tree. Ricky whispered something inaudible in her ear; her eyes widened and she gave him a funny look.

"Now do it!" Karvokono ordered.

"I . . ."

"NOW!"

And Karvokono reached over and backhanded his son across the face. Alyssa was confused. It looked as if Ricky was being tortured just as much as Hazel.

Ricky yanked his knife out of his pocket and cut open his own finger. As blood began to drip from it, he held his finger over the rope. But the drops of blood didn't stain like they should have. They appeared on the surface, then soaked into the rope and disappeared. After an encouraging kick from his father, he said a couple words in a strange language Alyssa didn't recognize. Not Sunolian; these words were no doubt darker and older. Then he stood and hurried back toward the castle, cradling his wound.

"What did you do to him? Don't hurt him!" Hazel demanded.

"Nothing, child, nothing. If you're still so worried about him, don't be. He is my son, so I may do whatever I want with him. And technically, he hurt himself. I didn't touch him."

At the look of surprise of Hazel's face, he doubled over in a cruel, cold laugh.

"You liar! You monster! You . . ."

"Now, now, there's no need for any of that. You just sit here quietly and be a good girl and I *might* think about feeding you." He laughed maniacally and Bella saved Alyssa's life by grabbing her and holding her back.

"Let me go," Alyssa hissed. "I'll have a go at him. I can fight."

"No, you can't," Bella whispered, tightening her grip on her older sister. "He'll kill you on sight. You have to stay here."

Karvokono kicked Hazel one last time before turning and striding off, not toward the castle like Ricky and Logan, but farther across the grounds away from the palace until he disappeared behind a hill.

Once he was gone, Alyssa and Bella dashed out from their hiding place. When Hazel saw them, her face broke into a smile, and she looked so happy Alyssa almost cried.

"Alyssa, oh, thank God! What is going on? They tortured me and my family. These are terrible people. Oh, Alyssa, they want you, they've been looking for you. Why do they want you? And Ricky . . . oh God, Alyssa, Ricky . . . he's . . ."

"Shh, calm down, Hazel. Please keep your voice down or we'll get caught," Alyssa said, fumbling with the ropes, frantically trying to untie them.

"Caught doing what? Alyssa, please tell me what's going on," Hazel pleaded.

"Shhh, I'll tell you later. Where is the rest of your family? Dang it, why can't I untie this rope? I spent, like, an hour just learning how to tie and untie ropes!"

"I don't know where my family is," Hazel answered. "My brothers have been running around like slaves doing what that horrible man tells them to. I haven't seen my parents in weeks, but Aiden says they're alive. I think they're being kept somewhere back there." She nodded in the general direction Karvokono had gone.

"How did you get here?" Bella asked, still panting.

"Well, I don't really know. I just woke up one morning a couple weeks ago chained to this tree. They feed me half a piece of moldy bread and about half a cup of water every day. Most of the time I just sit here bound to this tree. Every once in a while the man or Ricky or this other terrible woman makes me beat someone—there are lots of other servants here—but usually I just sit here."

"Sorry it took so long for us to come. We just had to . . ."

"Ugh!" Alyssa cried. "I give up! This rope is not coming undone!"

After failing at untying it, Alyssa had retrieved her dagger and begun sawing away, but it was no use.

"I don't understand!" she cried. "Why can't I cut them?"

"Because," came a voice from behind her, "those are enchanted bonds."

Alyssa and Bella jumped up and whipped around, drawing their weapons.

"You! You traitor! You nasty, rotten, lying little . . ."

"Good to see you too, Lyssie," said Ricky King.

"Don't call me 'Lyssie'!" Alyssa screamed.

"Shh, keep it down. I'm trying to help you."

"Yeah, I'm not falling for that one again. How dare you even speak to me after what you've done?"

"Listen, I know it's hard to believe, but I'm on your side. My parents . . . well . . . they force me to do what they say. If I don't, they beat me. They torture me. I don't get grounded. I get clubbed in the back of the head until I'm unconscious, then starved for a week."

Bella, ever the sensitive one, gasped, "That's awful!"

Alyssa rolled her eyes. "Please, you believe this guy? Ugh!"

She tore forward and raised her hand, ready to strike his face, but before she could, he grabbed her wrist with lightning-fast reflexes, pulled her in, and wrapped his arms around her.

At first, she started to squirm and fight her way free, but then it hit her. There was something very familiar about his tall, muscular figure. Even though she knew he was dangerous, she somehow felt safe and secure all of a sudden.

And then a whirlwind of memories hit her.

She was six and he was eight. They were sitting in her living room, just playing and laughing. Then, there was a sudden, loud thunderclap. Alyssa screamed and threw herself into those arms.

She was nine and he was eleven. She ran out of school crying because she'd gotten into a terrible fight with Hazel.

There he was, soothing her, putting those arms around her.

She was fourteen and he was sixteen. She jumped off a seven-story building and he wrapped those arms around her . . . steered her fall . . . saved her life.

"Oh my God."

Alyssa shoved Ricky away from her.

"You saved my life! Back at the mall. Why?"

"Because I'm your best friend. I told you, I'm not betraying you. I never was. I can't help who my parents are. I'm a Meladynian. I'm bound to this place. I can leave, but the second I fall asleep, I wake up back here."

"Oh, come on, Alyssa! He's telling the truth!" Bella insisted.

"Well . . . I . . ." Alyssa refused to believe him, but . . .

"Trust me, Lyssie. If I wanted to kill you, I could've a thousand times by now. I'm trying to help."

Alyssa wasn't giving in that easily. She crossed her arms and kicked him hard in the shin. "Well if you want us to trust you, you can start by getting us the heck out of here!"

"Unfortunately," he said, rubbing his leg where there promised to be a bruise, "there is only one way to break those bonds. The person who tied them has to . . ." He took a shaky breath. "The person who tied them has to die."

Alyssa's eyes widened. "And your own father . . ."

"Forced me to tie the ropes and enchant them. My life is bound to the ropes now. It's like a voodoo doll. Whatever happens to them happens to me."

"But . . . why?" asked Bella.

"I told you. My dad doesn't love me like yours does. I'm nothing more to him than a small pawn in his huge plot to conquer the world. Do you know why my name is Ricky, Alyssa? It means powerful. My father uses me to gain power. That's why I was born. Because my dad needed more soldiers. I mean nothing to him. Do you know what your name means? Truth. Because your parents trust you with their lives. You'll never back out on them, or lie to them, or betray them. My parents wouldn't trust me with a pen. My dad hates me."

Alyssa suddenly felt a pang in her heart for him. She didn't want to. He was so obviously a traitor! But still, she couldn't shake the nagging possibility that he might be telling the truth.

There had to be another way to get Hazel free. She couldn't kill Ricky, Meladynian or not. He was her best friend, and she loved him.

"Which is why he won't care if I do this." Ricky King unsheathed his sword, its wicked blade gleaming in the faint light. Alyssa realized what he was going to do a split second before he did it, and lunged to grab the weapon. But it was too late. Before she could take it from him, he had thrust it into his own gut and was on the ground, blood seeping from the fatal wound he had inflicted on himself.

CHAPTER 15

"RICKY! NO!"

All three girls screamed hysterically. "AAAHHHH! NO! RICKY!"

Ricky collapsed to the ground. He removed the sword and blood instantly started pouring from his wound. He scooted over slightly to be sure the blood stained the rope. Hazel's bonds loosened a bit; he was dying.

Alyssa dropped to her knees at Ricky's side. "No! No, Ricky, look at me! Look at me, Ricky, you're gonna be okay . . ."

But she could feel him going cold. She was losing him, and she knew it.

"Alyssa," he moaned. "Be strong. Untie her and get out of here. Her family is over that hill. Don't worry about me. Just go."

Tears welled up in Alyssa's eyes. "No," she pleaded. "No, don't talk like that. You're going to be okay. You are."

"Alyssa." It was even more difficult for him to speak now. "I love you. Will you go out with me?"

Through her tears she gave a half smile. "You bring it up now?" She leaned over and gently kissed his cold lips. She'd wanted to do that for so long. But she didn't feel happy now, the way she'd always imagined she would. She was more brokenhearted than any girl had ever been. She watched him struggle, watched the agony in his eyes, the violent jerks of his body. It tore her apart, but what could she do? She just pressed his hand against her heart, holding tight to it like she could hold him in this world, weeping uncontrollably. Then, with a final, laborious breath, his arm went limp against her and his body relaxed, no longer suffering.

Hazel slipped herself out of the bonds and they looked on in disbelief for a minute. Alyssa opened her mouth to speak, but all she could manage was a whimper. She couldn't bring herself to let go of him. Alyssa didn't know how much time had passed; each moment felt like an eternity. Her heart felt as if it were being ripped from her soul. It was so unreal. He was gone. How could he just be *gone*? He had saved her life multiple times. He had always been there for her. And he had died for her. It was her fault. She didn't feel sad or angry anymore. She just felt numb. Hazel finally mustered enough strength to place a hand on Alyssa's shoulder, speaking gently, her voice barely more than a whisper. "Alyssa, we have to get out of here. He's gone. Don't let him die in vain. We have to find my family."

Gathering all the strength in her, Alyssa finally dropped his hand, forcing her numb body to her feet, blinded by tears, nodding as years of memories with him flashed behind her eyes. She took several steps forward before realizing the others weren't following. "What . . . what are we doing?" Alyssa sniffled, blinking the tears out of her eyes in order to see. The sight before her was so petrifying she stopped abruptly in her tracks, and her brain almost couldn't comprehend what was happening. The cold eyes, the dark clothes, the evil smirk.

"Alyssa McCaw," he snarled.

"Karvokono," Alyssa whispered.

Chapter 16

"Why is my son dead?" He asked the question in a calm, controlled manner, as if he were asking why the pizza hadn't come yet: no misery, no rage.

Alyssa glared at him, nothing but pure fury in her eyes, fists clenching until her fingernails dug into her palms. "I killed him," she said without the slightest stutter.

"With his own sword?" he asked, raising an eyebrow.

She nodded.

"You're not as bad as I thought, kid. Though I must say, it is a shame you had to kill him. He proved quite useful, at times. But, of course, his main purpose was to keep an eye on you, and as you have wandered so naively into Meladyne, untrained and barely armed, I have no more use for him. Anyway, back down to business. Here's the deal. You give me the Key, you and all your little friends go free. You don't, I kill you and all my slaves. My slaves, as I am sure you know, are all people who I have snatched from families all over the world in attempts to find the Key. If you don't give me the Key, they die. If you do, they go free, and I never touch them again."

"We don't have the Key. Now leave us alone!" Bella shouted.

There was no fear left in either of them. Only hatred.

"Ah, you must be the little one. Isabelle, was it? Grab her." He snapped his fingers and two Meladynians appeared, seized the little girl roughly, and held their swords to her throat.

"Hey, let me go!" Bella squirmed, but could not break free.

Alyssa crossed her arms, remembering what the queen had said about not killing the bait.

"She's right. We don't have the Key. Search me."

"You don't have the Key? Well, then, I have no more use for you." He snapped his fingers and three more Meladynians seemed to materialize out of the darkness, forcing and pinning Alyssa, Hazel, and Bella to the ground, each with knives pressing into their throats.

"Kill them."

Alyssa closed her eyes and held her breath, whole body trembling violently in fear, and . . . nothing. No cold slit across her throat. Slowly she opened her eyes, almost too afraid to hope. And there they were. Oh no . . . Selena, Maegan, Caleb, Violet, Sylvie, Malcolm, all of them.

They all drew weapons, and with a battle cry in Sunolian that probably meant something like "we're gonna beat you!" charged down toward them. The Meladynians leapt off of the girls and prepared to fight. Hundreds more Meladynians appeared out of nowhere, swords at the ready.

Alyssa and her sister scrambled to their feet. Alyssa pulled her staff off her back.

"Hazel!" Alyssa shouted. "You have no weapon! Run! Find your family!"

"But . . . but . . . I . . . you . . ."

"Go!"

She stumbled to her feet and ran toward the hill, away from the battle.

As Alyssa charged down the hill, she let out a cry of anguish, putting all of her fear and rage and pain into it, no doubt sounding to those around her like a crazy person. She swung her staff around, whacking the Meladynians, knocking them unconscious. She felt a blade cut into her calf. She screamed, and stumbled, but forced herself to keep going. Her friends weren't doing badly, but there were too many Meladynians. Alyssa knew they couldn't take them all down alone. Then she realized she'd let her guard down thinking, and the Meladynian she was fighting cut a huge gash in her side. Screaming in pain like she'd never before felt, she fell to her knees. She had to keep going. Blinking black spots out of her vision, stumbling to stand back up, she was saved by Caleb, coming up from behind and killing her opponent.

"Never really liked him," he muttered. "You owe me one," he said, and ran off.

Alyssa had to do something. Her people were falling like dominos. The Key! She scanned the battle and quickly spotted Malcolm. He had the Key around his neck.

Malcolm, you idiot! she thought. But as Sylvie ran by her, she caught a glimpse of something silver around her neck. Could they really have . . .

"Selena, cover me!" Alyssa yelled.

Selena quickly obliged, dancing around her opponents like a ninja, bringing them quick and clean ends. Alyssa flew toward the tree Hazel had been tied to and climbed halfway up, hoisting her aching body with her arms, pushing upward with her legs. Blood continued to pour from her wounds, and she felt dizzy and lightheaded, but refused to stop, refused to be afraid. Surveying the scene, she realized everyone from Sunolia had a Silver Key chained around their necks. They were geniuses! Karvokono would never be able to tell which was the real Key because they had duplicated it so perfectly somehow. *Caleb,* Alyssa thought. *He's great with that stuff. Told me the first day I met him.*

She winced as she watched Maegan take a hard blow to the back and fall down. She could already see Sylvie on the ground. The false Keys had been torn from their necks. They couldn't fight forever.

Suddenly Alyssa knew what to do. Scurrying out of the tree, her feet slipping on the branches in her haste, she moved a fair distance from the battle, Selena still covering for her. Taking a deep breath, she held her hands up, palms skyward. Clearing her mind during this wasn't easy. Think about light. Only light.

Focus, Alyssa, focus, she told herself. *Breathe, relax. Get into the Neutral Zone, think about the ball of light. This isn't real, this battle isn't happening. There's no such thing as magic.* But try as she might, Alyssa was bursting with so many emotions clearing her mind seemed impossible. The thing she kept coming back to was Bella. She was so worried about Bella. *If only we were still at home. If only Bella and my parents and Hazel's family and Ricky were all at home right now, wrapped up in blankets, celebrating the New Year. We would be laughing and joking and singing. There would be good food and games and bright colors. They could be so happy* . . . Suddenly Alyssa felt a power surge. Her body filled with warmth and strength. She could feel it tingling in her fingertips, stronger than she had ever felt before. All the love and laughter and light in her mind seemed to melt into a radiance, a beautiful, astonishingly bright, shining light. The burning in her wounds seemed to dissolve, Alyssa felt amazing, better than she ever had in her life. She felt like she could rule the world.

Alyssa opened her eyes and thrust her hands forward. For a minute, she could see nothing. Only a blinding luminescence. Then, faster than she could blink, the light seemed to be sucked from the air and every last Meladynian lay on the ground, motionless. Karvokono was thrashing around on the ground, struggling, crying out in agony. Everyone watched as his pleas for help grew weaker, his twitching smaller, until his body lay still. The silence seemed to ring through the air, the tension so heavy it was nearly tangible.

And then a cheer broke out among her friends. It was over! They were free! They began to run toward each other, embracing and kissing and crying. The wounded were lifted gently off the ground and whispered to soothingly. Alyssa spotted Bella pushing herself up off the ground with effort. Alyssa's face broke into a relieved smile, and she took a step forward. But the second she shifted her weight, her legs gave out and her whole body collapsed. She remembered Malcolm's warning about using too much magic too quickly. The spell she had conjured had drained all the energy in her body, and now that the adrenaline had disappeared, the fatigue washed over her almost instantly. The world became fuzzy, and suddenly she was aware of a hand grabbing the back of her neck and dragging her away from her friends. A woman's hand. A cold hand. She knew who it was without even looking up.

Marvalonna.

All of her friends were already halfway out. *Good*, she thought. *Run. Go free. All of you.*

Violet turned and saw Alyssa, struggling relentlessly in Marvalonna's grasp, being hauled away. She shouted to her friends and they all turned around, saw what was happening, and started running back toward her. But halfway there, Violet stumbled backward like she had hit an invisible wall. All the others did the same. They couldn't get through to her.

Her friends banged on the invisible wall, yelling, but their voices were muffled as if on the other side of a glass window. Eventually they began looking at each other, shrugging, and turning away sadly.

But not Bella. She stood there staring blankly at her sister, a face that made Alyssa feel broken. She knew it was better this way; Bella would be safe in Sunolia. They would take the Key, kill Alyssa, and leave her sister alone. But she still couldn't bear to watch Bella like this. She was always so happy, so lighthearted. Never like this.

Sylvie put her hands on Bella's shoulders. Bella didn't move. She was just standing there, staring at Alyssa. Alyssa knew that feeling all too well, the feeling of utter hopelessness. No one could produce a spell stronger than the one Alyssa had. Alyssa was supposed to be their hope, their salvation. If she couldn't defeat Meladyne, no one could. And Alyssa could see that in Bella's face more than anyone's. Bella had been counting on her more than anyone ever had. Silent tears slipped down the little girl's face. Alyssa felt like she was watching her sister's heart break through her eyes.

Sylvie bent over and said something in her ear, but Bella shook her head, tears streaming down her cheeks. Caleb gestured backward and said something, and at that she ran up and banged on the wall, screaming hysterically.

The other two began dragging her backward, but she fought back with all her might. Alyssa couldn't hear her voice clearly, but she knew exactly what she was saying.

"No! Alyssa! Nooo! We can't leave her! Nooo! I want my sister! Give her back to me! No, Alyssa, no!"

This was the last thing Alyssa heard before the fuzziness in her head overcame her senses and she slipped into darkness as Marvalonna dragged her forcefully into Meladyne. Alone. Terrified. Weak. And completely helpless.

PART 2

CHAPTER 17

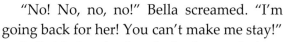

"No! No, no, no!" Bella screamed. "I'm going back for her! You can't make me stay!"

Bella McCaw lay beside the fire pit, kicking and screaming and clawing at the dirt with all her strength. Tears streamed down her face as she fought, her voice growing hoarse from screeching. "No, no, no!" was all she could say anymore.

She felt Sylvie's gentle hand stroking her cheek, but smacked it away. Bella leapt up and, once again, tried to make a run for it, but Violet thrust out her palm. Bella, once again, collided head on with the invisible barrier Violet had been using to trap her for the past thirty minutes.

"Bella, please calm down," Sylvie begged. "Shh, shh, we'll go back for her, I promise, but not now, dear. We're not strong enough yet."

But Bella refused to stop fighting. Sylvie glanced around hopelessly at her friends. Violet nodded toward Malcolm, and with a snap of his fingers, Bella's head hit the ground in an instant sleep.

* * *

Bella awakened in her sleeping bag, head throbbing. She let silent tears roll down her face for her sister. Oh, Alyssa! What could have happened to her? It was all Bella's fault and she knew it. She'd watched helplessly as she was dragged away and hadn't done anything to stop it.

Bella took a deep breath and shakily got to her feet. She exchanged her dirty, bloodstained clothes for fresh new ones and strapped her knives to her belt, one on each hip. She couldn't be afraid anymore, couldn't continue to feel sorry for herself. That wasn't what Alyssa would do. For once in her life, her older sister needed *her*, and she didn't intend to let her down.

I am going to learn to fight, and I am going to save my sister. And if it kills me . . . well, then, it kills me.

* * *

Outside her tent, Bella found Caleb, Malcolm, Violet, and Sylvie crowded tightly around a Sunolian speaking in hushed, urgent tones. Standing a bit outside of the cluster was Silent Selena, her stance tall and strong, gazing off into the distance. If only Bella could fight like her! Selena was like a ninja in battle, dancing around her opponents and shooting arrows through their hearts, then yanking the arrows out and reloading. She hadn't received even a scratch and still stood as beautiful as ever, black hair blowing around her in the gentle breeze, toned body outlined by her dark clothes. She was without a doubt Bella's role model.

Bella approached her slowly like one might approach a sleeping lion, as if there were a way to startle this young woman of steel.

"You were . . ." Bella cleared her throat. "You're an amazing fighter."

Selena nodded, slowly turning her head to lock eyes with the little girl. Her gaze was empty and blank, no trace of emotion anywhere in her eyes. Bella knew that look. It was the same one Alyssa had worn when Ricky had died. It was the same one Bella herself had made when Alyssa had been taken from her only hours ago. It was that feeling of complete numbness. When you've cried every tear out of your face and screamed until your voice is hoarse, you feel absolutely nothing. Because when given the choice between feeling the pain and feeling nothing, numbness suddenly sounds better than anything else. Bella hadn't realized it before because she had never felt that way, but now she could see it in Selena's eyes. What kind of life had this girl known before she came to Sunolia? What kind of horrors did she witness that would crush all the emotion out of her forever?

Bella cleared her throat, realizing she was staring. "Do you think you could help me find my sister?"

Something crossed Selena's face, something Bella had never seen there before. Just a flicker in her eyes, nothing more. Understanding. Sympathy. No, not sympathy— *empathy*. As if she knew how Bella felt, like she actually understood. She reached forward and touched the little girl's heart with her hand. Bella placed her tiny hand over Selena's, and for a moment they just stood there, searching each other's eyes for something deep inside that couldn't be found on the surface.

Then she heard a tiny sound from behind, like a clearing of the throat, and Bella turned to find all the others staring at them, the little Sunolian in front. Bella leapt back, looking around awkwardly as Selena resumed her blank stare at the mountains. Bella clearly wouldn't be receiving any more emotion from the older girl, but was glad they had connected. Now that Bella had been through a traumatic experience herself, she was beginning to see Selena as more of a human being and less of a stone-cold warrior princess.

"Good morning, my children. For our new young recruit," the Sunolian gestured to Bella, "my name is Morosa. I am one of the queen's most trusted advisors and have been appointed to watch over Aquamarinia. Keep an eye on things, so to speak." She looked identical to the other Sunolians except Morosa wore her hair in a high ponytail rather than two braids. "I've heard, obviously, of the awful event that occurred last night, and I am here to help in any way that I can. But first, I must ask; Caleb, where is your lovely girlfriend Maegan?"

Bella hadn't noticed her absence in all the chaos she had been causing. "She's in the infirmary," Caleb replied with difficulty. "She was wounded, maybe fatally, after the battle with Meladyne. The Sunolians are taking care of her, but we don't know if she'll make it yet." He turned away from the group, taking deep breaths, trying to fight the tears. Violet wrapped a comforting arm around his shoulders. It hurt Bella to watch him suffer, but at least Maegan had a chance. At least she wasn't in Meladyne being tortured or killed, like Alyssa was.

"I'm very sorry to hear that, Caleb. She's a kindhearted girl. Wish her my best, would you? Perhaps I will stop by to visit her later. All right then. Enough of that. Now I want to talk about the Silver Key. I have been informed that Malcolm currently possesses the Key. It needs to be kept somewhere safe where Meladyne cannot reach it."

"The Garden of the Dawn," Sylvie jumped in. "There's no safer place in the world."

Malcolm shook his head. "The Garden is the first place Meladyne will expect it to be. It needs to be kept somewhere unpredictable, somewhere they wouldn't think to look."

"As long as the queen resides there, the Meladynians cannot enter the Garden of the Dawn," Caleb pointed out.

"Only creatures of light can enter it. Everybody knows that."

"How difficult do you think it will be for Meladyne to penetrate the borders of the Garden if they unlock the power of the universe?" Malcolm argued back.

"If I may point out," Caleb said, "Meladyne can't gain that kind of power without the Silver Key. The walls of the Garden of the Dawn are completely impenetrable to them with the Key inside. They will never reach the Key there, and we can rest assured that it is safe."

"Touché," Malcolm gave in. "Garden of the Dawn it is."

"All right, then," said Morosa. "Are there any other objections?" No one spoke. "Very well then. Miss Rosa, if you would be kind enough to carry this to the queen." She handed the Key to Violet, who took it gingerly, the way one might handle a newborn child.

"Finally, we must decide what our next course of action will be. We can protect this Key, but Meladyne is at an advantage right now. We must get on top of Meladyne to discourage them, to convince them they could never win a war against us. Any suggestions?" It was quiet for a moment. This was the first time anyone had really said that word, the one everyone was thinking but no one had really managed to bring up: war.

Bella couldn't stand it any longer. "We have to save Alyssa!" she blurted out. "She's our best chance. Please."

Everyone turned to look at her. Blushing, she took a step back.

"Um, sorry," she said apologetically.

Morosa spoke gently to Bella. "Isabelle, we will do everything in our power to get your sister back, but you must understand that many great warriors have fallen in an attempt to rescue loved ones from Meladyne. I am told your sister is one of the most powerful warriors Sunolia has ever seen, and even she was ensnared by the same trap that defeated so many others. Right now, we must have a direct course of action to get us ahead of Meladyne. You mustn't forget—you are a child of light and dark too, and you are just as strong as she is. We still have hope. All right?"

"But . . . but Alyssa could put us ahead," Bella whispered, tears in her eyes.

"I'm sure she could. And I promise we will bring her back at any cost. You must have hope. Without hope we are nothing, Isabelle."

Bella nodded, and Morosa gave her a weak, sympathetic smile. Then she straightened and addressed the others, but Bella wasn't paying attention. She was staring up at the blue sky above. She couldn't cry anymore. Something changed inside of Bella that day; it was as if she grew twenty years older in that one moment. She would go to any lengths, kill any number of people, sacrifice her very soul to get her sister back. She wasn't Bella McCaw, first-grade ballerina anymore. She was Isabelle Dianna of Sunolia, young warrior, sister of Alyssa, daughter of Rebeccina and Perseus, the darkest and the lightest creatures ever to walk the earth. She was Isabelle—a revenge-hungry monster.

CHAPTER 18

Alyssa awoke with a start, gasping. A cold cloth touched her forehead.

"Shh, shh," a gentle voice soothed. "You're all right now. Don't be afraid."

As her vision slowly cleared, Alyssa could make out a young freckled face with pale blue eyes leaning over her.

"Matthew!" the child shouted in a high-pitched voice. "She's awake!"

Alyssa tenderly pushed her upper body off the ground into a sitting position, arms shaking with the effort. A very young girl knelt before her, tight, golden curls hanging around her thin, pale face. A tiny, clearly underfed body was covered in loose-fitting rags, a piece of the torn skirt in her hand. Alyssa figured that had been the cloth used to wipe her forehead.

"My name is Seraphina," she said, her voice soft and soothing. "Who are you?"

"Um . . . Alyssa," Alyssa replied.

Looking down to check for injuries, she found herself dressed in rags similar to Seraphina's. The wounds on her side, calf, and arm were wrapped in the same cloth.

"I'm sorry we had to change your clothes, but they made us. And there wasn't much left of your other clothes anyway. I bandaged your wounds too. They don't seem to be getting infected, which is good. The one on your side and leg are clearly from a sword—I've seen tons of those. But what is this little one on your arm? It looks kind of like a needle. Oh, Matthew! There you are!"

A boy, or really young man, rather, appeared at the little girl's side. His skin was naturally tan, very dark in contrast to Seraphina's snow-white complexion. His body, like the little girl's, was thin from lack of food, but muscular from years of hard labor. His sandy hair was long and wild, obviously needing a haircut, and he wore only raggedy shorts made of the same fabric as Alyssa's shift.

"Matthew, this is Alyssa," Seraphina informed him. "Alyssa, this is my older brother Matthew."

Alyssa nodded to acknowledge Matthew, then answered Seraphina's question. "Marvalonna put this thing in my arm, some kind of control device. Is there any way to get it out?"

Matthew offered a strong hand and helped Alyssa to her feet. He examined the scar on Alyssa's arm. "Possibly. If you had a sword, or a knife. But there's no way you could get your hands on one of those, trust me. I'm sorry this happened to you, Alyssa. I don't want to say I'm unhappy to meet you, but it's too bad we had to meet here."

"Matthew, she's different," Seraphina said urgently.

"What do you mean, she's different?" he asked, turning to his sister.

"She's not mortal. She's powerful. She's made of magic, blood and soul. And I can *see* her, Matthew. She shines brighter than anyone I've ever seen. But she also casts a shadow. A very dark shadow. I've never seen anything like her before. It's like she's half-light and half-dark or something."

"But that's impossible. She's mortal, just like us."

"No, Matthew, she isn't. I don't know what she is, but she's not mortal."

"Hey, uh, mind clueing me in here?" asked Alyssa, feeling awkward.

"My sister can tell when people are light or dark," Matthew explained, as if it made perfect sense.

"Once I've touched someone's skin, I can see it around them. Most mortals have almost no glow at all, especially nonbelievers. Students in Sunolia glow, as do all light magical creatures. Or at least they should. I was born here, you see."

"You were *born* here?" Alyssa asked incredulously.

Seraphina sighed. "Yes, and my mother died right afterward. My father might have returned to Sunolia, or he could have stayed at home, but I really don't know. He could be anywhere in the world. Matthew and my mom were captured before my mom even knew she was pregnant. My father doesn't even know I exist. Matthew's raised me for seven years, since he was ten."

The story made everything Alyssa had been fighting for seem so real, so important. This child was living proof of the cruelty of Meladyne.

"Well, anyway, light creatures glow. But Meladynians suck the light out of everything. This place is so dark I can hardly see anything. Flashlights, torches, fire; none of that stuff works for me. These dark people suck up all the light. I've been as good as blind my entire life."

She was American, Alyssa could tell now. Maybe Southern, but the accent was so faint she wasn't sure. Alyssa figured it must've been acquired from Matthew when she'd learned to talk. But she wasn't really American— she'd never *been* to America. She'd never seen anything outside of this place, had never felt anything but pain and suffering.

"But . . . but can you see now?" Alyssa wondered.

"Yes. You shine, you shine brighter than the sun Matthew's told me about. There's light radiating off you. It's amazing."

No wonder she's so pale! She's never even seen the sun.

Alyssa made a silent vow to herself to make sure this girl got to see the sun someday.

"But you said I cast a shadow."

"Yes, you do," Seraphina agreed. "Behind you there's a shadow. A real, real dark shadow that follows you around everywhere trying to absorb your light. Even darker than Marvalonna's. And then there's one part of you that's not light or dark, just mortal."

"And . . . and what part of me is that?" Alyssa asked, afraid of the answer.

In response, the little girl reached up a hand and pointed to Alyssa's heart. "You don't believe in magic, Alyssa. Not really. You're made of nothing but magic, but you try to tell yourself you're not. Somethin' inside you is holding you back. Your heart will never really be magic, dark or light, until you convince yourself you're not dreamin'. You'll never be as powerful as you could be because you don't believe, Alyssa—not really."

Alyssa looked at her confusedly. "You can tell all that just from looking at me? How?"

"Don't know," Matthew replied. "My sister was born that way. My mother could do it too. It's a gift that's been in our family for generations. My father told me our great-great-great-grandmother or something like that was a Sunolian who had a child with a mortal. My mother says it was given to our ancestors by Solaris herself in order to help people. No one really knows. She's just different. Just like you."

"But why, Matthew, why do we have to be different?" Alyssa begged.

He shook his head. "I don't know, Alyssa. I just don't know."

"Did you feel weird when you got here? Like you were really angry and sad and miserable all at the same time?" Seraphina inquired. "Like you wanted to kill someone?"

Alyssa furrowed her brow. "Yeah, actually, I did. Why?"

"It happens to me, on and off. Something about the magic inside you. It reacts to the magic in this place."

Alyssa thought back to the first time she'd entered Sunolia. "You know, something like that happened to me in Sunolia. Except it was the opposite. There, I felt really happy and content, like everything would be okay."

Matthew nodded. "That's magic for you. I'd like to go to Sunolia. My family has been trained there for centuries. My parents told me they'd take me there when I turned sixteen, but they never got the chance. I've heard so much about it."

"It's pretty cool. But—"

All of a sudden, a sharp, unbearable pain shot through Alyssa's head, cutting her off midsentence. Screaming, her knees buckled, her body smacking the cold, hard ground. She began to thrash around uncontrollably, the pain blinding her. It throbbed like nothing she'd ever felt before, allowing her only one clear thought: *make it stop.*

"Alyssa!" Seraphina cried, sounding terrified.

"Oh no," Matthew moaned. "What has Marvalonna done this time?"

All Alyssa could feel was pain. Her vision began to go blurry. *I'm dying,* she thought miserably. *I'm really dying. Oh, why can't I be dead yet? Please, just let this end, no more pain, please, please . . .*

Suddenly Alyssa found herself on her feet, though she couldn't remember standing up. Her vocal cords were muttering foreign things in a harsh language, words she'd never heard and didn't know the meaning of. A sword appeared in her hand, a long, gleaming, silver blade. The thing was so heavy, Alyssa shouldn't have even been able to lift it, but her arm held it with ease. Her legs were running toward Matthew at speeds even she shouldn't have been able to manage.

No! What am I doing? Alyssa tried as hard as she possibly could to stop, but she had no control over her legs anymore. Black spots appeared on the edges of her vision. *I'm going to die, why can't I just die? What am I doing?*

No doubt recognizing the wild, terrified look in Alyssa's eyes (the only things she seemed to have control of), Matthew grabbed his little sister's hand.

"Run, Phina, run!"

Seraphina fought against his grip, trying to reach Alyssa.

"No! Alyssa!" she cried, tears streaming down her face.

"There's nothing you can do for her anymore!"

No, don't leave me, Matthew! I'm dying! You have to help me!

Panicked, he scooped his sister into his arms and took off in the opposite direction as fast as he could, Seraphina kicking and fighting like a toddler the whole way.

Alyssa's arm raised the sword, her mouth opening to yell "*wan aga saku,*" completely alien words. Upon her command, the sword transformed into a beautiful silver bow. Reaching behind her back to the quiver of arrows her arm knew would be there, she loaded her bow. She'd always sucked at archery. She had never once hit a target. But this time, still running, her arm pulled back and released the arrow at Matthew.

The arrow pierced his calf, and he fell to the ground, his little sister tumbling out of his arms. He desperately tried to stand up, clawing at the hard ground, but Alyssa was on him in seconds. Another stab of pain burst through her skull, so violent her vision went dark. She couldn't see a thing but could still feel the bow in her hand, still hear the terrified, panting breaths of the children. But just as quickly as it had appeared, the pain vanished, and Alyssa began to speak. But it was the Dark Queen's voice that escaped Alyssa's lips, not her own.

"About time I killed you," Alyssa said icily. Even without the pain, she wished she were dead. She knew what was going to happen, what Marvalonna was going to make her do. "You should consider it an honor to be this darling little girl's first kill."

"Stop it, Marvalonna," Matthew begged, a hard edge in his trembling voice. "Please, Alyssa, I know this isn't you. Focus. Listen to my voice. You can fight this. Do you have a family? Think about them. Think about getting back to them. I know, Phina, but please, you have to run! Leave me, I'll be fine. Go find Miss Brynn, she'll take care of you." He took his sister's hands and looked her in the eye, pleading, his voice cracking from the tears. "I can't lose you, please, you have to get away! I've lost everything else already. Please, you're all I have left! Run away, run for me!"

Alyssa fought against the force inside her with all she had. Seraphina was so little . . . as little as Bella. How was she supposed to fight herself? It was inside her. *Get out of my head, get out of my head, get out of my head,* she begged. But it wasn't enough. She had learned to oppose physical forces with physical strength, but she had never been taught anything like this. She simply couldn't hold up. *I'm sorry, Matthew, I'm so, so sorry . . .*

Marvalonna laughed from within her. "You can't do anything about it. Unless, of course, you want to kill Miss McCaw for me. Then you could go free."

Yes, Matthew. Just kill me, I won't mind. Kill me and go free. Tell Bella I love her. But of course she knew that Matthew wouldn't hurt her. He'd let her take his life to spare her own. How many people would she hurt for herself? She knew whatever she was doing now wasn't voluntary; it was Marvalonna working through her. But still, Alyssa had to notice—everyone kept sacrificing themselves for her, even people she had just met.

"Free to do what, witch? Be your prisoner? At least if I'm dead I'll be free. And come on, Phina, run! You'll get out of here eventually, just run!" Matthew cried.

"No," the girl stated firmly. "I'm not leaving you, Matthew. You're all I have."

Oh, Bella . . . I'd die before I willingly hurt this girl. But the monster controlling her had other plans.

"Aw, isn't that sweet," she purred. "He wants to save the little girl. 'Run, Phina, run,'" she mocked. "Alyssa has a sister too. Isabelle, isn't it?"

No! Don't you dare say Bella's name! You have no right! Alyssa wanted to hurt her now more than ever. But the words were coming from her own lips.

"You know what? Change of plans, Matthew Cade. You can watch your dear little sister die first. Then you can go with her."

"No!" Matthew cried.

"Oh, don't worry, dear," Alyssa snarled. "I know you wanted to go first, but life just isn't fair sometimes, is it?" She felt herself giving him a mock sympathetic look. The bow in her hand molded back into a sword. Every molecule in her body fighting, struggling, screaming, she advanced in the direction of Seraphina.

Alyssa could hear Seraphina's tiny footsteps fleeing, stumbling away, but she should have done that a long time ago. It was far too late for that. Taking advantage of all those years of track, Alyssa chased blindly after the girl, caught her arm, threw her forcefully onto the ground, and stabbed the knife into her in one swift motion. Matthew and Phina both released the most tortured, heart-shattering shrieks Alyssa could ever have imagined in her worst nightmare. Seraphina's high-pitched cry of pain mingling with Matthew's miserable, nothing-to-live-for wail of loss created a piercing sound powerful enough to make the devil himself cry. It rung in Alyssa's ears, carving into her heart, eating away at her soul, refusing to cease. Still holding the handle of the sword, she twisted it, and the cry of pain out of Seraphina compared with nothing.

Tell me I'm dreaming, Alyssa thought. *I did not just kill a little girl.*

Heart throbbing, Alyssa's legs carried her toward the sounds of Matthew's uncontrolled sobbing on the ground. She could tell he was looking at her, could feel his dark eyes on her light ones. *I can't see though, no—I can't see anything but darkness.*

"Go ahead," he croaked miserably, choking on every word. "I have nothing to live for anymore. She was all I had."

Alyssa couldn't even describe in words the hurt she felt as she jabbed the sword into his gut. There was no need for twisting this time. There was no way she could've possibly hurt him any more than she already had.

The pressure in Alyssa's head finally ceased, and she fell to the ground, gasping for air. She could once again see her surroundings. She looked up and watched the last trace of life slip from his eyes. His body went limp, just like Ricky's had. *At least he can't feel any more pain. He's with his sister and mother now. He can be somewhere that's light again, just like he wanted. Seraphina will see light more beautiful than the sun now. They won't suffer anymore.*

Alyssa tried with everything in her being to make herself believe that, but she just couldn't. Maybe it was true, but that didn't help her feel better. Influenced or not, willing or not, it was *her* hand that had killed them. Children. The sword disappeared from her hand, and she collapsed to the ground, sobbing. Seraphina, who was so young, had an entire life ahead of her, who had never even seen the sun. Matthew, who had raised his sister from a baby in this horrible, dark land. There was a girl for him somewhere he would never marry, children that would never be born. And she had killed both of them. Firsthand. And she hadn't been strong enough to resist the control.

Sobs still racking her body, she forced herself to her feet, picking up Seraphina's limp body. She weighed so much less than Bella, having been starved her whole life. Alyssa laid her down beside her brother. She folded the little girl's hands over her chest and ran her fingers gently over her eyes, closing them. She spread the little girl's hair around her shoulders, making her look like Sleeping Beauty. She placed one of Matthew's arms to his side and the other under his sister's cheek. Then she closed his eyes too.

* * *

For what felt like hours Alyssa sat there, sobbing. Anyone could've told her it wasn't her fault, but anyone would've felt the same in her place. Well, not *anyone*. Not Marvalonna. *I am going to kill her,* she swore, once again looking at Seraphina and Matthew.

And then she was there. Marvalonna. She appeared out of nowhere, looming over Alyssa's weak body.

"Well done, Miss McCaw. Well done indeed. I see you're not as strong as they say. But that's good though, dear. That's very good."

Alyssa went at her with both fists. Something inside her had snapped. She no longer cared what happened to herself; all she wanted was to kill Marvalonna. In all her rage and adrenaline, she punched upward at the queen, striking her jaw, the hardest she had ever hit anyone in her life, screaming in anguish and fury. Without a second's pause for reaction, Alyssa's left fist followed her right, slamming into the woman's nose. It hurt Alyssa's hand, and she could hear her knuckles make a sick cracking sound, but Alyssa couldn't feel the pain. Marvalonna winced, holding up a hand to stifle the blood leaking from her nose.

"*Pyra radona!*" Alyssa screamed, remembering a spell Sylvie had taught her.

Little fireballs the size of baseballs shot out of her palms directly toward Marvalonna. The queen simply held up the hand that wasn't on her nose, creating a magical shield between herself and Alyssa, vaporizing the fireballs.

"Oh, you are a dark one when you let it take over you. Your mother was like that. She was beautiful. It's too bad she ran away with that foolish man. You might've been beautiful too, had your father not given you that dreadful light hair. But no matter. You can be like me too. You have darkness in you, Alyssa, my niece. Don't be stupid like your mother was and deny power. Embrace it, Alyssa. Let the darkness into your heart and show the world what you can do. It is your destiny, your birthright."

"My mother was never like you, you demon!" She pointed at Matthew and Seraphina, her voice shaking with rage. "Look at them. Look at what you've done. To children! How can you live with yourself? You deserve to die; you deserve something worse than death."

Marvalonna didn't look affected by the outburst. In fact, she probably got this kind of reaction all the time. But Alyssa was fired up now that she'd started. She couldn't stop yelling, and she had no reason to. This woman had taken her friends, her family, her life, her hope. And Alyssa wasn't going to lie down and take it anymore.

"You aren't even human. Humans have souls. *Humans* cannot *kill* innocent children! You are no person. You are a monster! I will never, ever do anything that might benefit you in any way, let alone join you! You'll regret this. Just wait. I'M NOT AFRAID OF YOU!"

"Yes, yes, that's very nice, dear. Now, if you're finished condemning me, I have a proposal for you," Marvalonna replied calmly, speaking as if to a small child.

"Propose away, then, because I have better things to do than listen to you!" Alyssa cried. She wasn't scared anymore, just filled with rage, and it was all spilling out now onto this woman—this *thing*—who deserved it more than anyone.

"Now that you've had a taste of what it's like to be controlled, I give you two options. One: I continue to control you and kill everyone in my path until I find the Key. Or two: You return to Sunolia, get the Key, and bring it back to me. I remove the device from your arm, and you and your dear little sister go free, unharmed. I'll never bother either of you again unless you come to me first. Consider wisely."

Alyssa thought it over, trying to restrain her burning anger for long enough to make a rational decision. Of course she didn't want to give Marvalonna the Key, but she couldn't be controlled again like she had been today. And going back to Sunolia, seeing real light again, sounded like heaven.

"Fine. But I have two conditions," she replied.

Marvalonna raised an eyebrow. "Oh? And if I don't meet these conditions?"

Remembering the spell Alyssa had cast when being controlled, a deadly Meladynian sword appeared in her hand. The girl held it out, the point toward her own throat. "Then you lose your primary weapon." Alyssa wasn't bluffing, and Marvalonna knew it too. There was nothing Alyssa wanted more at that moment than to die, and the only reason she hadn't sliced her own throat yet was because she needed to protect Bella.

An amused look danced in the monster's eyes. "Well played. Name your terms."

Alyssa wanted so badly to attack the Dark Queen with her sword, but she knew Marvalonna could reject it with simple magic. She couldn't beat Marvalonna in a fight, especially with her minions all over the place.

"I want my staff back." Instantaneously, Alyssa's wonderful, old, familiar staff appeared strapped to her back. "And I want them," she gestured at the children, "to be revived. I know you can do it. Bringing back the dead is dark, dark stuff. Your specialty."

She waved a hand dismissively. "I have no use for them. I can't believe they survived, especially that baby, after I killed their mother, but oh well. They were too small anyway."

She held out her hand and a small flask appeared in it, filled with a blood-red liquid. "Put a drop of your blood into this and pour it down their throats. You have magical blood from your parents. It will restore life in them. With the help of a dark spell and my influence, of course."

Alyssa cut open her finger with the sword and did as she'd said. Seraphina bolted up gasping, the wound on her stomach growing smaller and disappearing. "Alyssa? What? How? I don't understand . . ."

Matthew's eyes flung open, gasping as well. "Alyssa, what—Phina!" He pulled his sister into his arms, tears running down his face. Relief flooded through Alyssa as she watched the color return to their young faces.

"All right, go now. And take them with you, I don't need them anymore. But you'd better not fail me. I'll know, Alyssa. I will."

With one more death glare and swear, Alyssa headed back to Sunolia with her newly revived friends to retrieve the Silver Key.

CHAPTER 19

Isabelle pulled her arrow back. Steady, aim, fire! Miss. Steady, aim, fire! Almost. One more time. Steady . . . aim . . . fire! Bull's-eye!

"Beautiful, Bella, beautiful!" Violet cried. "You've improved so much! Excellent!"

"Wow, Bella, you're doing great," Caleb commented. "I wish I could shoot like that."

"It's Isabelle," she spat coldly with a glare.

She fired a bull's-eye into Caleb's target, turned on her heel, and strode off, ignoring the fact she was supposed to be practicing.

Caleb turned to Violet, who was standing beside him supervising with her arms folded. "What is with her lately? She's acting like you."

"What's that supposed to mean?" she snapped, giving him a threatening look.

"I mean she snaps at everyone who talks to her, she won't let anybody call her 'Bella' anymore, she stays out here training after we're asleep and before we're awake, and she won't even smile. What's up with her?"

"I do not act like that!"

"Uh-huh. Of course you don't. But that's not the point. I'm worried about her."

"She just misses her sister. Give her a little time, Caleb. We've all been through this."

Caleb shook his head. "It has to be more than that."

Isabelle made her way to the opposite end of the training field, where she found Malcolm and Sylvie engaged in an intense duel of swords. Isabelle watched intently as Malcolm slid his sword down Sylvie's blade, flicked his wrist, and in one swift motion held both weapons in his grasp. Sylvie bent over, panting, wiping the sweat off her face with a washcloth. "Nice one, Sylvie," Malcolm praised, grabbing her hand and giving it a friendly shake. "You wanna go again?"

"Yeah, sure, okay. Give me a second."

"You ready? Three, two, one—go!"

They raised their swords, and Malcolm advanced, swinging his forward at Sylvie. But Sylvie didn't move to defend herself; she didn't even blink. The blade slashed a deep cut in her cheek, and Malcolm stumbled backward, puzzled. "Sylvie, are you all—" It was then that he spotted Isabelle, standing, palms forward, glaring at him.

"Whoa, Bells," Caleb praised. "I didn't know you could do freezing charms already. Cool."

Isabelle turned on her heel and strutted off, leaving a puzzled Caleb behind. *Ugh, this is boring,* she thought. *I wanna go somewhere with some real competition.* She glanced at the thick forest looming over her, remembering Violet's strict insistence to stay on the path and to go straight to the arena without stopping or looking around. *Hmmm . . .*

It didn't take long. Almost immediately after Isabelle's foot had left the path, a hound twice the size of a wolf with a hideous, snarling face vaulted out of a nearby bush. It bared its sharp, deadly fangs at her, growling in the back of its throat. It had the build of a wolf with muscular legs and a strong body. Its head was almost the size of Isabelle's entire body. A *necron,* she suddenly remembered it was called. Sylvie had told her stories about them. She had used the word *big. Big* didn't even scratch the surface of this beast.

Suddenly realizing this was a bad idea, the girl began to back away meekly toward the arena. She could hear her heart pounding in her ears. There was a rustling sound and she whipped around to face another necron behind her. She held up her knives weakly, but dropped them and screamed as two more appeared on either side of her. There was no hope of running or fighting. This was the end. She had gotten herself killed for no reason. *Stupid.* She just hoped the others would go back for Alyssa . . .

Just then an arrow soared downward at an angle, seemingly coming from the sky. It hit a necron straight through the eye—a perfect shot. For a moment it stumbled, confused. The creature stared at her for a moment, blinking huge, puppy-dog eyes, and she almost felt bad for it. Then, to Isabelle's utter confusion, the creature disintegrated before her eyes, crumbling into thousands of miniscule particles until all that remained was a small mound of dust at her feet.

Bewildered, Isabelle watched as three more arrows whistled through the air, one after the other, hitting each of the other three monsters in the eye. They all crumbled the same way the first one had. Then she stood alone in the woods, stunned.

She heard a small noise behind her, like a chipmunk had leapt from a tree. Isabelle whirled around to meet an arrow aimed straight at her nose, so close she had to cross her eyes to see the tip. Frightened, she held her hands up and froze. Whatever had killed the necrons had perfect aim. It wasn't going to miss two inches from her face.

Then the arrow lowered and Isabelle stood staring into the dark eyes of Silent Selena. Selena frowned at her, retrieved her arrows, and trotted deeper into the forest, not making a sound as her feet hit the ground.

Isabelle dashed back across the arena and to the relative safety of her small tent, still gasping for air.

She ate dinner alone on the hill, denying all her friends' requests to come sit with them around the pit. Then she crawled into her sleeping bag miserably, pretending she was sleeping as she listened to the others squealing with delight in the rain.

Hours after her friends had all fallen asleep, her strength finally gave in and the little girl closed her eyes.

* * *

Meladynians were riding bareback on necrons. There were millions of them chasing Alyssa through the downtown mall.

"Bella!" she was screaming. "Help me!"

Isabelle stood to the side, watching helplessly as Sylvie held her back.

"We have to help her!" Isabelle screamed.

"No! It's too dangerous! Bella, no! There's nothing you can do for her!" Sylvie cried, holding her back firmly.

She watched as the hounds chased her sister off the balcony, and as she fell, Isabelle could hear Alyssa's piercing screams . . .

Isabelle awakened in the middle of the night, still screaming and crying. Throwing her shoes on, she rushed out of her tent, just wanting fresh air on her face. She couldn't let anything happen to Alyssa. She just couldn't. She made her way to Caleb's tent and let herself in without even knocking.

"Caleb," she hissed, shaking him awake.

"What are . . . Bella? Why are you in my tent?"

"Put a shirt on, Caleb. We need to talk."

CHAPTER 20

Alyssa stood in her front yard regarding the small, wooden trapdoor lodged in the ground. She hadn't even considered the fact that, as she no longer possessed the Key, she couldn't enter the only place she was really safe.

She glanced longingly back at her house, the one she'd lived in for so long. It was so painfully familiar—old green shutters, cherry-wood siding, windows shut and locked firmly in order to keep out the cold. It was so close . . . Though her new friends were alive again now, she still had tears brimming in her eyes threatening to spill over just from the thought of what she had done to them. But what about her parents? They were okay, weren't they? What if Meladyne had gotten to them? All heredity set aside, they were still her parents and she would never stop caring about them. Oh, forget it! She obviously couldn't get into Sunolia, and there was no point staying out in the cold, so Alyssa resolved to spend what little time she had left in what she considered the most wonderful place on earth—home.

"Come on, you guys," she said to Seraphina and Matthew behind her. "We're going to my home now."

But when she turned to face them, Seraphina and Matthew stood gazing up toward the sky, eyes fixated on the light, appearing mesmerized. The sun was just beginning to rise, picturesque pinks and purples and oranges streaking across the heavens like a perfectly shaded painting.

"So that's the sun," the little girl whispered, entranced.

Her brother put an arm around her, pulling her in close. "It's never looked more beautiful," he agreed.

"At the end of every day the sun goes down and there are beautiful colors in the sky," Alyssa explained, remembering what Seraphina had said about being born in Meladyne and never having seen the sun.

"But where does it go?" she inquired, looking a bit worried.

"To the other side of the world so the other people can see it. That's when it gets dark outside and we go to sleep. But then the next morning, the sun rises again here and the people on the other side of the world go to sleep and we wake up. The sunrise is even prettier than the sunset sometimes," Alyssa told her.

"Really? It does that every day?" Seraphina asked, eyes sparkling in wonder and amazement.

"Every day," Alyssa said, smiling herself and brushing away tears. "Now come inside with me. This is the house I usually live in. You can meet my parents. Don't stare at the sun for too long, Phina. It's bad for your eyes."

"It's been seven years," Matthew whispered, tearing his eyes from the sky with difficulty. "Alyssa, do you think we'll be able to find my dad? As far as I know, he's still out here in the Mortal World. He doesn't even know Seraphina exists. He has no idea where we've been. Anything could've happened to him."

Alyssa put a hand on his shoulder, a comforting, sympathetic look in her eyes. "Matthew, we can go find your father when all of this is over. But right now it's not safe out here for anyone. You'll have to come to Sunolia with me once I figure out a way to get in. You and your sister will be safe there. I'm sorry."

Matthew nodded. "It's okay, I understand. We're free. I can't complain now."

Alyssa gave him a weak smile, squeezed his shoulder, and flung the door open, letting the warm feeling spread over her. *Yes.* How wonderful it looked! There was the TV her father had bought without her mother's permission, the living room decorated by deep-red paint and dark-brown furniture, the pet turtle Bella had received for her birthday, the dining room table that proudly wore a winter-themed tablecloth. She'd never seen a more welcome sight.

"Mom!" she yelled, overjoyed voice echoing off the walls. "Daddy! I'm home!"

And then there they were. Brown hair, dark eyes, young, beautiful. Bags under their red-rimmed eyes from sleep deprivation and weeping. Her parents. Not her biological parents, but her *real* parents—the ones who'd raised her, fed her, driven her, loved her. The ones who'd come to every track meet, who'd returned home every day for her, who'd kissed her before bed every night. Her parents, who'd never leave her for anything.

It really wasn't fair for Alyssa to blame her actual, biological parents for leaving, and she knew that. But at that moment, she didn't care in the slightest.

The next few minutes were a blur of hugs and kisses and tears and relief. Alyssa had never felt so happy in her life, and she didn't think she ever would again. It was as if a million weights had been lifted from her chest, as if she had been drowning but hadn't realized it until she could breathe again. Never before had she understood exactly what her parents meant to her.

When they broke apart at last, still laughing with joy as tears leaked out of the corners of her eyes, Alyssa introduced her new friends. Her parents seemed confused but not concerned about their presence, acknowledging them only with a nod. Her mother, turning her attention back to Alyssa, took Alyssa's face in her hands and looked hard into her eyes. She spoke with a slow, calm voice, though Alyssa could hear an edge in it. "Alyssa, where is your sister?"

"She's safe for now," Alyssa assured them, thankful she didn't have to lie. "But I need to get to her."

"But where *is* she, Alyssa?" her father persisted, worry lines forming on his brow. "What do you mean she's safe *for now*?"

"It's a very, very long story and I will explain later," Alyssa replied, taking her father's hand reassuringly. "But Bella is safe and I will get to her, I promise."

"Alyssa, please," her mother begged, beginning to break. "You have no idea what I've been through worrying about you two! And you acted so strange before you disappeared. Please, where is Bella? You can tell me anything, don't be afraid. And what are you wearing? What happened to your leg? Where have you been for the past week and a half? You look like a zombie."

"That's part of the long story," Alyssa mumbled, growing weary of the questioning. Now that she'd overcome all her emotions and knew she was safe, she realized she was exhausted. Releasing her father, she grasped both of her mother's hands, controlling her tone as best she could. "Mom. I know you're worried about Bella. I get it. But you have to believe me when I tell you she is okay. I can't tell you anything now, but she's safe. She's with some really good people who are taking care of her, and they are going to bring her back unharmed. But for right now, I need you to trust me. I know it's hard. But you always said you trusted me, so for right now I need you to show me that trust. I will explain everything later. But right now I need to sleep. Please."

Alyssa could see the panic in her mother's eyes and couldn't even imagine how difficult it must be for her, not knowing where her little girl was. But something in her must have truly trusted Alyssa. Something in her knew that her practical, scientific, no-nonsense daughter would not make anything up, especially not something that serious. Martha sighed. "Alyssa, I am going to decide to trust you because I can't see what other option I have. You have never told me a lie. But just promise me you will explain everything in the morning. Promise me you will tell me where Bella is tomorrow. Okay?" Alyssa nodded. "Okay. Come with me and we'll get you fixed up."

"But my friends—"

"Can sleep in Bella's room. Don't worry about them. Just go with your mother, Lyssie. I love you," her father said, ruffling her hair like he had when she was little.

In a daze, Alyssa followed her mother upstairs. In the bathroom, as her mom peeled the bandage off her side, she jumped, placing a hand over her heart and gasping. Looking in the mirror, Alyssa winced. She hadn't realized how deep the gash was. The one in her leg wasn't much better.

"What happened to you?" she cried, an edge of hysteria in her voice.

"Sword," Alyssa muttered, really just wanting to go to bed.

"A sword!" She'd officially crossed over the hysteria line now. "Whose sword? Where'd you get this? Is Bella still there? Alyssa, talk to me!"

"Mom, calm down. I already told you Bella's in a very safe place, and I promise she'll be fine, and I'm fine now, so please just relax, okay?"

"And what's this for? A *staff*?! Is there a war going on that I don't know about? Alyssa! Who are those other kids? Tell me!"

Alyssa snapped then. It was cruel, and she regretted it instantly afterward, but after all she'd been through, she had not come home to be yelled at.

"Bella's in a magical sun-world under our front yard, and she's learning how to fight with kids and fairies and sprites and spirits and stuff. I was trapped in an evil moon-world that captured Hazel and me and my brother and a bunch of other people. I have a control device in my arm that's gonna kill me in twenty-eight days, and I can't get back to Sunolia because I don't have the Key, which I have to get back to Meladyne or they will kill Bella and my friends and my real parents, who are trapped in Sunolia. Now we're all gonna die and the world's gonna end, and everyone's counting on me and I can't do anything about it!" She was screaming now and crying, too. She'd never realized exactly how bad this all was until she laid it out in the open.

"Oh dear, what did they do to you?" Mom asked, crying herself. "Did they do something to your mind, too?"

"No, please! Listen to me! Mama, please, I'm not crazy! Please . . . just listen to me."

Alyssa slipped down onto the floor and sobbed out everything she'd been holding in. She couldn't be strong for everyone.

"I killed them, Mama. They're back now, but still . . . I killed them," she whispered. "Both of them. She . . . she's so young. She looks like me. If I hadn't been able to get that potion to bring them back . . ."

"Shh, shh," her mother soothed. "You're okay now. Come here."

Her mother clearly didn't believe a word she was saying, but it didn't matter anymore. Alyssa moved mechanically, just letting her mom guide her. She was placed in a tub of warm water, her hair washed thoroughly in soapy water. She slid down in the water, groaning because it felt like heaven. Her mother massaged shampoo through her hair, stroked her face with a washcloth.

Alyssa allowed herself to be dried and dressed and put to bed. The instant she was left alone to sink down into the first mattress she had slept on in weeks, she fell into a deep slumber. And she didn't awaken until she heard the bloodcurdling screams ringing through the house.

CHAPTER 21

Isabelle stood with every inch of her body covered by weapons. Knives in her boots, swords sheathed at her sides, spears in her jacket, and a *kan*—a type of twisted, deadly, poisonous blade—in her hand. Her backpack was stuffed with potions, antidotes, poisons, and remedies, as well as food, water, and first-aid supplies.

She stood with Caleb and Silent Selena, both of them equally well armed. Though the sky shone just as brilliant and azure as always, the tiny silver hands reflecting light back at Isabelle from her watch read 2:23 a.m.

"Everybody ready?" Isabelle whispered.

They gave silent, sleepy nods and followed Isabelle across the meadow, careful not to make any noise in order to keep from rousing the others. As they traveled, everyone ate a quick breakfast of granola bars from Isabelle's bag, and then paraded on in drowsy silence for about an hour. Eventually Caleb began to grow bored and decided to play with a potion he had in his bag. "It's called a Desirable Potion," he explained to the two girls, though he might as well have been talking to himself. "One drop of this and even a water spirit would fall for me."

"Mmhmm," Isabelle muttered, glancing at the map in her hands, not even looking up.

"You know what I think? I think you don't believe me. I'll prove it to you, just watch. I'm drinking it now."

Isabelle glimpsed Caleb for a second, and he did appear a bit more attractive, though not nearly enough to distract her from her mission. But it was Selena's reaction that bewildered her.

Selena dropped everything she was holding and gaped. For a moment, she just stood there, gazing at his face longingly. Isabelle had never in her life beheld such a broken expression, so much pain in one person's eyes. It was heart wrenching, as if all the torment in the world had been forced upon her shoulders all at once. Reaching a quavering hand out, Selena stroked her fingers lightly down Caleb's cheek, her breath growing ragged and forced, like she was battling everything inside herself not to cry. Caleb, like Isabelle, just stood stock still, perplexed. "Selena?" he whispered, trying to keep his voice gentle but unable to conceal the edge of incredulity. "Are you . . .?" Selena gasped, seeming to snap back into reality. Whipping around to hide her face from the others, Isabelle could swear she brushed a tear off her cheek.

What was that about? she wondered, as the young woman bent to retrieve her things. Selena—who'd never shown so much as a trace of emotion on her stone-carved face—crying because of a simple potion? Isabelle didn't know what her friend saw when she looked at Caleb, but there must have been a horrifically painful history there she didn't know about. Isabelle felt suddenly guilty for never having reached out, never having tried to help . . . But how could she have known?

They resumed their awkward, tense silence, padding along through fields and over hills for hours until at last they reached their destination: the Garden of the Dawn. By the time the trio stepped into the crimson forest, Isabelle's watch read 5:34.

"Ready?" Isabelle looked at Caleb.

"We'll get in *so* much trouble for this."

"Not if we succeed," she argued.

"Are you sure the queen won't just give us the Key?"

"We talked about this last night, Caleb. She'll never let us leave, not after what happened to Alyssa. This is the only way."

"Yeah, okay. I just wish we didn't have to do it like this," Caleb sighed, assuming his position before the weeping willow and retrieving a potion from his bag. Isabelle glanced up at Selena, who was crouching in a tree high overhead, looking ready.

"Three . . . two . . . one . . . go!"

Isabelle dashed into the garden, tears she'd been working up for a while running down her cheeks. The lovely queen rested in the grass, legs tucked underneath her, running a brush through her layers of golden hair. Upon seeing Isabelle's mock frightened face, the hairbrush fell from her hand, and with an elegant flutter of her dazzling, aurous wings, she was on her feet. Her action stance was delicate but determined, her arms slightly extended from her sides, weight resting on the balls of her small feet.

"Oh, dear queen, please help me!" Isabelle cried dramatically, clearly not at all worried about laying it on too thick. "It's Caleb, he's . . . he's . . ." She was all out sobbing now. "He's hurt so badly! Please, Your Highness, he needs your help! Please!"

Caleb, now lying on his back curled in a ball, Blood Potion poured all over his leg, let out a convincing moan and yelp of pain. Blood Potion wasn't the red paint you bought at Lowe's. This stuff looked, smelled, and tasted like blood. It also made the illusion of a very realistic deadly gash on his leg. Cressidalaina emerged hurriedly from the garden, for despite the queen's wisdom, age, and experience, even she could not resist the desperate pleas of a child. She rushed toward Caleb, still moaning and crying and making a scene of himself.

As the queen bent over the boy, Selena looked down to Isabelle, who gave a slight nod. She sprang from her hiding place and jammed a needle into the back of the queen's arm. Isabelle did her best to catch her as she fainted backward, stumbling a bit under her weight.

"Okay, well done. You two go look for—"

"Wait, it's around her neck!" Caleb announced.

Bending over, he lifted her head gently, unclasping the chain around Cressidalaina's neck. He tossed the Silver Key to Isabelle, and she smiled triumphantly at her prize. Then Caleb scooped the queen off the ground, cradling her like a baby, to carry her back into the Garden.

"Need any help?" Isabelle offered, clipping the chain securely around her own neck.

"No thanks, she's probably only ninety pounds."

Caleb disappeared behind the willow branches for a moment before returning, an odd expression of guilt and triumph on his face. Isabelle nodded her approval.

"Good work, soldiers!" Isabelle praised. "We've got about two hours before she wakes up. It'll take a good five or six to get to the portal, but at least we have a head start. Let's get going."

But before Isabelle could turn to go, Selena stepped in front of her, shaking her head.

"Selena, what's wrong? We have to go!"

Still she shook her head and held out her hand to Isabelle, like she should take it. A bit reluctantly, Isabelle complied. Selena nodded and offered her other hand to Caleb. The boy looked at it hesitantly. This was the most

Selena had ever attempted to communicate with anyone, as far as Isabelle knew.

Selena glimpsed down to where her hand entwined with Caleb's. A flicker of sorrow passed over her eyes, but vanished as quickly as it had appeared. *Maybe our stone-faced friend isn't as empty as we thought.*

As that passed through her head, her feet began to lift off the ground. Isabelle gasped and squeezed Selena's hand. She started kicking her legs frantically. Caleb didn't seem as alarmed; he was just staring at Selena in shock.

"That girl never ceases to amaze me," he muttered. "Magic as advanced as that . . . and nonverbal too . . . incredible. Bella, take my hand. We have to be in a circle."

Isabelle was hesitant, but she trusted the two of them, and there was no time to argue. The second her fingers gripped Caleb's, the group shot forward so quickly Isabelle could barely see the blur that was the trees. The wind blew so hard the rubber band flew out of her hair, leaving her shoulder-length brown locks to fly behind her. Isabelle screamed, gripping Caleb and Selena's hands like they were her lifelines, which, for all she knew, they were. It was maybe thirty seconds before Caleb's voice shouted, "Let go!"

"What!" Isabelle shrieked, but her voice was whipped away by the wind.

Caleb and Selena released her hands, and she stopped moving instantly, as if she had smacked into a wall. Then she hit the ground on her hands and knees, vomiting violently. The others touched down gently on their feet to her right and left with the grace and precision of an angel.

Caleb laughed, offering his hand to Isabelle. "Get up, Bella. Haven't you ever traveled by wind before? Nice job, Selena. That's really difficult stuff. I didn't know you had that in you. Only the best of the best can lead a group of people on a several-mile trail while traveling themselves on a nonverbal wind trip. That's unheard of, especially for someone as young as you."

Selena just nodded, the blank, distant look back on her face as if she were in another world, far away. *When she looks at you, it's like she's looking at your soul or something,* Isabelle thought. *Kinda creepy.*

Isabelle, snapping out of her thoughts, stood shakily, muttering, "Where *I* come from, people prefer cars or busses."

That was when Isabelle caught sight of the little wooden door, floating in midair above her head. She glanced around at the familiar landscape, frowning. "But that's—" she began, but stopped herself, reminding herself that *nothing* was impossible in his crazy, inexplicable place.

"All right, only two can pass though the portal at a time, so Selena and I will go first." He held out his hand for Selena to take. She stared at it, unmoving. When Caleb saw this, he took a step toward her, slipping his strong hand into her loose one. Hesitantly, she tightened her fingers around his and looked up into his eyes. A hint of a smile danced on his lips, but he didn't speak except to say the magic words *sic crestaes aloma.* The duo shot up out of Sunolia, and a second later, the Key was passed down to Isabelle. Soon all three stood together in the Mortal World, Selena having dropped Caleb's hand the second the trip had finished. She stood with her back to Caleb and Isabelle, taking deep breaths. Isabelle was tempted to say something, but figured they had pushed her too far already.

"Okay," Caleb started, taking the Key back. "We should be able to—"

"Wait!" a voice called from below.

"Oh, what now?" Isabelle moaned.

Malcolm was riding to the portal on the bare back of a beautiful, pure-white horse at top speed. The poor steed looked exhausted. "You're going to save Alyssa, aren't you?" he called.

"Shh, you're gonna give us away," Isabelle hissed. "Get up here."

Caleb tossed the Key down to Malcolm. He turned to his mare. "Go back now, Jordan," he told her, petting her mane affectionately. As he traveled up through the portal, his horse trotted off. After gaining his balance, he looked around the street, eyes wide, taking deep breaths through the nose. "I haven't been in the Mortal World for so long . . ." he breathed. "It's crazy the things you miss—cars, houses . . ."

Isabelle crossed her arms, cutting off his muttering to himself. "Don't you try and stop me, boy." She spat the word *boy* like it was an insult. "I'm not stupid. I know you think it's too dangerous to go to Meladyne, but I'm getting my sister back whether you like it or not."

"I'm not trying to stop you," Malcolm confirmed, focusing his attention on Isabelle and throwing his hands up innocently. "I'm coming with you. I heard you guys talking last night. I got up in the middle of the night to get here in time, but I had to stop and let my horse take breaks. There are lots of horses around here by the way. They live by the pond if you haven't seen them. We race them for fun on weekends sometimes."

"Why did you come?" Isabelle demanded. She didn't care where the horse came from; she wanted her sister back.

"Because Alyssa . . . well . . . I . . . uh, we . . . Because we're friends." The boy's face strongly resembled a tomato. Isabelle held back a smile. She would've laughed under different circumstances.

"Ah," Caleb stepped in. "Well, we can't be standing in the way of young love, now, can we? Welcome aboard, Malcolm."

"Okay, whatever. Everybody can come, I don't care. But after we get to Alyssa—"

But Isabelle never finished her sentence because she was interrupted by the bloodcurdling screams ringing out from the house behind.

"That's my house," Isabelle whispered.

CHAPTER 22

 Alyssa shot up out of her bed, instantly awake, and raced down the stairs. She saw her parents lying unmoving on the ground, swords protruding from their stomachs, and dark-red blood staining the carpet before she could believe it.

"Mom! Dad!" she cried, her voice coming out in a horrified sob. She dropped to her knees, pressing two fingers on each of their wrists. *No, no, please, not my parents* . . . No pulse. Cool skin. So much blood . . .

The Meladynian standing over her never knew what hit him. The knife that had been used to stab Alyssa's father was in the dark servant's throat before he could blink. The one behind her received similar treatment. It all happened so quickly Alyssa didn't have a chance to realize what was going on.

Alyssa had learned that in traumatic experiences, people often get a rush of adrenaline. They lose their minds for a moment and let it all go, running down everything that could be responsible—and sometimes things that aren't. Then came the break down after the storm, when they stop exploding and realize what's going on. Usually, this meant sobbing.

Her parents . . . dead. Murdered. It wasn't possible.

Out of the corner of her eye, Alyssa caught sight of Matthew tearing out of his room, Seraphina creeping out behind him.

"Alyssa . . .?"

And then she felt that excruciating pain shoot through her arm, her head, causing her to cry out in pain, dropping to her knees. That pain that meant the Dark Queen would take her over again.

But no. She lied to me and cheated me and killed my parents. No, Marvalonna, I don't think so!

She yanked the knife from the Meladynian, blood seeping from his lifeless body, and forced it into Matthew's hand.

"Cut it out!" she screamed desperately. "My arm, please! I didn't have a blade before, and I don't even know if it'll work, but I can't let this happen again!"

"But I can't—"

"Do it, Matthew! You have to! Now!"

Hearing the intensity in her voice, he locked eyes with her and drove the knife into the back of her arm. The pain was so bad she started to lose consciousness, but she fought it. *No . . . I can't black out . . . she'll take me over . . . Matthew . . .* Her friend reached tenderly into her arm, Alyssa gritting her teeth as his warm hand brushed over her raw skin. He jerked out the control device quickly, as if taking off a Band-Aid. It looked the same as it had before, still full of the sickly green toxin.

She stumbled forward, blinded by pain. Seraphina, obviously having learned a thing or two in Meladyne, hurled her knives with flawless accuracy into two more Meladynians. Both her friends preoccupied with enemies, she had almost reached the door when a floorboard directly behind her creaked. Alyssa whipped around to face one of the evil servants coming at her with a sword.

The girl looked around frantically, out of weapons. She was still holding the device. It had a small crack in it, and a tiny bit of the liquid inside was oozing out.

She held up her hands. "Wait! Please. Come here."

She'd manipulate him with words, charm, and lies, just as she'd been taught.

"Why should I listen to you?" he demanded.

"Because I have powers." She was completely improvising.

"What kind of powers?" He was interested now. That was good.

"What's your name?" Alyssa asked him.

He regarded her suspiciously, but answered, "Thomas. Why?"

"Does Marvalonna know your name, Thomas?"

"Well, um, no, I don't think she does. But what does that matter?"

"Well, why would you take orders from someone who doesn't care about you, someone who doesn't even know your name? You're not just a pawn in her plot to take over the world, but you're acting like it. You're more than that, I know you are. You could have a life, a school, a home, a family, a girl. Aren't you tired of doing what Marvalonna tells you all the time when she wouldn't even notice if you were dead?" She gestured at a boy she'd flung the knife at, lying dead on the floor. "You think anyone's gonna have a funeral for him? You think anyone's gonna care? All he ever did was do what other people told him to because he was afraid of them. Do you really want that to be you? Are you going to stumble around through life like a zombie, following orders for the rest of your life?"

Might as well lay it on thick. She could see it getting to him. Thomas shifted uncomfortably, considering her words. It hurt her to even look at his face since every Meladynian was an exact copy of Ricky. *Ricky wasn't a pawn. He was a hero . . .*

"So what are these powers you were talking about?" he wondered.

"Well, um, my father is the king of Sunolia." That part was true. "So there's magic inside me that can turn people light. If I turned you light, you could live in the Mortal World. You could have anything you wanted."

Oh, that was good, Alyssa. Well played.

"Okay, so what's the catch?" he asked.

"Drop the sword. That's the catch."

"Done. Now how does this work?"

Alyssa couldn't believe the boy was so stupid. She almost felt bad for him. Almost. She tapped her lips.

"Just one kiss," she said. "But it's gotta be a good one or it won't work."

She slipped the blood-covered device into the band in the back of her pants, careful not to stab herself, so he couldn't see it. *Come here, boy.*

"Oh, fine. Come here, then."

He leaned toward her. Head tilted, eyes closed, lips slightly apart . . . She caught him off guard, jabbing the device into the back of his arm. He screamed, clutching at it, but it was no use. The venom inside was poisoning his body, killing him quickly. Another thirty seconds of writhing and begging and he lay still, dead on the ground.

"Sorry, Tommie," Alyssa whispered, a sick, guilty feeling beginning to grow in her stomach. "You weren't really so bad."

It was difficult for Alyssa to kill people, especially people who looked like her recently departed best friend. But she had to remind herself that they weren't Ricky, they weren't sixteen, and they weren't innocent. *What if he's the one who hurt Maegan?*

"You guys okay?" she asked, turning to the other two. Her friends nodded. They were alone now, just the three of them. "Let's get outta here. We'll find somewhere safer."

After tossing a few necessities into a bag and pulling the front door open, Alyssa smacked face first into . . .

"Bella?"

"Alyssa!"

Alyssa embraced her sister tightly, relief washing over her, momentarily forgetting all her misery. She began to sob with relief, grief, exhaustion, pain.

"Oh, Bella, thank God you're okay!" she cried, pulling away from the hug but still gripping her small hands.

"How'd you get here? We were coming to save you!"

"It's a very long story. I'll tell you later. This is Matthew and his sister Seraphina. I rescued them from Meladyne."

For the first time, she noticed Selena, Malcolm, and Caleb gathered behind Bella, shivering in the cold. Alyssa was so touched by the scene before her she was crying. Her friends had come for her. What had she been so worried about? These strangers she didn't even know, these friends she'd endangered and nearly gotten killed—they had risked their lives to save hers. Again. Would she ever stop owing these people?

That was when Bella, peeking around Alyssa into the house, noticed her parents lying on the floor, motionless. "Mom? Dad? Are they . . . ?"

Bella looked up at her sister with tears brimming in her eyes, and Alyssa knew she couldn't tell her, not now.

"I think we might be able to save them. But only if we hurry. Come on, guys. These are the people who raised me. Please help me save them," Alyssa begged. "My mom doesn't weigh that much, me and Selena can take her. Caleb, Malcolm, you think you can get my father?"

"You . . . you took out all these Meladynians?" Bella asked, amazed, looking around at the twenty-something bodies lying on the floor.

"Matthew and Seraphina did most of it. And I, um, had an adrenaline rush. Now come on, we're wasting time!"

Alyssa ran to the mantel and grabbed her staff, feeling much more secure now that she was armed with her best weapon. *How* did *I throw those knives?* she wondered. *Must've been some adrenaline rush.*

Once Alyssa's parents had been hoisted into arms and carried outside, the group began toward the portal.

"Alyssa," Malcolm said, glancing forlornly down at Lukas, who was cradled awkwardly between the boys, "he's not—"

Alyssa shot him a look and jerked her head toward Bella.

"Ahem. He's not gone yet. Don't worry. There's still time."

Out of the corner of her eye, she saw Bella relax a little. Alyssa shot Malcolm a grateful look. He nodded back at her. Bella would find out about her parents soon enough. No need to make her upset about it already. Let her hope for a little while.

"Where do we go?" Bella asked. "Back to camp?"

"No," Malcolm replied. "Too far away. There's a Sunolian village about a mile that way. We'll take them there."

They steered their course left and followed Malcolm, tense silence hanging heavy in the air. It took only about fifteen minutes before they came upon the miniature town. Alyssa recognized the village; it was the same one she and Bella had found together just two and a half weeks ago.

Malcolm headed directly to one house in particular on the end of a row. He tapped lightly on the door, and it was answered a moment later by a Sunolian. Malcolm leaned over, conversing quietly with the Sunolian. They seemed to come to an agreement, and he turned around, announcing, "We'll stay here for the night. My friend Cadia here will see what she can do for anyone who is injured. If you are in good condition, go inside and you'll find food and water. Leave the injured here on the ground and they will be helped."

Alyssa's parents were laid gently in the grass while everyone else piled into the small space inside the house. The Sunolian, Cadia, stepped out of her home and knelt before Alyssa's lifeless parents. Unable to watch, Alyssa turned her back on the trio.

She found herself in a cozy little gold-and-brown-toned living room, complete with a fireplace, couches, and wooden floors. A tiny kitchen containing only a dining table and small cupboard was connected to the room, and two doors in the back likely led to a bedroom and bathroom. A window provided a perfect view of the surrounding meadows and cottages. It strongly resembled a small cabin one would stay in at summer camp. It was warm, small, and comfortable.

"All right," Caleb said, dropping his stuff on the floor like he owned the place. "There's not a lot of space here, but we'll make it work. We'll stay on couches, the floor, chairs—anywhere will work. We've all slept in worse places, so you will survive. In the morning, we can make the call on what we're going to do based on the state of the McCaws. There's food in the kitchen, and you can find a shower and clothes in the bathroom. Yes, the clothes will fit; they're magically altered that way. Make yourselves comfortable, and I'll go help Cadia with the McCaws."

Alyssa, having been voted most deserving of the first shower, let the warm, sudsy water rush over her skin, closing her eyes and moaning like she was in heaven. There was so much to worry about, so much to cry about, so many questions to ask. But she didn't want to think about any of that. She was giving herself five minutes to just be thankful for warm water and shampoo. But her five minutes soon ended, much to her displeasure, and she was forced back into the harsh light that was reality. She found a yellow sundress exactly her size in the closet with a brown belt around the waist. Once her hair was brushed and braided and she had a bit of food in her stomach, she felt calmer, more prepared to face her problems. She left the small kitchen full of people to find Malcolm, sitting all alone on a couch, reading a book. His hair had been cut to shoulder length, a tough style for a fifteen-year-old to pull off, but he certainly managed. He wore a black dry-fit shirt flaunting his muscular arms, making him look like a teenage Chris Hemsworth. Upon seeing Alyssa, he dropped his book and gaped.

"Whoa, Romeo," she teased. "Looking pretty hot."

"Not so bad yourself, princess," he replied, coming out of his daze.

She curled up next to him on the couch, thankful for someone who could joke so lightly in such desperate times.

"I'm really sorry about your parents," he said, serious now. So much for lighthearted conversation. Reluctantly, he put his arm around her. Alyssa leaned her head against his chest. She could feel herself relaxing, grateful for someone to just hold her.

"Well, they were good people," she replied. "They didn't deserve to go that way. But I guess that's just all the more reason to fight. Do you think we could bring them back? Marvalonna brought back Seraphina and Matthew for me. Do you think we could do the same with them?"

Malcolm's eyes widened. "You let her bring them back from the dead? Do you have any idea how dark that kind of magic is?" He pulled away from her, glaring.

"What was I supposed to do, Malcolm? Leave them to die?" She raised her voice a little, frustrated.

"Yes! You can't fight fate, Alyssa. Or death."

"Don't talk to me about fate. *Fate* killed my parents. *Fate* made Ricky die. *Fate* made me not even know my birth parents. Do you expect me to just sit here and let your stupid *fate* take over everything I love? Fate isn't on our side, Malcolm."

"Every time someone comes back to life, someone else dies, Alyssa. You can't just bring people back from the dead and expect not to pay a penalty. Somewhere in the world, a seven-year-old girl and a seventeen-year-old boy died the minute you used that potion. *Because of you.*"

"What? It's not fair, it's not fair, it's not fair! All I ever do is mess things up and get people killed when I try to help! I'm going home, Malcolm. You all made a mistake, nobody needs me, just leave me alone!"

She leapt up from the couch and ran toward the front door, not even knowing or caring where she was going. Throwing it open, she had taken three steps out the door before Malcolm grabbed her arm.

"Alyssa, I'm sorry—"

She yanked her arm away. "Don't touch me! Get off me, Malcolm! Let me go!"

"No, Alyssa, come on—"

They struggled for a minute, and then Alyssa somehow ended up in his arms, crying into his shirt.

"Hey, hey, hey, I'm sorry. I'm sorry."

She clenched balls of his shirt in her fists, sobbing, "No, no, no."

"Alyssa, look at me. It's gonna be okay."

"No, it's not," she whimpered. "It's never gonna be okay again. I didn't ever want anything to change, and now Ricky is dead and Hazel might still be in Meladyne, and my parents are dead, and it's just never gonna be okay! What about you, Malcolm? Where are you from? What happened to your family?"

He sighed. "I'm from northern Switzerland. That's where the accent comes from. My dad abandoned me when I was two. My mom and my sister went out shopping five years ago. They never came back. Lily was only three." His voice cracked a little. "A Haven Portal led me to Aquamarinia. I have lived here ever since, training. I just can't stand it anymore. I've been here since I was nine years old. You are the first light person ever to return from Meladyne. And with so little training . . . you gave me hope, Alyssa. You still do. You have shown me that you can win against all odds if you really have something worth fighting for. You're my inspiration. You're *everyone's* inspiration. There's not a single person here who hasn't lost something. You are their living hope, Alyssa."

"But what if I can't do it? I got lucky, nothing more. All I can do is run fast, Malcolm. They can't look up to me. In fact, I'm short enough most of them literally look *down* at me. I can't help them," she moaned into his shirt.

This was too much. All these people were depending on *her*? These people could've hit a moving target on a sprinting horse when they were two years old. How could they depend on *her* when a month ago she'd refused to believe in magic? Alyssa couldn't let all these people down. They were all younger than twenty. They needed a real leader, not her.

"The way you win a battle is the way you win a war. If you won a battle by running fast, teach me how to run fast, too."

Alyssa knew that wasn't entirely true. If you won a battle by running fast, during the next battle they would already know you could run fast, so they would make sure you couldn't run again. But her friend was only trying to make her feel better, so she kept this fact to herself.

"You really think there's gonna be a war, Malcolm?" she asked instead.

"We've spent too many millennia being afraid. We need to fight, we need to win, and we need to stop living in fear. So yes, I think there will be."

She bit her lip and stayed quiet for a minute, looking down at the ground.

"Hey, you're bleeding," he noticed.

Though it throbbed, Alyssa had grown so used to hurting everywhere all the time she had completely forgotten about the cut on her arm. "Here, let me help you. What happened?"

"Long story. I don't really want to talk about it right now. I have one on my leg and my side, too."

Malcolm pulled away from her and picked up his backpack. He rummaged around in it for a second, then pulled out a bandage. He gently wrapped her arm until the bleeding was stifled. Then he handed her two more. "For your leg and your side," he told her.

"Thank you," she murmured.

"Sure," he replied, looking down at her.

Alyssa looked up into his deep, brown eyes. They weren't like Ricky's—cold, hard, intense. They looked safe, they looked warm, they looked like . . . home. She wrapped her hands around his neck and pulled his face down to meet hers. Pressing her forehead against his, she could feel his breathing, hear his heart beating.

"Stay, Alyssa," Malcolm whispered. "They need you. *I* need you." His hand traveled to her face and brushed off the remaining tears.

He wrapped his arms around her waist. Something inside Alyssa was screaming at her, telling her, *This is wrong, this is wrong, what are you doing? You just lost Ricky, how can you just forget about him this quickly?* But Alyssa hadn't forgotten about Ricky; she would never, as long as she lived, forget about Ricky. But she needed this right now, she needed someone to hold her. She couldn't do this on her own. *Ricky would understand that.* For a half second, her lips met his, but before Alyssa had time to select an emotion from the endless, unorganized supply swirling through her head, Caleb appeared in the doorframe, right next to where they were standing. Startled, Alyssa let go of Malcolm's neck and took a step back, eyes flicking to the wall, the floor, Caleb, anywhere but on Malcolm.

"Alyssa, Cadia says—" he faltered, seeming to realize he was interrupting something. Caleb's face reddened.

"Oh, uh, sorry. Alyssa, Cadia says . . ." He took a deep breath. "Your parents . . ." He shook his head. "I'm sorry."

CHAPTER 23

 "Today we are gathered here to recognize the all-too-early deaths of Lukas and Martha McCaw. They were good souls, innocent people who never did anything but good. It was not fair for them to go this way, but there's nothing we can do about it now. However, we can be sure their souls will rest peacefully in heaven and will watch us and guide us as long as we live."

Alyssa stood, once again sobbing into Malcolm's chest, something she seemed to be doing a lot lately. Caleb stroked her hair from behind as she held Bella. They were all gathered in a lovely garden about the size of Alyssa's school cafeteria, every spare inch packed to the brim with hundreds of exotic trees and flowers, before Alyssa's parents.

"Alyssa, Bella, would you like to say anything?"

Bella shook her head miserably.

Caleb gently took Alyssa from Malcolm and led her up to the front. There they lay—her parents, looking young and peaceful in their bed of flowers. She felt as if her heart were being torn to shreds, as if the last thing she'd had to hold onto was gone and she was free-falling endlessly into darkness . . .

They're sleeping, she told herself. *In a minute Dad's going to wake up and say, "Lyssie, would you mind telling me what I'm doing in this corny little flower bed?"* But they didn't wake up. They never would.

Caleb steadied her, then took a step back. Alyssa looked at all the grim faces around her with her bloodshot blue eyes that once sparkled with a cheerful light. She cleared her throat, trying to keep her voice from cracking.

"My parents that you see here were not my biological parents. They were not famous, or rich, or magical. But they had hearts like none I've ever known. When my real parents left, they took us in, my sister and me. For nine years, they raised us, fed us, loved us. We were their children and they were our parents, no matter what anyone says. And they never did anything in their lives to deserve deaths like this."

Her voice cracked on the word *this* and it took her a moment to regain her composure.

"But as a friend of mine told me, we can't fight fate, nor can we fight death. Death wanted them, and Fate gave them to him. But it is God who will rescue them from Death's cold and heartless embrace and accept them in his eternal heaven, where they will never again have to worry. And they will stay there, waiting for me. And one day, I will be there waiting for my children, and they will wait for theirs. Maybe lowercase-d death has taken them, but capital-d Death will never conquer them because they will live forever in our hearts. Our love is what keeps them alive. And only when we forget them will they really be capital-d Dead. So please help me remember them not as Dead, but as Alive. Thank you."

She stepped down and let the tears flow again as her sister came over to be held. She had made all that up on the spot, but God, it was beautiful. She had surprised herself; public speaking had never been a strength of hers, but losing people was bringing things out she didn't know were in her.

Falla stepped forward next. "Since these people were good and gentle and light, we will do the standard procedure of turning their best qualities into something new and beautiful."

Alyssa noticed the Sunolian's hair had been let out of its braids and turned black. Unlike the usual cheery little outfit, she wore a black dress with dark tights. The only thing that remained colorful were her solemn golden eyes, and they weren't shining like they usually were. Even her light freckles had disappeared. The usually bubbly little girl had been replaced by a solemn, sophisticated, wise, immortal woman.

Falla placed her arms over Alyssa's mother, palms down. She spoke softly, gently, as if whispering a story to a baby. "She shines bright and she is light, peaceful as a dove. Turn her strength and all her might into something we will love."

With those words there was a flash of light, and where her mother had previously lain stood a beautiful little flower, healthy pink petals bursting in every direction. Written across the gold center in shimmery black letters was the name *Martha* and underneath the word *Lady*.

"As you can see, I have taken the light in her and turned it into something beautiful. Even 'capital-d Death,' as Alyssa refers to it, cannot kill light. And *light* doesn't mean *magic*; it just means good intentions, a good heart. And then of course, *lady*, the meaning of her name, important because our names tell us who we are. What is the first thing you ask someone when they have a new baby? *What is her name?* How do we tell each other apart when people are calling for us? Our names.

"Now we will move on to this handsome young man. How old is he? Can't be a day over thirty."

"Thirty-five," Bella choked out.

Thirty-five, Alyssa thought. *They took us in when they were twenty-six years old, only a few years out of college. They gave up the lives they could've had, their dreams that could've come true to raise us. And now they're dead. Because of me.* Alyssa remembered attending their wedding when she was six years old. She had never thought anything of how young her parents were. She'd always just figured they'd had kids when they were young, in college. But now she realized she had no idea how old her biological parents were. Actually, she didn't know anything about her biological parents. Not that it mattered. *They aren't here. They never were.* Once again, she felt bad about blaming her parents for their absence. But not really all the way to *guilty*. Not yet, anyway.

Falla placed her arms over Lukas. The language sounded different this time; her voice was strong and firm rather than tender and peaceful. *Always strong, always bold, always helping little ones. So now forever you may hold, our faith until the world's gone cold.*

Alyssa watched in awe as her father's body morphed into an enormous, sturdy apple tree, shading her mother's flower. Falla reached up and plucked a picture-perfect apple from a branch. She handed it to Alyssa, who took it with trembling hands. She tried to read it, but her tears were so blinding and her hands shook so violently she almost dropped it. Caleb cupped his hands underneath hers to hold them steady. Alyssa blinked, letting the tears roll down her cheeks, and examined the apple. It looked like Snow White's poisoned apple—perfect and smooth and glossy and red. Alyssa knew apples never looked this perfect on their own, but this was magic, after all. She slowly turned it over and discovered a name in shimmering golden letters written on the skin: *Lukas.*

And underneath was the word *light,* the meaning of his name.

Why can't this just be over already? Alyssa thought, fighting every urge in her to collapse to the ground and sob.

For a moment, everyone was silent. But Alyssa, left only to her own miserable thoughts, felt suffocated by the silence, and eventually reached the point where she could no longer stand it. She had to say everything now, get rid of everything that had been weighing down on her heart while her life was already at the lowest it had ever been. "When I was in Meladyne . . . Marvalonna made me kill them." She nodded toward Matthew and Seraphina; her voice was small and uneven, but everyone turned to her. "I couldn't help it; she was controlling me with a device she shoved into my arm. But she gave me a potion to revive them at my request. I didn't realize the risk at that time, so I used it. But now another girl and boy somewhere in this world are dead. Now somewhere someone else is sobbing over their losses. And I just wanted to . . . well, I don't really know. I just wanted to say it, to let someone else know."

Falla nodded somberly. "Don't blame yourself, Alyssa. Things happen. You didn't know."

Alyssa didn't quite agree with that. Eating too much food and getting a stomachache *happened.* Watching a movie late at night and scaring yourself to death *happened.* Falling and scraping your knee *happened.* Kids dying didn't just *happen.* But like she often had to, she kept her mouth shut.

"Do you think we could make a flower for my mother Elizabeth?" Matthew asked, speaking up for the first time. "She died years ago in Meladyne when my sister was born, but we never got to have a proper ceremony for her."

"Well, I don't have a body, but of course I could make a flower for you."

A wave of the Sunolian's hand and another flower appeared next to Alyssa's mother, only this one bore sky blue petals and read *Elizabeth, Oath of God.*

Another silent moment, and then Bella asked, "Were all these trees and flowers people?"

"Yes," Sylvie replied. "People that don't hurt anymore."

Alyssa looked down at her sister. Nine years old and in the middle of a war. Related to the main cause of that war. Watching her parents die. Learning how to kill. This wasn't right, none of it was. Suddenly that broken feeling of misery and pain and mourning melted into a cold one of hatred and determination and revenge-hunger. And suddenly her cheeks were dry, and her face was set. She shoved Caleb's comforting arms off her and stepped forward. She turned around and faced the sea of black clothing and grim faces.

She took a deep breath and spoke, projecting her voice across the garden, across all of Sunolia. "My parents were the kindest, gentlest people in the world. Ricky was loyal to me my whole life, even when I didn't realize it. I didn't even know Elizabeth or the two kids that almost died because of me, but I can tell you right now they didn't deserve to die."

The anger was building up in her now. The longer she talked, the more fired up she made herself. "Now tell me, good people, did they die in vain? Did they die for no reason, for nothing? Did they die so we could stand on the sidelines biting our nails?" She was shouting now. "How many millennia have the Light let the Dark take away our children and our brothers and sisters? It's time to put an end to that! We must fight!"

There were scattered cheers of agreement, uncertain murmurs, and cries of resentment.

"If we don't fight, they'll just take more people we love! They are winning just by being alive! This won't end unless we end it! We are losers in a losing game!"

This brought a bigger, louder roar, mostly filled with cheers. Alyssa knew the insanity of all she was saying but didn't want to stop. Her parents' deaths had opened her eyes and made her see the situation clearly. She had turned a funeral into a pep rally.

She spotted Violet shoving her way forward through the crowd. Her olive skin looked lighter than it usually did against the darkness of her dress and curly hair. She was stunning in that dress; it tightened and loosened in all the right places on her.

When she'd reached the front, she turned to face everyone, her voice hard and determined like Alyssa's. "This girl is like nothing I've ever seen before. She walked into and out of Meladyne and lived to tell the tale. She was alone and lost and scared and confused and untrained, and *fourteen flipping years old*, and she escaped all on her own. I vote that Alyssa McCaw be put in charge of this group, or army. Because let's face it, if we want to accomplish what she is suggesting, an army is what we'll have to be. She will be the general and we the soldiers. This is the way it must be and you know it. Now who's with me?"

Alyssa felt dizzy. *General?* Was she insane? All Alyssa had done was hide and run fast, get lucky and be saved. Now she was expected to lead an *army*? When she couldn't hold a sword properly or hit a suicidal elephant with an arrow?

She stumbled backward. "Violet, I—"

But she was cut off by the outburst of voices.

"Yes! I'll follow Alyssa anywhere!"

"I second that!"

"She's the one we've been waiting for!"

"She's the first to make it out of Meladyne alive! Imagine what we could do if she trained us!"

Alyssa couldn't believe all these people had such strong opinions about *her*; she, who a month ago had been fighting for no more than a chance at being her school's Snowflake Dance Queen? Who had cared about nothing more than winning events at track meets? *Do they know? Do they know how little I can do? How scared I am?*

The uproar was broken by a flash of light. It was blinding, and for a second, Alyssa could hear nothing due to the ear-splitting, high-pitched sound that had erupted out of nowhere, like a piccolo playing the highest note in the world. She felt momentarily lost and panicked. What was happening? Then the light dimmed and the sound faded away and Alyssa could see a Sunolian standing beside her, holding her hands skyward. She was dressed the same as Falla, and all the Sunolians for that matter, but it was clear she had more authority just by the confident way she carried herself, the dignified look on her face.

"Miss McCaw," she began, in a voice much older than the seven years she looked, "cannot simply take over Aquamarinia. Though brave and honorable her actions were, as leader this division belongs to me. Sunolia has never been a dictatorship but—"

"But what?" Sylvie, ever the defiant one, shouted from the back of the small crowd. "This is a democracy, is it not? What do they say in America? Of the people, by the people, for the people! We are the people, are we not? If we say Alyssa's the leader, then, by God, Alyssa's the bloody leader! We've spent thousands and thousands of years getting beaten down and kidnapped and killed by Meladyne! Now here—here, I see a strong young woman who will lead us into battle with her head held high. Alyssa will be our savior, and denying her would be denying our lives! I say let the people choose! Let them stop dying so they can start living. I am for Alyssa!"

Oh Sylvie, stop! I'm not what you think I am, I can't handle it, you'll get all these good people killed! Alyssa opened her mouth to protest, but Malcolm stepped up first.

"I am for Alyssa," he said sincerely, unsheathing his sword with a soft *shing* and raising it above his head.

Alyssa looked him in the eye and pleaded with hers. *Stop, I can't do this,* she mouthed.

Yes, you can, Lyssie, he insisted.

Lyssie. The last person to call her that had been her father. Seeing it on her friend's lips stung like salt in a cut. The memories it sparked were painful, but it still made her feel a bit better to hear Malcolm say it. Like she had lost her dad, but still had someone to depend on, to protect her. Funny how something as little and ridiculous as a nickname could break the floodgates and release a tsunami of sentiment.

"For Alyssa," Violet echoed, raising her own sword as Alyssa came back to her senses.

"For Alyssa," Bella agreed.

"Alyssa."

"Alyssa."

"Alyssa."

Soon every sword was raised, and Alyssa knew she'd have to train like a crazy person, because these people all believed in her, were all depending on her. She couldn't fail them. If they wanted a leader, then a leader she'd have to give them.

"Very well," resigned the Sunolian. "Alyssa McCaw will temporarily be given my position. You may train the students however you choose. Would you like to say anything? And I am Morosa, by the way."

Alyssa was nervous, but she took a shaky breath and steadied herself. If they believed she was strong, she'd have to act strong, even if she had fallen off the stage and ended her acting career in fourth grade. She took a shaky breath.

"I will not pretend I am as strong as Violet or Selena. I am not as clever and creative as Caleb or Malcolm. I am not as good with weapons as Bella. I am small, weak, and inexperienced, and I will not try to hide it. But if there's one thing I am, it's determined. I will not fail you or betray you or give up on you. I will stop trying when I'm dead. And I expect you all to do the same. But you won't die because I will train you until you collapse. Anyone not willing to train with me can leave now."

The silence was almost tangible as Alyssa waited for someone to say something, but no one spoke. That was the moment Alyssa first felt true confidence. It was when she realized that every single person there was going to back her up to the ends of the earth. And, for the first time, Alyssa thought they might possibly even have a chance of winning.

"Wonderful," Alyssa said, letting the confidence solidify into a smile. "Now, everyone, here is what I propose. We train for a year. We forget all extra studies that won't be effective in battle. We'll train six days a week, harder than ever before. We will work in groups sometimes and all together sometimes, but we must learn to work together as a united army. If you have a weakness, find someone who can help you with it. One year from today we will meet back up and discuss what our course of action will be. Are there any questions? Comments, objections?" No one spoke. "Good. Tomorrow you'll have a day off, then training begins the day after."

And then Alyssa once again broke down into tears, crumpling to the ground. She felt Bella curl up next to her. They held each other and cried. She let the misery envelop her, the loneliness pressing down on her from all sides. Tears flooded her whole world, and she felt as if she had no desire to ever move from that spot. *I have to get it all out now*, Alyssa told herself. *I'll cry now for as long as I want, then I won't cry anymore.*

Once Alyssa had sobbed out all the tears in her eyes and the pain had died down to a dull numbness, she got shakily to her feet, looking down at the young faces surrounding her, still watching expectantly. "All right," she said, her voice weak and raw. "Let's do this."

CHAPTER 24

"Down, up, one! Down, up, two! Down, up, three!" Alyssa screamed at her new students. Seven thirty a.m. and she had them outside doing push-ups in the grass. She herself, in order to set a good example, had arisen at five thirty to get her own workout in. She had promised the others she would never make them do anything she wasn't willing to do herself, and she planned to stick to that. She wasn't very used to being in charge; before Sunolia, she'd always kind of tried to keep a low profile. But she had to admit, she was kind of enjoying it. If she was going to be famous anyway, she might as well enjoy herself.

"You call that a push-up, Bella? Get down farther! Down, up, thirty-eight! Down, up, thirty-nine . . ."

* * *

". . . and Alyssa, you're partnered with Matthew."

Alyssa watched as Violet demonstrated the sword-fighting techniques again.

"All right! Now, three, two, one . . . Thrust, parry, lunge . . ."

* * *

"Can you believe we've been here for two months?" Caleb asked. "The time has gone by so fast!"

"That's debatable," Alyssa mumbled.

"What's that supposed to mean?"

"It means this has been the longest, hardest two months of my life," Alyssa cried.

"Oh, come on. We're not that bad."

"Again, debatable," Alyssa teased. Caleb shoved her playfully, and Alyssa giggled.

"Okay, water break over. Go on, get up, you lazy people. We're doing solar magic again today." Sylvie's statement was met by a collective groan. "Shut up, would you? I was *going* to say we're doing solar magic again today *and then* we're going to teach Alyssa and Bella some earth magic. But if you don't quit your whining, we'll do solar magic til the sun falls out of the sky. Okay? You people complain more than anyone I have ever seen. On your feet now, hands up. Get in the Neutral Zone."

"Maybe we could if you'd stop talking," Alyssa mumbled to Caleb.

"What did you just say?" Sylvie snapped. "You think the Meladynians will all stop attacking and be real nice and quiet so you can perform a spell? No! You have to be able to clear your mind on the spot, midbattle. I will talk as much as I want. Stop complaining!"

"I already did magic in battle! After only two weeks of training!" Alyssa cried.

"Then I should think you could do magic with me chatting a bit, don't you?"

"Fine then." Alyssa closed her eyes, raising her arms. Remembering the strategy she had used with Violet, she let the anger she felt toward Sylvie envelop her, and released it all in a flash of light and heat. The orb shot through the air, smacking into a tree and lighting the thing on fire.

She gave Sylvie a satisfied smirk as Malcolm rushed to extinguish the flames licking up the tree bark. Sylvie just glared back at her, sighing in frustration. Tension hung in the air for the rest of the hour, and by eleven thirty everyone was drained and ravenous. It was a relief when Sylvie announced it was lunchtime.

Rather than making a mad dash for the fire pit with everyone else, Alyssa hurried to catch up with Sylvie. "Hey, Sylvie. Look, I didn't mean—"

"Whatever, girl. We're all on edge. It's okay. We all see each other at our worst and our best. Don't worry about it. That was some pretty powerful magic, though. How do you do it?"

"It's all in emotions. Anger is the strongest. Whenever I get all fired up, it just happens," Alyssa explained.

Sylvie shrugged. "Whatever works for you."

The two girls loaded their plates with sandwiches and chips and took a seat beside Violet.

"Hey, Alyssa?" Malcolm called across the pit. "I've got a question. What time zone are we on?"

"Ummm . . ." Alyssa hadn't really thought about that one. She glanced down at her watch. "US central? Who cares?"

"But we're doing, like, combat and stuff. Wouldn't that make it military time?"

"I don't know, Malcolm. What did you do before?"

"Before I had this watch we went by, but it got destroyed in the battle. So could you just tell us what time it is now, and we'll go from there?"

"It's eleven forty-three. Sunolian central military time," she decided. "Any more questions? Good. Don't forget we're doing physical combat at twelve, so everyone finish up."

"God, I feel bad for Caleb. I've never seen him like this," Violet muttered, leaning close to Alyssa. Alyssa glanced over at him, sitting alone several feet away.

"What happened to him?" she inquired

"It's Maegan. She has a serious head injury. The Sunolians are afraid she won't make it. It's crushing Caleb. He would have no one left without her."

The words cut deep into Alyssa as she looked on with pity. "I wish there was something I could do."

"Yeah, me too. But it's no one's fault, we have to remember that. Come on, it's twelve o'clock."

Upon returning to the arena, Alyssa found the grass almost completely covered by a blue and red mat, like one that would be used for wrestling or gymnastics, only much, much bigger.

"Welcome to Physical Combat," Malcolm greeted, trotting down the remainder of the trail and into the arena. "Now, I know you may be wondering why, in a world of magical combat, you would need to be able to do anything like this. But let me show you something."

It happened so fast Alyssa didn't have time to react. One moment, he was standing there—the next, she was on the ground, arms pinned down, Malcolm on top of her. Startled, she struggled against him, but his grip was too strong. What was he doing? She squirmed around and bit at his arms, frustrated, but it did nothing.

"You can't move. You are in so much pain you can't think straight. Tell me, Alyssa. Can you perform any magic right now?"

"No, but I've got a wand up my sleeve and as soon as you get off me you better believe I'm not afraid to use it," she spat back.

He leaned down until his lips were inches from her ear. Her heart was pounding so hard she was afraid he could hear it. "You're not wearing sleeves, we don't use wands, and you can't focus looking at my face."

Her racing heart stopped dead in its tracks.

"Yeah. I saw that."

Dang it! Did everybody see that?! That was months ago! Alyssa glared up at him, wishing her skin wasn't so ghostly pale that it brought out the red in her cheeks. There wasn't much opportunity to get a tan in Chicago in winter.

"So," Malcolm continued, once again addressing everyone. "The only way she could possibly win this fight would be to physically force me off her." He stood up and held out a hand to help Alyssa up. Smacking his hand away, she picked herself up. "Thank you, Alyssa, for volunteering to help me."

"I don't remember the *volunteering* part," she grumbled, going back to stand by Violet and Selena at a safe distance from her teacher.

"All right, let's have some more volunteers! How about you two in the back, what are your names again? Violet and Matthew—yes, perfect."

Rolling their eyes, the two made their way toward Malcolm, an overenthusiastic, stupid grin on his face. He was still thrilled about the fact that Alyssa had granted him permission to start this class. "You two will be paired up for demonstration. Of course, you won't really hurt each other, because what is the point of wounding your own soldiers?"

"Oh, quit with the theatrics, Malcolm. Just do it," Violet said, arms crossed.

"Okay, okay, chill. Violet, you will play offense, so you will strike first. Matthew, you will be the defense, so you wait until she hits you to go at her. So Violet, if you were making the first move, what would it be?"

"Um . . . find out if he's single?" she joked.

The corners of Malcolm's lips curled upward a bit. "Bella, do you have a guess? What should she do first?"

"A kick?" Bella sounded uncertain.

"Okay, a kick. That's a good start. How would you do that?"

She snapped her leg forward in a simple kick.

"All right, and Matthew, how would you react to that?" He grabbed Violet's leg at the shin. "Okay, good. Grab the shin first to stop her leg, but then grab it higher, right above the knee. Good now, you want to twist it back this way so she can't hold her balance," Malcolm explained, gently demonstrating to be sure he didn't hurt Violet. "But Violet, you don't want him to do that. If he twists it far enough, you'll have a broken hip, and then you'll be all but finished. So Bella, what should she do first instead of kicking?"

"Punch?"

"Very good. Right on the nose. There you go. Now, Matthew. One of the most important things to remember is to keep your hands in front of your face. There. So what will you do about her fist?"

"Block it?" Alyssa was not impressed by Matthew's physical combat skills. She didn't claim to be an expert, but she could've fought better than that when she was Bella's age.

"No. If you block it, she will just bring the other arm around and punch you there. Then you will block that fist and she is free to kick you like she tried to before since your hands are full. You getting all this, Bella? Because if Violet's opponent makes one slipup, she has to jump on it and use it to her advantage. Matthew, you will catch her fist with your right hand and then bring your left around to punch her in the ear.

"But Violet, before he can punch you, you will twist your hip around and kick him in the waist here, hard as you can.

He should stumble or fall, and then you jump on him and attack. Got all that? Good. Let's run through it a couple times with your partner, and then tomorrow I'll teach you exactly what to do after that waist kick. Dismissed."

After inflicting considerable damage on Sylvie and receiving her fair share, Alyssa made her way back toward camp, massaging an aching shoulder. Half way down the trail, Alyssa felt Malcolm slip his hand around her waist. She stiffened and stopped walking as he bent down to whisper in her ear, a sly grin on his face. "Volunteer again tomorrow, will you?"

Alyssa shoved him off and stormed back to her tent, cheeks burning. Why did he have to get to her like that?

* * *

Strategy, Alyssa found, was one of her favorite subjects. Sylvie was a great teacher; she was absolutely brilliant. The class was spent making battle plans—when to fall back, when to attack, where to attack from. A lot of it was maps and vulnerable places and good routes to take. Then there were scenarios with little figurines and problems to work out. After nearly four months of combative training and pushing her body to its physical limits, it felt good to sit down in Sylvie's little tent and just think something through logically. While Alyssa wasn't as bright as Sylvie, she had a quick, sharp mind and began picking out the good strategists in her group. She soon found herself looking forward to it every day.

* * *

It was almost a month later when Alyssa sat, leaning against a tree, talking to her sister and braiding her hair.

It had been a long, hard day of training, and she was soaking up all the free time she could get before having to return to combat. She caught sight of Caleb moving toward the forest, and thought nothing of it until he disappeared into the trees, nowhere near the path.

Frowning, she stood up and began to follow him. "Stay here, Bella. I'll be right back. Caleb!" she called after him. "What are you doing? You could get eaten out there!"

"I'm not going to get eaten. Now are you going to follow me or not?"

Sighing and shaking her head, Alyssa stepped off the path herself, keeping close to Caleb, her eyes darting around the trees for impending danger every few seconds. "Where are we going?"

"I have this secret hideout. I found it and built it up a couple of years ago. I've never told anyone about it, not even Maegan. But I feel like I can trust you. Will you promise not to tell anyone about it?"

Alyssa drew an X over heart. "Promise. You wanna spit shake on it?"

Caleb smiled, ducking behind a tree and into a clearing. Opposite the two of them in the clearing stood an immense bush, at least twenty feet tall. There was no way around it, at least as far as Alyssa could tell; it traveled left and right as far as she could see.

Unable to think of anything more intelligent to say, Alyssa asked the obvious. "What's with the bush?"

Caleb pointed at a hole in the ground leading under the hedge. "We have to crawl under it. If you don't like it, you don't have to come."

"Tell you what. You go first, and if you don't die, I'll come too."

He grinned. "You've got yourself a deal." He dropped to his stomach and scooted under it until his feet disappeared. Alyssa waited for him to say something. "Caleb?" she called. Silence. "Caleb?" Alyssa yelled, feeling a little panicked. "Are you okay?"

For a moment he said nothing, then there was an agonized scream. "Help me! Please!" his voice cried.

"Caleb!" she screamed. Without thinking, she flattened onto her stomach and dove into the hole. *I'm not losing Caleb too.*

The hole was small and very uncomfortable. It would've made anyone feel claustrophobic. She had no idea how Caleb had fit through here—her skinny little self had to wriggle around, army crawling her way through with her elbows, but it didn't matter now. The tunnel wasn't long, only about ten yards, and she soon found herself at the end of it. Alyssa placed her palms in the dirt above her head and pushed her body up, the way one would get out of a swimming pool. The second her entire body was above ground, she yanked her knife out of its sheath where it lived on her side, prepared to fight, but what she saw wasn't a monster. It was Caleb, standing with his arms crossed, grinning.

"What are you . . . what . . .?"

Her friend bent over laughing, and then Alyssa realized what he was doing.

"Hey! Don't make jokes like that in the times we're in! You almost gave me a heart attack!" She punched him, but couldn't suppress her own smile.

"You definitely passed your test, though, McCaw. You came running, hardly took you any time, and already armed. Not bad. Not bad at all. You are either the bravest or the craziest person I know. Probably both."

She opened her mouth to give him a piece of her mind, but a question surfaced in her mind first. "Why can't we just go through?" Alyssa asked. "It's a bush. It's not gonna kill us."

"Oh yes, it is," Caleb corrected, directing her over to the bush. He pointed out a thorn, dripping with a thick, syrupy, black liquid. "It's a Darkkeshade bush. You are not going to want to touch these thorns. Poisoned. Instant death."

"I will keep that in mind," she said, eyes widening a bit.

"Turn around, Alyssa," Caleb commanded.

"Oh give me a break. I'm not falling for—"

"Oh, Alyssa, just turn around."

Alyssa did, and she found her mouth hanging open. The clearing was huge, even bigger than the arena. She couldn't even see the whole thing. She assumed the Darkkeshade bush wrapped all the way around the clearing, but it stretched so far in both directions, she couldn't see where it ended. And she couldn't even see the hedge in front of her. But the size wasn't the amazing thing. It was the weapons that filled it.

It looked like a blacksmith's shop in an old movie. There were beautiful swords, knives, and spears lined up on the ground, hanging from racks, and lying on shelves, as well as unfinished ones scattered all over the place. There were also some odd sort of guns lying on a table, but they looked experimental and unfinished. An outdoor fireplace blazed with hot coals in the corner, and scraps of shiny new metal littered the floor. Alyssa stared in astonishment.

"Caleb where . . . where did you *get* this stuff?" Alyssa stuttered.

"I made it," he replied proudly. "You like them?"

"Like it? It's incredible! How did you do this?"

Caleb shrugged. "I'm good at making stuff. It's a hobby."

"This is not a hobby, Caleb," Alyssa told him. "It's a gift. Why didn't you tell us you could do this?"

"Didn't want to brag. And I didn't think it was that big a deal."

"Not that big of a deal?" Alyssa cried. "You can't let something like this go to waste!"

"It doesn't go to waste. My dad showed me how to do this when I was little, before Meladyne took him. He made fencing swords. When my portal appeared and I came here, I found this clearing and started building things. I showed them to Cressidalaina, and she told me I should keep it a secret because if Meladyne found out, they would want to use me. So you have to promise never to tell anyone anything about this. Okay?" Alyssa nodded. "And like I said, it doesn't go to waste. Let me see that knife." She handed him the dagger, which she found she was still clutching in her hand. After careful inspection, he carefully chose a knife off a rack and held it up next to Alyssa's. They were absolutely identical.

"You made that?" Alyssa asked, amazed.

He nodded. "I make most of your weapons, except those staffs of yours. These creatures—dryads—make those."

He was blushing, and he was making a failed attempt at hiding it. While it would have been entertaining to watch him stutter all day, Alyssa decided to come to his rescue. "Can you teach me to do that?"

Caleb nodded. "Yeah, sure. Meet me back here tomorrow during practice time. I can teach you how to mold swords and everything."

"What are those?" Alyssa asked, nodding at the guns.

"Oh, um, nothing, they're just an experiment," he said quickly. "You're just starting out on swords. Don't worry about that. Oh, and rules. Don't touch anything unless I tell you to, and under no circumstances should you ever touch the bushes. Like I told you, Darkkeshade kills you in seconds, so fast you don't know what hit you."

"I got it, Caleb. I've faced worse than bushes, trust me. I'm gonna go now. You wanna come?"

"No, you go ahead. I'm working on something."

Alyssa had nothing else to do, so she decided to go visit Maegan. She felt guilty because it was kind of her fault she was hurt so badly, and because she hadn't gone to visit her once in the near six months she had spent in Sunolia. She had just been so caught up in the training, she had never gotten around to it. She started to walk, but then realized she had no idea where she was going. She spotted Malcolm leaning against a tree, sharpening a knife. "Hey Malcolm, where do they keep the injured? I want to go see Maegan."

"Through the woods over there, straight line to the right about five minutes. It's a big tent, you can't miss it."

"Okay, thanks."

"Alyssa, you want me to come with you?" Malcolm called.

"No thanks. I want to do this on my own."

The tent was bigger on the inside than it appeared on the outside. It was filled with rows of white cots, each of them surrounded by a curtain and most of them containing a patient. The patients were of all different species; some Sunolian, some dryads, some water spirits, some little sprites, some creatures Alyssa had never heard of. Everyone seemed to be in a different state; some appeared to have nothing more than simple viruses, others were completely covered in bandages and were moaning as if they were dying. Alyssa had always hated hospitals. It just killed her, looking at all the innocent creatures suffering.

She remembered the time her grandmother had been in a hospital. She had only been seven years old and had run from the place in tears. Hospitals make you start to ask those unanswerable philosophical questions that make people go crazy. It starts out simple: Why do they have to suffer? What did they do to deserve this? Then it evolves into, What am I here for? Why should I care about life? Why shouldn't I just give up? She couldn't stand thinking like that.

"Hey, Alyssa!" a young female voice called. Alyssa turned to see little Seraphina standing in a white skirt, blonde curls swept back into a ponytail. She had been helping out in the hospital the past couple months, wanting to get as far away from fighting and violence as possible. Bella, who had been sharing a tent with her, always talked about how happy she was. Every little thing in Sunolia excited her, the same way it did Bella. Seraphina loved to work in the hospital, helping out sick and wounded creatures. She spent so much time there that no one saw her very often, except at mealtimes and bedtime, and even those she didn't always show up for. But her cheeks had color in them, and her eyes sparkled with enthusiasm, so there was no question about her happiness. "Do you need something?"

"Hey Seraphina, how have you been? I'm looking for Maegan Copperfield. Can you help me find her?

"Oh yeah, that poor girl. Come with me."

Seraphina led Alyssa past rows and rows of cots until they reached the very last one in the corner. The curtains were hanging around the bed, concealing it, and Alyssa suddenly felt nervous.

"Now, I've gotta warn you, she's in real bad shape. I've seen worse, of course, in Meladyne, but are you sure you wanna do this?"

The real answer was "no," but she swallowed hard, took a deep breath, and nodded. Somehow she felt she owed it to Maegan, to Caleb, to everyone.

"All right, then." Seraphina drew back the curtain, and Alyssa gasped. The girl lying in the bed was nowhere near the girl Alyssa knew. Her face was pale—too pale—and the usually cheerful freckles were faded. Her lips were dry and cracked, her long, dirty-blonde hair tousled like she never would've allowed it to be. And normally, she was a healthy, muscular kind of slim, but not now. No, now she was skinny, miserably, hardly-eaten-anything thin, not unlike the way Seraphina and Matthew had been when Alyssa had found them. There was a bandage wrapped around the top of her head, though Alyssa could see no injury. She appeared to be fitfully sleeping; her friend kept making violent movements and muttering "Caleb."

"She hasn't woken up since she got here. That's all she says. 'Caleb,' over and over and over again, all day, all night. That poor boy. Comes in here for hours every day, sometimes even sleeps in that chair right at her side. I've never seen somebody so heartsick."

Alyssa sat down on the edge of the bed, smoothing out Maegan's hair. She ran her fingers over her face slowly, gently tracing the side of it. She leaned down next to her ear and whispered, "This is my fault. I'm so, so sorry, Maegan." Then she sat up, letting gentle, silent tears slide down her cheeks.

"My father once told me that pain is like being stuck in the middle of an ocean," Caleb's voice said from behind Alyssa, startling her.

"Yeah? How so?"

"As soon as you can stand, as soon as you can breathe, as soon as you think you'll be all right, the waves drag you back under and don't let you go, almost drown you. But you never do drown, you never are freed from the pain. Because at the last second, you surface, sputtering and coughing again, wondering how you ended up in the middle of the ocean and when you will ever get out of it. And then it drags you back under again."

"I'm sorry, Caleb."

He sat down next to her on the bed. "It's not your fault. Quit beating yourself up over it. This war was bound to happen sooner or later. You just sped up the process. Sure, a lot of us got hurt, but just think of how many of us are still here."

Alyssa nodded, but her heart wasn't in it. "What happened to her?" she asked.

"Real hard blow to the back of the head," he told her. "I think it was the butt of a sword. Cracked her skull and damaged her brain a bit. Bad concussion. The Meladynian who hit her must've had an awfully strong arm."

All she could do was nod again. "She must really love you. All she says is your name."

"Yeah, I know." They sat in silence for a minute. "Come on, Alyssa. That's all the excitement you'll get from her. Come back with me, it's almost dinnertime."

Reluctantly, she took his outstretched hand and stood. They'd taken only a few steps before Alyssa heard a sound behind her, a ruffling of the sheets and a bed creaking. She turned to see Maegan sitting straight up. There was a crazed look in her eyes, and they were glowing green. Not like figurative pretty green—*glowing,* as in emitting bright light.

Alyssa yelped and jumped back, grabbing Caleb's arm. He whipped around and gasped. "Maegan . . .?" he asked, looking half-scared, half-relieved. "It's me. Are you okay?"

"Caleb . . . her eyes . . ." Alyssa stuttered, eyes wide.

"I know. What's wrong with her?"

Then she spoke in a raspy, miserable voice that didn't belong to her. "You're not safe. You're dead. You're all dead. It's coming for you. It's coming soon. Don't trust the little one. It's dangerous." The nurses standing around her began trying to tie her down, to drug her, to knock her out. She began yelling. "It's dangerous! It's dangerous! It'll kill you! It'll kill you all! Don't trust it!"

She fell down, squeezing her eyes shut, writhing around as if fighting some invisible force. She screamed at the top of her lungs, a horrible, terrified shrieking sound. She pressed her hands over her ears, as if trying to block out the noise she was making. There were tears streaming down her face. Seraphina finally managed to jam a needle into her neck, and the girl slowed down gradually and stopped moving, curled up in a little ball.

"Maegan!" Caleb rushed to her side and took her face in his hands. "What happened to her? Is she okay? Her skin is cold! What's wrong with her?"

"Move over," ordered Seraphina, in a commanding tone Alyssa had never heard from her. "Eyes like that could only mean one thing. She had a vision of the future."

"The future! What? That's impossible! How could that happen?"

"I learned about this when I first started working at the hospital. You see, there are invisible little spirits flying all around here called Chronicles. The Chronicles can travel in time and space as quickly as they want. If they see somethin' bad goin' on in the future, they might go back in time to try to prevent it. But here's the thing. Chronicles are forbidden to make direct contact with humans 'cause we humans ain't supposed to tamper with time. But every once in a while, they will find a human on the brink of death that's not gonna make it anyway. They can possess these people and use them to warn the others of what's gonna happen in the future. That's what happened to Maegan here. What did she say? You oughta listen to her."

"I don't care about the future! What is going to happen to my girlfriend?" Caleb demanded.

Seraphina looked solemn. "Chronicles are dangerous things, and time is very powerful. Having that kind of power in your body for more than a second will kill anyone."

Caleb fell to his knees and put his face in his hands. "No," he moaned.

"Wait . . . time. What about the Lake of Time?" Alyssa realized. "It healed my sister once, why won't it work on her?"

"Already tried it. Time is a very strange thing, not to be messed with. The future wants some people, and others it has no use for."

"Then what's with these Chronicle things? Are they good or bad?"

"Chronicles aren't definite things. They are just a theory to explain things like this. They aren't good or bad, just do what they want. They're helpful and harmful. All we really know is that they're powerful. Kinda like water, yeah?"

Alyssa stared at Maegan, watched her face rapidly grow paler. Caleb held it, stroking her hair, kissing her lips, sobbing. Alyssa felt bad for her friends, but more than that she couldn't stop thinking about what she'd said. "It'll kill you. It'll kill you all. Don't trust the little one. It's dangerous." The words gave her chills.

"Save her!" Caleb shouted through tears. He pointed at Alyssa. "It's your fault! You did this to her! Now save her!"

She took a step back, a little afraid. Holding her hands up, she said gently, "Caleb, I can't save her. You can't fight time, that's what Seraphina was just telling us. I don't—"

"AAAHHH!" He threw himself at her, pinning her to the ground, yanking out his knife, and pressing it up against her throat. Shocked, she struggled against him, but of course she couldn't fight him. Drops of blood appeared on her neck as he pressed the blade into her skin. She tried to yell, but could only make a strangled sound. All the nurses rushed to drag him off her, but it took almost all of them to pull him off, and they just barely managed to restrain him. As soon as he was off, Alyssa tore away from him, taking off at top speed out the door. *He's lost his mind,* she thought.

"LET GO OF ME!" he screamed. "YOU KILLED HER! YOU KILLED MY GIRLFRIEND! I TRUSTED YOU! IT'S YOUR FAULT YOU—"

She didn't slow until she reached the fire pit, then she doubled over gasping for air.

"Alyssa?" Violet asked, jogging to her from her tent. "What happened? Come on, sit down."

She let Violet lead her into her tent, sat down, and explained the experience to her, sipping water from a bottle nervously.

"I just don't understand," Violet said, brow furrowed in confusion, wiping a tear away from her eye. "It's not like Caleb to act like that. He's always been able to handle things so well. I don't think he would've actually killed you. But why would he threaten you?"

"I don't know," Alyssa replied. "Grief makes people do crazy things. I guess before it didn't seem real, and he was just trying to stay calm. But after she died he couldn't believe it. He needed someone to blame. I can understand that. But he's got a whole armory full of weapons that he made himself. If he wants to kill me, I'm already dead."

CHAPTER 25

Alyssa didn't have to worry about Caleb for long. The next morning, upon emerging from her tent, she found him poking the fire with a stick, looking anxious. When he spotted her coming his way, he leapt from his chair and launched into an explanation.

"Alyssa, oh my God! Look, I can explain, what happened yesterday . . . what I said to you . . . what I almost *did* to you . . . I swear, I've never done anything like that before. It's just that after my family disappeared, Maegan was all I had left. She meant the world to me. I tried to tell you before that it wasn't your fault, but after she died, something inside me just snapped. I wouldn't have really killed you, you know that, right? I would never hurt any of you. It's just that in the moment . . ."

"Shh, Caleb, Caleb, relax, I understand!" Alyssa stopped him, placing a finger over his lips. "It's okay. I know you wouldn't have killed me. And I know what grief is. My parents just died, and when they did, I killed every Meladynian in that house. I know it's hard, but we've gotta stick together. We're already outnumbered a million to one, and if we start fighting amongst ourselves we're dead. You are a great person with an amazing talent and you didn't deserve to lose her. But she's gone now, so we have to keep going, all right?"

"I . . . I don't understand. You're *forgiving* me? After what I did?" He looked bewildered.

"Of course I am. I understand. It'll be okay. I just need you to trust me. Can you do that?"

Caleb nodded, and Alyssa gave him a quick embrace.

"Hey, Alyssa!" Sylvie yelled, hopping her way out of her tent. "You busy? How's a swim sound?"

"A swim? Do you have a pool?"

"That depends. Do you want to swim?"

"Yeah, of course. It's miserably hot today. But I don't have a suit."

Her friend tossed her a beautiful one-piece, thin-strapped swimsuit; a rich blue color with silver weaved throughout it, making it appear shiny. "Happy birthday."

Alyssa smiled. "Thanks."

"It's your birthday? I didn't know that! Happy birthday, Alyssa!" Caleb cried.

"Yep. May fourteenth."

"How old are you again?" Sylvie asked.

"Fifteen."

"Fifteen? Awesome. I remember being fifteen. It was awkward. Good luck."

"Uh, thanks?"

Sylvie laughed. "Meet us at the pond in ten, birthday girl."

"Sounds great."

Alyssa jogged back into her shelter and began to peel her clothes off. The suit fit perfectly; it was probably magically manufactured to do that. She let her hair loose around her shoulders and yanked a towel from a pile of toiletries beside her bed. On her way out, she caught a glimpse of light reflecting off a smooth surface. Bending over to pick it up, she discovered a small mirror, formerly concealed by her towel. Frowning, she flipped it over. A sticky note stuck to the back read, in loopy handwriting:

You have changed, Alyssa McCaw. You wouldn't believe me if I told you, so I want to show you. Just look.

There was no signature, and Alyssa couldn't think who would've given it to her. She flipped the mirror over and looked at her face.

She *had* changed since she'd first come to Sunolia. Her hair and legs were a bit longer, her face a bit older—normal aging things. But she was also very muscular now, not only in her legs but in her arms and abdomen as well. And she looked so much *older.* Older because she had grown a bit physically, but mostly because she'd had so much stress beating her down for the past couple months. Before coming to Sunolia, she had never been expected to lead anything. She had been perfectly happy just living life as it was, accepting the way things were, not caring what anyone else was doing. But now she was so different. *It's strange how one person can become a completely new person just because of circumstances,* she thought. The odd thing about it was, it also made her feel better about herself. Before, she'd always looked in the mirror and thought, *Well, I'm okay, I guess. Not ugly, not pretty.* Even though she looked nearly the same as she had six months before, for the first time she looked at the freckles scattered across her nose, the bright blue eyes, the waves of her hair and thought, *Wow. I'm beautiful.* She stared at herself a moment, shocked that she would even think that. Her grandmother had taught her many years ago that vanity was dangerous. *But what the heck,* she thought. *Grandma's not here and this is my life, and I can think I'm beautiful if I want because I am.* And having proved that point to herself, she set the mirror down gently and dashed barefoot outside, across the field, down the path, and into the pond, where her friends were waiting for her.

* * *

"Your chariot awaits, Miss McCaw," Matthew said, gesturing at a cloud hovering a few feet off the ground in front of Alyssa.

She glared at him. "Are you serious?"

He shrugged. "Bella's idea."

Alyssa turned her glare on her little sister, who just smiled and said, "Happy birthday," with an innocent little wave. Alyssa stuck her tongue out, and Bella laughed.

"Come on, you," Matthew urged, offering his hand.

She took it with a sigh and plopped down on the cloud. It was soft, like a comfy chair. She looked up at her friend. "I thought clouds were made of water vapor," she protested.

He just smiled his charming little smile and said, "That's what the clouds want you to think. You think they enjoy people riding them around?"

Alyssa rolled her eyes. "You have my halo and my harp on you as well? So I can properly be an angel?"

Her friend leaned in to her ear and whispered, "Not all angels have halos."

She looked at him. "What's that supposed to mean?"

He just winked and gave the cloud a little push. She shrieked as she lurched forward and began going forward toward the mountains. "Where am I going?" she yelled back to her friends, but they were just cheering.

Alyssa sighed and shook her head. *This place is weird. One minute they're trying to kill you, the next you're riding clouds to some unknown place playing a harp.* That's when she noticed she was going not only forward, but rapidly ascending. Her palms began to sweat as she looked down and saw the ground falling away from her. The last time she'd been up this high, she had been otherwise occupied with fighting Meladynians and jumping off of balconies in downtown Chicago. But now that she was just sitting here on her own with plenty of time to think about the distance between herself and the ground . . . *What if physics decide to kick in and this cloud drops me because it realizes people can't ride clouds? Oh, shut up, conscience, I can handle this.* But she couldn't stop looking down and found herself clenching fists until her knuckles turned white and her fingernails dug into her palms. Her forehead broke out into a cold sweat. She was nearing a mountain—was that where she was going?—and as the air thinned, she began to hyperventilate. She gave up on keeping herself calm and all her thoughts blurred into *I'm gonna die I'm gonna die I'm gonna die.* Just as she was writing a will out in her head, she heard a familiar, amused voice call out through the wind.

"What's this, then? The legendary Alyssa McCaw, afraid of heights? I simply refuse to believe it."

"Malcolm, get me off of here!" she screamed. He was standing atop the mountain directly in front of her. The cloud finally came to a halt, and Alyssa jumped off it as quickly as she possibly could. But she'd underestimated the distance between herself and the mountain, and as her foot slipped, she tumbled off the cliff, screaming. It was because Malcolm's reflexes had been carefully trained since he was a child that Alyssa didn't fall to her death at the base of the mountains. At the last second, he gripped her hand. Alyssa's shoulder made a violent snapping sound, and a searing pain shot through it. Her legs dangled dangerously over the side.

"Malcolm, help me!" she shouted.

"Hold on, I got you. Give me your other hand."

She struggled to hold on to Malcolm, her arm trembling terribly from the terror of her impending death and the injury in her shoulder. "I can't," she moaned. "I'll fall."

"Alyssa, look at my face. You are not going to fall. I won't let you. But I need you to give me your other hand. Okay?"

She took a shaky breath and nodded. Squeezing Malcolm's hand, she swung her body back and forth like the pendulum of a clock until she was able to swing her left arm up and grab her friend's other hand.

"Okay, hold on, I got you." He shifted awkwardly into a squatting position and slid his hands down her arms until they rested under her arms. Then he stood, pulling her along with him like she weighed nothing. He set her down, but her legs were unsteady and she fell on him. Suddenly Alyssa found herself unexpectedly on top of Malcolm, her face in his chest. He looked down at her, and for a second they just stared at each other, breathing hard. Then he cracked a little half smile at her, and they were laughing. Hysterical, posttraumatic laughing, but still laughing, absolutely cracking up uncontrollably. They didn't stop until a loud, booming sound was heard above them. At first Alyssa thought it was a gunshot; she jumped and looked around quickly. But then she saw the colors explode above her head. *Fireworks. They're actually freaking fireworks.* She rolled over so she was lying in the grass side by side with Malcolm and noticed the sky was black, like a normal, mortal nighttime sky. Sure, it was nearly ten o'clock, but it was always bright in Sunolia. It made the colors pop in contrast.

"Wow," she whispered. "Look at that."

"Yeah, Caleb's idea," he replied.

"Why is the sky dark up here?" Alyssa asked.

"It just is. Same way it looks like a sunrise in the Garden of the Dawn. We have all the seasons and every time of day here; they're just all in different places. You can't sit in one place and watch time go by the way mortals can. You have to look for the summer, search for the night sky. But it's still there."

For a while they just lay there peacefully on the mountaintop, watching the light show. Alyssa's arm was still throbbing, of course, but she was used to pain enough at this point she could bite her tongue and keep her mouth shut about it. She didn't want to be in pain. Not on her birthday, with Malcolm. She just wanted to feel the moment. After a few minutes, Malcolm commented, "You know what's amazing? There is absolutely nothing magical about fireworks, and yet they are more spectacular than so many things magic can do." Alyssa nodded in agreement. She winced at this small movement from the pain that stabbed through her right shoulder. Malcolm noticed.

"Are you okay?" he inquired, looking worried.

"Yeah, I just—" She had to yell over the fireworks. She made an attempt to sit up, but the pain was so unbearable black spots appeared on the edges of her vision, forcing her back down. "I think I dislocated my shoulder."

"Oh. Ouch. Come here." He moved over and grabbed her arm gently. She tried to fight the pain, but couldn't help crying out when he lifted it. "Sorry. Okay, my mother used to be a doctor. I know how to do this. I'm going to have to pop it back in."

"You're going to have to *what*?" Alyssa cried. She felt like little shards of glass were being shoved into her arm from the inside.

"It's the only way to fix this. It'll hurt, but it'll be over fast if you hold still. And if you're good, you get a sticker and a lollipop at the end. All right?"

"Okay." Alyssa closed her eyes and waited. *The anticipation is the worst part,* she told herself.

"You're too tense. Relax," Malcolm ordered.

"I'm sorry, I'm having a hard time relaxing due to the knives slicing through my shoulder right now!" she cried, frustrated.

"Okay, okay, I know. Just do your best to sit still." He put one hand on her elbow and the other gripped her hand. "Ready? One, two, three!" He yanked on her arm. It made a sick cracking sound and a pain shot through her so fast she shrieked. And then it was over. Her shoulder still hurt miserably, but not excruciatingly. She could handle pain like this. "See? No so bad, huh?"

"I guess not. But can you just promise me on my next birthday you'll just get me a cake?"

He laughed. "You got a deal. And that reminds me. Did you like my present?"

She looked confused. "The mirror?"

Malcolm frowned. "What mirror?" Alyssa gave a brief description of the mirror and the note she had found in her room that morning. "Hmmm. Well, it wasn't me. Sounds like something Violet would do. Or maybe even the queen. But I don't know."

Alyssa considered this for a moment before rendering it unimportant and placing it carefully into the back of her mind to think about later. "Okay, but what present were you talking about then?"

"The simple joy of my presence, of course," he joked, spreading his arms humbly. It was Alyssa's turn to laugh. "Hey, that's not funny!" Malcolm nudged her shoulder playfully.

And then she got the strangest fluttering feeling in her stomach. Like she was nervous about something. At first she didn't understand it, but then a thought popped into her head out of nowhere. *I want to kiss him.* Where had that come from? But suddenly she *had* to kiss him; she had to so badly.

"Malcolm?" Alyssa said, looking up at him.

He'd been watching the fireworks; now the boy shifted his eyes down to her. "Yeah?"

She took his face in her hands and pulled it down to her own. She was so close she could feel his breath . . .

"Alyssa!"

Really?

She let go of him reluctantly and turned to face Violet standing behind her, looking awkward.

"Can I help you, Violet?" Alyssa asked, annoyed.

"Um, sorry to interrupt, but we have a problem I thought you should know about."

"Ugh. We always have problems. Malcolm just relocated my shoulder. Can it wait for one freaking day?" Hey, it was her birthday. Why should she have to deal with everybody else's problems on her birthday?

"Uh, yeah, sorry, but this is kind of a major problem."

"Okay, fine, what is it?" she demanded.

"You should probably come with me," Violet suggested.

Alyssa and Malcolm grudgingly climbed onto the cloud Violet was standing on and rode back with her. They mostly sat in awkward silence, everyone avoiding eye contact with everyone else. Alyssa, very aware of how close Malcolm's hand was casually lying beside hers, noticed the sky gradually growing lighter as they descended. The trip seemed endless, but by the time they finally reached the fire pit, the sky was blue and bright again. When they climbed down, they discovered everyone crowded around next to the pit. Alyssa pushed her way through onlookers, trying to get a look at what they were watching. Nothing could have prepared her for what she found in the center of the circle.

It was Sylvie, holding a little bundle of blankets. At first Alyssa didn't believe what she was seeing, but as she moved closer, she caught sight of a tiny hand and gasped. It was a baby. An infant, no more than a few months old.

"Whose . . . where did you . . . *what?*" Alyssa stuttered, unbelieving. Perhaps it was ridiculous to be so surprised over an ordinary baby, given all she'd been through the past few weeks. But it was just the absolute last thing she was expecting to see.

"I found him," said Violet. "I was just taking a walk in the woods and found him lying there on the ground. I have no idea where he could've come from. Nothing like this has ever happened before. This is really no place for a baby."

Alyssa took the infant from her, cradling it in her arms. It was a little boy, wrapped in a baby-blue blanket. He couldn't have been older than two months. The name *Jasper* was stitched into it in white cursive letters. She bounced up and down gently, rocking him until he calmed down. He looked up at her with huge brown eyes that made her smile.

"We need to have a meeting about this. Sylvie, go gather everyone up," Alyssa ordered.

Sylvie looked around the group. "Um, Alyssa, we're all gathered here already."

"Good, this will be easy, then. So, this baby," she gestured at the infant in her arms. "They said he was found in the woods. Obviously we can't just leave him, though I have no idea where he came from. If you ask, though, he was probably brought here through a Haven

Portal by Cressidalaina. What are we supposed to do with him?"

"We could send him back to the Mortal World," Bella suggested. "He'd be safer there."

"No," Sylvie declared. "This is the safest place he could possibly be. If he's here, it's for some reason. We can't send him back."

"We can't trust it!" Violet cried.

"He's only a baby! We have to help him!" Matthew said. "My sister's been that baby before, and she would've given anything to have a bunch of people help her. You can't leave him anywhere! We have to take care of him!"

There was pain in the boy's face, and Alyssa knew what he was saying was true. They had to help him somehow. "All right, calm down!" she yelled, as everybody was just arguing now. "We will keep the child here for the rest of the night. In the morning we will find a safer place for him, okay?"

"A safer place like where?" Caleb demanded. "Like Sylvie just said, you're not going to find a safer place than this."

"Yes, there is a safer place," Bella corrected. "The Garden of the Dawn. It's where the Silver Key and Cressidalaina are. If he's not safe there, he's not safe anywhere."

There were murmurs of consent, and it was decided. "He will stay with us tonight, and first thing tomorrow we will take him to the Garden. Who will look after him?"

"I will see that the child is cared for," Morosa replied, stepping forward from the back of the crowd. "He will be safe with me, I assure you. We will try to identify his parents."

Alyssa nodded. "All right. Any other concerns while we're all gathered already?"

"Let me see him," said a young voice. Alyssa turned to see Seraphina emerging from the crowd. "I'd like to check to see if he is light, dark, or mortal." Morosa looked at Alyssa inquiringly, and Alyssa nodded. Seraphina gently touched the baby on the head with two fingers, closed her eyes, and reopened them. Then she furrowed her brow, a confused look on her face.

"There's something odd about him. I can't tell exactly what it is. Like he's almost mortal, but not quite. I don't know. I just have a weird feeling. Maybe it's because he's so young, though. I've never tried to read a baby's magical energy before." The inconclusive reading made Alyssa feel uneasy, but still, it was an infant. She could hardly just leave him alone in the middle of a war.

"Okay, then. Morosa, take him to the Garden first thing in the morning. The queen will be able to handle him. Okay, that's it for now. Everyone to bed now. And the fireworks were cool, by the way."

CHAPTER 26

Alyssa opened her eyes the following morning to white cotton sheets and curtains. The infirmary. She was confused for a moment before remembering Malcolm had talked her into going there last night in order to let her arm heal. "I popped it back into place, but it still needs to be looked at by the Sunolian nurses. They can give you medicine for the pain and wrap it up," he had insisted. She had been too tired to argue, so she now found herself wrapped in soft, white blankets on a small cot. It had been a long time since she'd slept in a bed, even a small one. She moaned and rolled over. Stretching, she propped herself up on her good elbow and pushed back the thin curtains. She jumped upon seeing Seraphina nearly two feet from her face.

"Seraphina! What are you doing? How long have you been sitting there?"

Her face looked relieved. "Alyssa! Thank God you're awake, I couldn't wake you up! I have to tell you something!"

"Whoa, whoa, slow down, sister, what's going on?"

"You remember the baby you sent to the Garden with Morosa?"

"What about him? He's all right, isn't he?"

"All right!" the girl cried. "He ain't all right! That's the darkest little thing I've ever seen! Cressidalaina . . . she's dead."

"WHAT!" Alyssa screamed, shooting up out of bed so quickly it made her dizzy. "What do you mean, she's dead?"

"You know the power I have, the one where I can tell if people are light or dark just by looking at them? I tried it on the baby last night, and it didn't work that well, right? That's because it was a concealer spell!"

Alyssa shook her head. "Seraphina, you're not making sense. Why is the queen dead?"

"It's Marvalonna, Alyssa! Marvalonna disguised herself as a baby in order to slip past our protection spells! And it worked; I couldn't tell she was dark, and the amount of darkness in her usually gives me a headache. This morning, Morosa took her out to see Cressidalaina and Marvalonna killed her!"

"How could she get into Sunolia? The queen has the Key, there's no way to penetrate those borders!" Alyssa cried.

"I don't know. I guess the amount of raw power she has combined with the power the other three Keys are giving her is enough to get through. But she's here now, and if she's been to the Garden, that means she has the Key. She's brought her army here; all of Meladyne is attacking us. We can't hold up for long, Alyssa."

The look of terror on her face was like nothing Alyssa had ever seen. This girl had grown up in the darkest place on earth, and she looked horrified.

"What . . . what are we supposed to do about it?" Alyssa stuttered.

"You have to get to Meladyne before Marvalonna does and get the Silver Key back. Have you heard of the Twilight Hollow? It's like Meladyne's version of the Garden of the Dawn, the heart of all darkness. Once the Key is there, it will be too late. Marvalonna will release more power than the world has ever seen and the earth will fall. It's up to you, child of light and dark! You have to get that Key back! You have to save us!"

Alyssa sprinted for the door of the infirmary, feet still bare, body still covered by a hospital gown, heart racing. What she saw outside killed her inside.

The whole place had been transformed as gray as Meladyne. The sky had turned from its shade of bright blue, the grass from its green, the flowers from their gold. The only color other than gray was the red of bloodshed. The place was packed with Meladynians battling Sunolians, spirits, magical creatures, and Alyssa's friends. Everything inside her fell to the ground as she gazed around at her friends falling, the friends she had trained for so long, whom she'd grown so close to. In their midst stood Marvalonna, sending out waves of darkness, killing everything in her path while laughing maniacally.

This is good, Alyssa thought, trying to have a little hope. *If she's still here, that means we can beat her to Meladyne.*

"Find them!" the Dark Queen ordered her servants. "Find the McCaw children and dispose of them! Then the Key will be ours!"

"Oh no, Bella," Alyssa muttered.

"I told you," Seraphina said. "She's coming for you. We have to protect it, Alyssa. It's our only hope!"

The words of the Chronicles echoed through Alyssa's head. *It's coming for you. It's coming soon. Don't trust the little one. It's dangerous. It will kill you all.*

"I know. Phina, where are my weapons? I need a sword, a staff, and two knives. And see if you can find me some shoes. It has finally begun. The war has begun."

PART 3

CHAPTER 27

"Bella!" Alyssa screamed, making her way around the chaos. "Bella, where are you?" She ran into Matthew, who had just finished off a Meladynian, breathing hard, sweat soaking through his shirt. "Matthew, have you seen my sister?" she cried frantically.

"Alyssa!" He looked relieved. "She was with Malcolm last I saw her. They were going to find you."

"Thanks," she replied, and turned to run back toward the hospital. But Matthew caught her arm first. "Wait, Alyssa. What are we supposed to do?"

Oh, right. Army general and whatnot.

"Ummm . . . well, we aren't prepared for this fight. It's the middle of the night and most of us are still in our pajamas. We've got to get out of here," Alyssa decided.

"How much time do we have?" he demanded.

"Why do you keep asking me questions like I know something you don't? Um, okay, if Marvalonna penetrated Sunolia's borders, that means the portal is open. So I need everybody to get out of here as fast as possible."

"But what about Aquamarinia? What about the Garden? We can't just leave them here!" he panicked.

"We don't have a choice. It's already destroyed. We're not ready for this fight; we don't have a chance. Have everyone meet at 8342 Summer Breeze, that's my friend's house. Save everyone you can, leave the bodies. This is a war now, and the Battle of Aquamarinia is a hopeless fight."

"But—"

"Do as I say!" Alyssa hadn't exercised her power as the leader much before, and she hated yelling at people, but she needed everyone to cooperate without question if they were going to have a chance. "And if you find Caleb, send him to me."

The sudden burst of authority seemed to startle him, and he rushed to oblige. It almost felt good bossing people around, if he wasn't her friend and they weren't in the midst of a battle.

"Bella!" she cried again. "Bella, where are you?"

This time she heard a reply. "Alyssa!" It sounded far away, but it was definitely her sister.

"Bella, are you okay? Follow the sound of my voice."

"I'm here, Alyssa!"

Alyssa could just barely make out a little brown ponytail hopping around over the crowd. Sighing with relief, she shoved her way through everyone, swinging her sword as she needed to, and pulled the little ten-year-old into her arms. "Are you okay, Bells? Are you hurt?" she asked.

"I'm fine, I'm fine!" Bella replied, shoving Alyssa's arms off her. "But they have it, Alyssa. They have the Key!"

"Yeah, I know they have it, but we've got to get out of here. I've given orders for everyone to evacuate to the Mortal World. We can stay at Hazel's house and regroup. We'll get weapons and armor and food together to strengthen our forces. We don't stand a chance right now. You need to help me get everyone there safely. Salvage any weapons you can, and leave the rest here."

"But, Alyssa—"

"No buts, Bella, I need you to listen to me! Get out!"

"No, *you* listen to *me*," she commanded, grabbing Alyssa's arm and staring hard into her eyes. "We don't have time to regroup. If they have the Key, they'll use it as soon as possible. We need to go after it *right now* or we're all done for! Don't you understand that? We can't just abandon this place. What about the Sunolians? This is their home! And the water spirits? They can't even leave! We can't run away now. Alyssa, be the leader. You need to take charge and get that Key back *now*."

She had a point. Once Marvalonna got the Silver Key to the Twilight Hollow, they were all finished. So they didn't have much time.

"Okay, you're right. But how are we going to catch up with Marvalonna? She's got to be almost there by now."

"Leave that to me. I need you to find Selena."

"Silent Selena? She could be anywhere! How are we going to find her in this?" Alyssa gestured at the havoc around her.

"I don't know, but *hurry*. Meet me at camp. Bring as many people as you want, but this is going to be dangerous."

Alyssa nodded and turned to run. "Oh, and Alyssa?" Bella tossed her a small bag. "It has supplies in it. I got it together months ago. Figured we should have it just in case. There are about twenty more in my tent."

Alyssa shook her head in disbelief. She hadn't realized how clever her sister was. As the leader, Alyssa should've thought of preparing this way. But here was her baby sister outsmarting her. She kept discovering more in that kid than she ever would've guessed.

Finding Selena took nearly twenty minutes. She watched with pain as her friends fell, but was impressed with how well they were doing. Meladyne outnumbered Sunolia several hundred to one, but it looked as if their training had paid off. Sunolia was almost winning. Everyone and everything seemed to be helping—Alyssa's friends and

Sunolians fought side by side with swords and knives and magic and other contraptions Caleb had invented. Dryads melted out of trees and played magical wooden flutes until everyone around them collapsed—asleep or dead, Alyssa didn't know. Water spirits and naiads dragged the enemy under the water and drowned them whenever they stood close enough to the lake. Sprites had tiny pea-shooters full of salt that they were pelting people's eyes with. Some people were wearing armor, most of them pajamas. The eternally blue sky above had turned black. And it wasn't black like a normal night sky. It seemed to radiate dark magic, sucking the life out of everything. The flowers on the ground withered, and the grass had turned a sickly yellow. In the center of everything was Marvalonna, who seemed to be the source of all the darkness. And that sparked an idea in Alyssa's head.

The Meladynians were mostly mindless drones, zombies stumbling around taking orders from their queen. If Alyssa could manage to take her down, their main power source, they'd be done for. But how . . .? She was the most powerful person in the universe, but she wasn't even a human being. She was a child of darkness, the night's daughter. The only one who could possibly match her would've been Cressidalaina, who was dead now. Alyssa didn't know how, but there was no doubt now. The best way to stop them would be to take out the queen bee.

But Alyssa had no time to make plans. She just had to trust Bella. There! Across the distance, on top of a ruined hill, was the beautiful warrior princess she was looking for. Selena was wearing a bronze breastplate over a black tank top and combat boots over yellow plaid pajama bottoms, not an unusual style among the fighters at the moment. Her hair was in a single braid down her back, and she had her infamous oaken bow in her hand, shooting arrow after arrow and never missing her target. Alyssa had always admired her, especially watching her in battle.

She knew calling out across the battlefield was pointless, so she made her way across, avoiding fights as much as she could. She earned a cut on her cheek and a gash in her thigh, but was still able to make it without any fatal injuries. The second she was within earshot, she called out, "Selena! Selena! I need you, come here! Selena!"

Eventually, she seemed to hear Alyssa. She didn't turn her alert eyes off of her target, but began moving toward Alyssa. Most of the Meladynians seemed to have decided standing within shooting distance of Selena was a bad idea, so she didn't have as many people to shoot. Alyssa figured getting her off that hill was a good thing, though. Yes, it gave her higher ground, but she didn't want Marvalonna to see her as a threat. Selena might give Marvalonna a run for her money, but the silent young woman would surely lose in the end.

They met up eventually somewhere in between the ground and the hilltop, and Selena fixed her gaze on Alyssa, a questioning look in her dark eyes.

"Meladyne has the Key, and we have to get it back right now, or we're all dead. Bella says you can help us. Will you come with me?" Alyssa inquired in one breath.

Selena gave a nod and began toward camp with her. Halfway there, they discovered a Sunolian on the ground, writhing in pain and clutching her leg. Alyssa knelt beside her, unable to leave her alone, and examined the wound. She gagged looking at it; there was a knife in her leg so deep she could see the bone. Liquid gold poured from the wound—the blood of the Sunolians. On the handle of the knife, Meladyne's name gleamed in silver letters.

"Can you hear me? What happened?" Alyssa cried, not sure what to do. Selena crouched down beside her to help. The Sunolian only mumbled inaudible, pained words. "What did you say?" She began to speak again, louder, but in a language Alyssa had never heard. *Marvalonna destroyed the magic of this place,* Alyssa realized. *We can't communicate with each other anymore. The magic that translates our languages must be gone.*

"Okay, Selena's going to pull the knife out for you, okay? I'll hold your hand. You're going to be okay, I promise." She tried to twist and see her leg, but Alyssa caught her head before she could fall back on it. "Don't watch, okay? I want you to look at me, just me, okay?"

She nodded, seeming to understand. Alyssa grasped her tiny hand, looking into her golden eyes. The little girl looked back at her, focusing on her eyes as she'd told her to. It made a disgusting noise when Selena pulled the dagger from her leg, and the Sunolian cried out in distress. When Alyssa had enough stomach to look back at Selena, she was wrapping a piece of cloth tightly around the blood-spurting wound. She ran out, though, and seemed to need more. But where else were they going to get cloth?

And then Alyssa remembered the bag Bella had given her. She quickly snatched it up off the ground and dug through it. It contained a water bottle, pack of crackers, flashlight, walkie-talkie, knife, compass, blanket, towel, and bandage. Marveling at the amount of useful supplies, she yanked the bandage out and handed it to Selena. The girl wrapped it around the Sunolian's leg and expertly tied it off. Then she looked around, as if trying to find someone. Alyssa understood. They needed to get her to the infirmary as quickly as possible. Alyssa jumped up and grabbed the nearest person she could find, which happened to be Matthew.

"Matthew!" she called. "I need you to take this Sunolian to the infirmary. She's hurt."

Matthew nodded, lifting the tiny body with one arm with ease. Then he ran off with her, bashing a Meladynian in the head with a giant rock on the way. Alyssa looked up at Selena and said, "We have to keep moving. Let's go."

Selena nodded, and they took off across the land, shooting and stabbing as needed, earning a few more injuries. Alyssa took a blow to the back of her head, making her so dizzy she nearly blacked out, but Selena picked her up and carried her until she could walk again. Another five minutes and they'd reached the fire pit. Every tent surrounding the pit had been burned to the ground, leaving nothing but a few charred pieces of clothing and flaming sleeping bags. It hurt Alyssa to look at; it may not have been much, but it had been her home for nearly six months.

The fight was even thicker there than anywhere else. Dark Ones rode on the backs of sleek silver wolves, and the strongest creatures with the most powerful magic cast spells eliminating everyone around them.

"Pretty bad, huh?" Bella commented, suddenly beside her. Violet and Sylvie were also there, panting and looking exhausted with mud streaked across their foreheads, hair plastered to their skin with sweat.

"This is insane," Alyssa agreed, taking it all in and trying to explain to her unwilling mind that it was real. "Bella, where are we going to go after the war? We don't have a home anymore."

"None of us have homes anymore. But we can worry about that after the war—if there *is* an after the war, which there won't be unless we get moving *now*," Violet insisted. Alyssa knew this must be hard for her; she'd been more dependent on Sunolia for longer than most of them. But other than a flicker of sorrow in her eyes, she didn't let it show. If only one day Alyssa could be like that. Stonehard, able to turn her emotions off completely when it was necessary and focus on the task at hand. Absolute titanium.

"Selena?" Violet asked, holding out her hand. "We have to beat Marvalonna to Meladyne; if she gets the Key back to Meladyne before we get there, we're done for. Everyone else can stay here and fight the Meladynians, but we have to stop Marvalonna. We'll go together, just the five of us. Take us out of here."

Selena nodded, took her hand, and glanced at Alyssa expectantly. Bella clutched Selena's hand and held out her own to Alyssa. Alyssa gave them a confused look. "It's okay," she encouraged. "We can get out faster this way."

"Okay," Alyssa agreed hesitantly.

"Oh, and you might vomit, by the way," Bella added at the last minute, when they were all in a line holding hands like kindergarteners ready to cross the street.

"Wait, *what?*"

"Three, two, one, go!" Violet shouted, and Alyssa didn't have time to back out.

The two people on the ends of the line joined hands as if they were getting ready to play ring-around-the-rosy. Alyssa's feet slowly began to rise off the ground, and she started to get that fluttery, panicky feeling in her stomach that could be induced not by bad guys or monsters or wolves, but by the feeling of her feet being lifted up and the view of the ground falling away below her. Beside her, Bella squeezed her hand.

"It's okay," she whispered. "You won't fall; don't be afraid."

"What?" Alyssa attempted a snort, but it just made a weird squeaky noise in the back of her throat. "Why would I be afraid?"

"Be real, sister. Everybody knows you're afraid of heights."

Alyssa opened her mouth to spit something back at her, particularly Bella's fear of the dinosaur ride at the Animal Kingdom in Disney World, but before she could, the wind was sucked out of her. They were accelerating through the air so fast everything around them looked like a blur. Alyssa's hair whipped behind her, and she nearly blacked out from the speed. She attempted to scream, but all it did was dry out her throat and make it hard to breathe. It was not a pleasant ride, but it didn't take long. After a mere half minute, Bella and Sylvie both squeezed her hands at the same time, and then let go. There wasn't even time to panic before she stopped moving so abruptly it was as if she'd slammed into a wall. Her body dropped to the ground, and she landed hard on her back. Groaning and feeling sick to her stomach, she sat up and saw everyone else standing, looking down at her. "I thought," she moaned, "you said I wasn't going to fall."

"Well, I meant not fall while we were moving," Bella reasoned, as if that were perfectly obvious.

"Yeah, whatever."

But when Violet helped her to her feet, she was amazed to look around and find herself in her own front yard. They were back in the Mortal World again.

It was the middle of the night, so the road was empty. Streetlights illuminated the dark road. The air was warm with a summer breeze. It was a bittersweet feeling, seeing everything so quiet, so perfect, the way it used to be. In a few hours, the lights would turn on in the little houses and kids would walk to school, parents would kiss them goodbye and drive to work. For over half a year, Alyssa, Bella, their parents, Hazel, and Ricky had been gone, and yet nothing had changed in the town. But they needed to get moving, or there would be no town left. The world could end in a matter of minutes, and still the people slept, oblivious to the danger. Alyssa desperately wished she was among them, this responsibility on someone else's shoulders. As they paraded to Ricky's house, she took a deep breath through her nose. She would succeed, if only to save this little neighborhood, this town that managed to be peaceful even though it sat right on the outskirts of noisy, wild Chicago.

The door had been carelessly left open by the Meladynians, so getting in through Ricky's basement was no trouble. It was also completely deserted.

"The idiots," Violet mumbled. "They all left at once. The place is completely unprotected."

"Come on, we've got to wind travel again," Bella ordered, holding her hands out, but Selena shook her head and Violet told her, "Light magic is weaker here. The wind spirits can't help us. We have to travel on foot now."

"But the Meladynians have *wolves!*" Bella exclaimed. "And they must be ahead of us if they had enough power to get through Sunolia's borders. How the heck are we going to beat them there?"

"She's got a point," Alyssa agreed. "Traveling on foot is pointless. We might as well just kill ourselves now."

"All right, well what do you suggest we do?" Sylvie demanded, sounding annoyed.

"Uhhh . . ."

"We don't have a lot of time for 'uh' right now!" Sylvie cried.

"Guys, guys, we don't have time to argue! Now let's just run until we can find a better solution," Bella suggested.

Everyone grumbled in agreement and started jogging after her. But after a minute or so, Alyssa started thinking about her street again and an idea sparked in her head. What if . . .?

"Hey Violet, stop a second!"

She turned to face her. "Yeah?"

"Could you drive a car through here?"

"A car? Like, a mortal car? Uh, I don't see why not. But I can't drive."

"We have to go back outside. Follow me."

Alyssa took off at top speed back toward the portal, not believing how she hadn't thought of it before. What was the easiest way to get somewhere quickly? A car, of course.

They dashed back through the portal, up the stairs, and back down the street to Alyssa's house. Alyssa's house had a big "For Sale" sign in front of it; apparently people had become a little suspicious when they'd disappeared. Alyssa couldn't imagine what kinds of wild stories they were coming up with for all the disappearances, not to mention the twenty identical corpses she'd left in her house.

But the car still sat there, for whatever reason, right in the driveway where they'd left it. They must not have gotten around to selling it yet. The house still had half its furniture, including the kitchen table, upon which the car keys rested just like they always had. Alyssa snatched them off the table, tore outside, and shoved them into the ignition. "Everyone in," she ordered.

"Girl, you're serious?" Bella cried.

"Bella, if you can give me one reason I would not be serious right now, I'd love to hear it. Otherwise, *get in the freaking car.*"

Everyone obeyed without further question. Alyssa had never driven a car but, hey, how hard could it be? Just turn the keys, set the car in reverse, and push the pedal . . .

"AAAHHH!"

"Sorry!"

She crashed backward into the tree in her front yard, slamming her head backward into the headrest. It ached as soon as she sat back up. "Is everybody okay?"

"Dang it, move over, McCaw. We don't have time for driver's ed."

Violet shoved Alyssa off her seat onto Sylvie's lap and took control of the car. She drove the car straight through the wall of Ricky's house, then down the stairs and through the door in the basement, passengers screaming and shielding their faces from flying shrapnel. As Violet floored the gas pedal, they sped across the dirt like a racecar on a racetrack. Alyssa had no idea if they were even going the right way; everything looked the same. All she knew was they were going faster than the car should go. And then they could see it, looming on the horizon. The village of the Meladynians, full of old, rickety mansions, the dark, menacing palace glaring down at them all.

"Violet," Alyssa yelled over the noise, still sitting on Sylvie and gripping the sides of the seat until her knuckles were white. "We've got to get to the Twilight Hollow; that's where they're headed. Do you know where that is?"

"No, you want me to stop and ask for directions?"

"Vi, see what's over that hill," Bella commanded, pointing to the left at one of the only elevated places in Meladyne.

She veered left, and everyone was thrown against the walls and each other. Then she drove up the hill and abruptly stopped, forcing everyone to fly forward and smack their faces on something. Alyssa found herself on the floor under the glove compartment, her face in the carpet. The car, meanwhile, continued rolling, getting partway down the hill before it stopped.

Alyssa crawled out from under the compartment, tasting blood. Sylvie's nose was twisted in an unnatural way, but the others looked okay.

"Violet!" Bella screamed, peeling herself off the back of the front seat. "I said 'see what's over that hill.' *Not* do that."

She shrugged apologetically. "Sorry, I've lived in Sunolia most of my life. I never got to learn how to drive."

"Why did you stop?" Alyssa moaned.

Sylvie sat up, a look of disbelief on her now-distorted face. She was staring straight ahead, pointing at the scene before her. "That's why."

The place was a colony, thriving with people—men, women, and children, all different nationalities, sizes, and ages. Some had obviously been there for longer than others, judging by the state of their clothes and their worn bodies. Many even bore the marks of torture—slashes across their faces, gashes in their arms, limps in their steps. They were all keeping busy somehow; many people slept under rags, shivering on the ground. Some ate moldy pieces of bread or drank water from small tin cups. Women folded clothes, and men sharpened knives or polished swords. The community stretched out as far as the eye could see, packed to the brim with thousands of tortured, starving prisoners.

"What . . . what *happened* here?" Bella asked, all traces of humor gone from her face.

"It's a colony," Alyssa whispered.

"More like a prison," Sylvie figured. "It's where they keep their slaves."

"It's awful," Violet said, an edge of sorrow in her voice. "I can't even see where it ends."

"They've been building it up for millennia," Sylvie explained. "And this is what's going to happen to everyone in the world if they beat us to the Hollow with that Key."

"Do you think we're ahead of them yet?" Violet worried.

"Doubt it. But we might still catch up, depending on how they're traveling. We were going almost one twenty."

Alyssa gestured at the people below, who were starting to gather around and stare. "You wanted to ask for directions."

The second they piled out of the car, everyone backed away from them, afraid.

"Good people of Oz—" Bella started, spreading her arms out like she was ready to make a speech.

"Shut up, Bella, you just don't know when to stop. They're scared, can't you see that? Let me do the talking," Alyssa hissed, shoving her sister behind her. She looked down at all the gaunt faces looking up at her with confused expressions. "Um, ahem. My name is Alyssa McCaw, and um, you don't have to be afraid." There were a few whispers at the mention of her name. No wonder. Alyssa and her sister must've been on the front cover of the *People to Kill* magazine in Meladyne by now. "This is Bella, Sylvie, Violet, and Selena. We are trying to help you, but we need your help first. I need one of you to show us the way to the Twilight Hollow." A little shuffling and whispering, but no volunteers.

"Please, I understand you're afraid, and so are we, but the world will come crashing down at any minute if we don't get there before Marvalonna. Please, is it far from here?"

"It is not far," a raspy voice spoke up. Alyssa turned her head to see an elderly man step forward. What hair he had left was white and wispy, his skin dark and tough. He had a wild, unkempt beard like many of the other men she could see. His back hunched a bit, but he stood on his own. He had to be at least seventy or eighty. "I can show you the way if you like."

Alyssa wasn't sure what to say. He was so thin, so beaten. She tended to leave a path of destruction wherever she went, and she didn't want to hurt this old man. She had been looking more for someone young and healthy. He seemed to see her doubts in her eyes.

He chuckled. "Oh, I know what you're thinking. I'm an old man, yes? How could I be useful in a fight? I'll be killed. Well, let me tell you something. I've lived in this place for—what year is it?"

She told him, and after thinking for a second, he replied, "Well, I'll be . . . has it really been that long? I've been here for fifty-two years now. I can take care of myself. Don't you worry about me, kiddo. I'm stronger than you'd think, even if I'm not sixteen like all of you. Let me come. I know this land better than most."

"Works for me," Bella decided. "We've gotta go. Get in the car, Mister, uh . . ."

"Dale."

"Dale, right."

Alyssa held a hand out to help him, but to her surprise he stood up straight without assistance. "The hunch is just for show. They don't expect as much from old people."

He took a Meladynian knife from a young boy who sat cross-legged on the ground sharpening it and jogged back up the hill with amazing speed.

"Um . . . okay," Sylvie agreed. "Let's go, then."

Once in the car, Dale pointed them in the right direction, and Violet started off at eighty miles per hour. After a few minutes, though, Dale called from the back seat, "Is that as fast as this car will go? I thought we were saving the world! Even in the fifties we drove faster than this. Floor the gas pedal, girl!"

"Yes, sir," Violet obliged, looking slightly frightened.

"So, um, Dale," Alyssa tried, "you said you've been here for fifty-two years?"

"Yes, ma'am. When I was twenty years old, they captured me. I lived in Kentucky at the time, happy, just about to marry my girl Cecilia. They tied me up and dragged me here while I was sleeping. They wanted to know if I'd discovered some kinda Key or magic portal or somethin'. They tortured me, but I didn't know nothin' to tell them. Eventually they brought Cecilia down here too. They beat her too, but o' course she didn't know what they was talkin' 'bout. So eventually we were thrown back to the colony. They force us to work for them, torturing and starving us. Every couple months there's another person brought in, and when they don't know anything they get stuck here, too. We don't know the details, really. Just what we've been able to pick up. There are four Keys that have some kinda power in them, and the people here have three. So, they capture random people and torture them until they are convinced they don't know where it is, then the people get thrown into the colony. I've heard stories about a place called Sunolia, magic like this place, but good. I think that's what the

Keys unlock. Lately, though, the leader here, Marvalonna, has been getting restless, ever since her husband Karvokono died. Apparently, she found what she was looking for, but can't get to it. Kept talking about the McCaws. I have a feeling that's not too good for you."

"Yeah, me and my sister were protecting the last Key, but they have it now, and if they reach the Twilight Hollow before us, they'll have enough power to take over the world. Then everyone will be trapped here like you, slaves of Meladyne. The world will be nothing but darkness, just like they want it. That's why we have to get there first."

It was quiet for a few minutes, and Alyssa began to feel antsy and uncomfortable. So she tried to come up with something to say to keep her mind occupied. "So, your girlfriend, Cecilia. Is she still here?"

Dale shook his head. "She died a couple of years ago. I have a son and a daughter, though. They were born here, in the colony."

"It's incredible, how you all survived here for so long. You all have families and jobs and everything. You created your own community," Violet marveled.

The old man shook his head. "It's not like that, kid. We only survived because Meladyne wanted us to. We sleep on the ground, barely have any food. We don't get paid for doing the jobs we have. We just get beaten for not doing them. It was terrible, raising a family in a place like this. As soon as my children could walk, they had to learn to polish a knife, bow their heads when the monarchs passed by. They were tortured when they didn't do it right. It's not the way a person should live. I hope to God you kids save the world before they destroy it. I swear, people can't even kill themselves. If you're caught attempting it, and many have been, you just get put under constant supervision, and if you manage to get away with it, they hurt everyone that was close to you. Look at this. They've stolen our lives until we don't even want them back anymore; we don't even try. What I wouldn't give to see the sun again."

"You will see it, Dale," Alyssa promised. "We'll—"

"WE'RE HERE, EVERYBODY OUT!" Bella yelled, throwing her door open and leaping from the car before it had fully stopped. Everyone followed suit, tumbling from the vehicle and scurrying to their feet.

Alyssa took in her surroundings briefly. The sky above had turned from tornado gray to a deep, sapphire blue—the kind one would see just after sunset, before it was completely dark—giving the whole place an eerie bluish glow. Before her towered a colossal tree, so tall the top seemed to fade into the sky, and so big around she wouldn't be able to wrap her arms halfway around it. The branches were bare and twisted menacingly, like claws. Alyssa never would have thought she could be intimidated by a tree, but this one managed it. It was surrounded by a ring of fire, the flames no higher than her knees. There were two slots in the tree that she could see, one with a little golden Key protruding from it, the same size as the Silver Key, the same tiny crystals embedded in it. The other was empty. She slowly made her way around the tree, careful to keep her distance from the flames, amazed by its size, and found, as she had suspected, two more of the slots on the other side, both with Keys placed delicately in them. They were both the same size, same crystals, but one was bronze and the other a copper color.

"This is it?" Bella asked incredulously. "No guards, no magic barriers, nothing? This is the cause of thousands of people suffering, stuck in this tree, right where we can take it? You have got to be kidding me." She unsheathed her sword. "All right, come on then! Where are you? I know you're waiting somewhere! We're stealing the Keys! Come get us!"

Sylvie cried out, pressing a hand over the little girl's mouth. "Don't make this hard. We got this far." She gestured at their surroundings. "Look around. No leaves. No trees. No hills. No rocks. Just dirt. Where could anyone possibly be hiding?"

"Stop talking, you idiots!" Alyssa cried. "Forget the Silver Key, as long as we have these three, they don't have any power. We'll be stronger than them, and we can come back for the Silver Key later! We have to take these three and get the heck outta here!"

Without hesitation, Selena ran toward the flames, leaping over them as if clearing a hurdle. But rather than land safely on the other side, she seemed to slam into an invisible force field. She was thrown backward in midair and landed hard on her back on the ground.

"Look, Sylvie, there is a catch. Happy now?" Alyssa demanded, extending a hand to help Selena to her feet. The young woman looked up as if considering before declining the help and standing up on her own.

"How do we get past it?" Bella asked. "We've come too far to be topped by an invisible wall. There's got to be some certain type of person able to get through. That's how force fields work."

"As a matter of fact, Isabelle, there is." The icy voice hadn't come from any of Alyssa's friends. She whipped around to find Marvalonna standing before her, Silver Key in hand, a malevolent smirk on her face. "You must be dark. It must be in your heart, your soul, your blood. No spell will penetrate these walls. Only darkness."

Alyssa knew she wasn't lying. She didn't have to. It was impossible for any of them to take back any more Keys because they were all light. If Marvalonna had set it up, there was no defeating it. She was not ruthless and cruel the way Karvokono had been. She was clever and collected. There was no defeating her.

"Now behold, children, the day your world falls at my feet. The day dark magic envelops the earth and the humans bow to their rightful queen." She stepped into the circle, the flames parting for her like the Red Sea for Moses and closing back up behind her. "I have waited for millennia for this day to come. Behold! The start of the age of darkness!"

The cold, silent hands of fear seemed to wrap their fingers around Alyssa's neck, holding her in place, choking her, leaving her powerless to do anything but stand paralyzed as the Key neared the slot. Selena stood just inches away, her arm brushing Alyssa's, and though she showed no fear in her eyes, her body was tense and ready to move. Dale placed a hand on her back in a supportive, paternal fashion, as if to say, *It's going to be all right, honey.* But his hand trembled against her. Bella squeezed her sister's hand so tightly the circulation was cut off in her fingers. Violet put an arm around Alyssa's shoulders and held her close in a tight embrace. They all stood huddled together, heads down, eyes shut, blood pounding in their ears, waiting in anticipation for the world to crumble.

 They stood for a few minutes, frozen in fear, no one daring to speak, and still nothing happened. "Is that it?" Bella whispered. "I didn't feel anything."

And then they heard harsh cursing and spells, and lifted their heads to see Marvalonna trying to cast spells on the Key. It was inserted in the slot, just as the others were, but nothing was happening.

The Dark Queen whirled on Alyssa, a murderous look in her eyes, and Alyssa stumbled backward a few steps, afraid. "WHY WON'T IT WORK? I KNOW YOU KNOW! TELL ME!"

Alyssa threw her hands up, tears slipping from the corners of her eyes. "I don't know, I don't know, please, I don't know, let me go!" She racked her brain for any possible reasons it wouldn't be working. But it didn't make any sense. All four of the Keys of Power, united in the Heart of Darkness, should unleash a dark magic powerful enough to overcome everything light in existence. But somehow . . . it hadn't. For some reason, she was still standing there, alive and well. But why? Had Violet or Sylvie or Cressidalaina or any of her instructors ever told her about anything like that, any reason it wouldn't work? What about Falla . . .? And then, with a gasp, she remembered. *Because it belongs to you. No one else can use its power but the owner. And the only way to become the owner of a Key is to be willingly and consciously given the Key by the chosen owner, or to kill the owner*. And that was when she realized. She was the only thing standing between Marvalonna and her power. And she was standing five feet from where Marvalonna was.

It must have been the way the fear intensified in her eyes, but the queen seemed to understand as soon as she did. She narrowed her eyes and curled her finger in a *come here* gesture at Alyssa. In a panic and a rush of adrenaline, Alyssa shouted the first spell that came into her head, but nothing happened. She knew her mind wasn't clear enough, but it was impossible to stop thinking about how terrified she was. The place was too overrun by dark magic, anyway. She could feel it; it seemed to be pulsing through the air, held back by a thread, fighting to break through. Her life was so fragile, and so near to the end, there was hardly anything to stop it anymore.

But that was when she remembered. *Only darkness can penetrate the barrier. But I* am *dark. My mother was a Dark Queen, just like Marvalonna. My mother is dark, my father is light, and I grew up in the Mortal World, where everyone is a little bit of both. I have dark magic in me. I can do it.*

Squeezing her eyes shut and concentrating, she did everything she could to make herself dark in that moment. She imagined herself killing Marvalonna, tearing her apart, destroying everything she had, pounding her into the ground until the queen was crying and begging for mercy on her knees. She imagined bloodshed, every Meladynian in existence lying lifeless in the dirt. She imagined Karvokono, writhing on the ground, screaming in agony. And the light half of her whispered, *That's terrible, no one deserves that fate.* But the dark in her said, *Yes, she deserves it! Look what she's done to all those people! Make her suffer! Kill her!*

And for once, she stopped fighting the darkness; she let it in, let the anger and misery and hatred envelop her.

Reaching deep within, she extracted a spell. She had never heard it, never spoken it, and didn't even know where the words had come from. But from the darkest side of her heart, from millennia of black magic in her very blood, came the spell, full of harsh-sounding foreign words making hard sounds on her tongue and in her throat. Screaming these words, she thrust her palms outward at Marvalonna, and a storm of darkness erupted. Wind whipped around the Dark Queen and she screamed, the worst, most tortured of screams. It was a sound Alyssa hated to hear, but still she sprinted forward, leaping over the flames and landing within the circle just as she had known she would be able to do.

Feeling triumphant and more confident than she had ever been in her life, she reached for the Golden Key. Her fingers pinched the minuscule object, and she yanked on it as hard as she could, but it didn't budge. Frustrated, she positioned her feet on the tree and pulled with all her might, putting all her weight into it, but still it wouldn't budge. She inspected the little slot, trying to see what it had been caught on, but it was just sitting loosely inside. There was no physical reason it wouldn't move; it, too, was something magical. But Alyssa didn't understand why it wouldn't work. She was obviously dark enough to cross the force field and cast that awful spell on Marvalonna. But why couldn't she take the Keys?

"Alyssa, what are you doing?" Bella screamed over the queen. "We've won! Just take the Keys and we can get out of here. We can save everyone. We can meet our parents! Just hurry up!"

"I can't move it, Bella!" Alyssa called back.

"Pull harder! We didn't come all this way for nothing!" Violet insisted.

"It's enchanted, too, Violet, don't you see that? I *can't* move it. No amount of physical strength is going to help."

"Well, what are we going to do then? We can't just leave!" Sylvie cried.

"I've heard legends of a Light Queen from the others. A wise, beautiful, powerful queen, said to control your Sunolia," Dale said, and Alyssa whirled to face him, having completely forgotten he was there. "Is it at all possible you could ask her? She would surely know how to break this curse."

Alyssa shook her head. "She was killed by Marvalonna. How are we supposed to do this without her?"

Bella looked tentatively at the Dark Queen, still writhing and screaming, crying out, "Please, let me go, I surrender, just stop it, stop it, let me go, PLEASE!"

"Please stop it, Alyssa," Bella begged, and Alyssa could see tears brimming in her sister's eyes. "I thought we were the good guys. She surrendered, okay? You're acting like her now. We're not animals. Don't hurt her anymore."

But the hate Alyssa had conjured up in order to pass the barrier had consumed her and become something real and deep. She loathed Marvalonna wholeheartedly, and all the pain she was feeling she deserved. "Did you see them, Bella?" Alyssa shouted, enraged. "Did you see those thousands of people she's ripped from their families and tortured? There are children here who have never seen the sun, people who never got to have the life they deserved. They were all innocent, and she made them suffer. I won't stand for it anymore. For thousands of years we've let her do this. Well, I'm saying no. Let her feel what she has made others suffer." Alyssa drew another dark spell from inside, harsher foreign words. The second they were out, Marvalonna screamed even louder, and Alyssa could see her jerking body, her teary face, her tortured expression. She pleaded even harder, promising the people could go free, the recently deceased she could bring back, Alyssa could have all the Keys and all the power she wanted, her brother and her parents, but Alyssa was too angry to listen.

"You wanted so badly to get away from her, and now you're acting just like her!" Bella screamed. "This is exactly what she would do to you. It's over now, Alyssa. She'll cooperate. Let it go. You aren't dark, stop acting like it. It's in your blood, but stop letting it into your heart. Come back to me, okay?" Bella held out her hand. "Remember Hazel and Ricky, Alyssa? Remember Mom and Dad? Remember track and dances and boys and school? Remember home? Remember me? Please, it's still waiting for you. We can end this and go home and have a normal life, just like you wanted. Just let go and come with me."

Alyssa glanced down at Bella's small face surrounded by a puff of hair, her dark, pleading eyes, her outstretched hand, and the hatred melted away. "Okay. Okay, let's go home," she agreed, holding out her own hand to take Bella's. She stepped out of the circle of flames and pulled her sobbing sister to her chest, falling to her knees. "I'm sorry," she whispered. "I'm so, so sorry. It's okay now. We don't need the Keys. You're right, we've won."

She glanced down at Marvalonna, who had collapsed to the ground and was curled in a ball, breathing hard, no longer in pain but trying to recover. Letting go of Bella, she made her way to the queen.

"Alyssa . . ." Sylvie warned.

"It's okay, Sylvie, I won't," Alyssa promised.

She looked down on the pathetic woman crumpled before her with disgust, kicking her in the ribs with the toe of her boot. Marvalonna cried out, her body convulsing.

"You. I want you to let all those people go. I want you to slink back into the dark hole you came from. I don't ever expect to see your hideous, heartless face again. You need to go away now and never hurt anyone else. Because if you don't . . . well, you know what I can do. Do you understand me?" Marvalonna moaned. "I SAID, DO YOU UNDERSTAND ME?"

"Yes, yes, all right. Take the prisoners—all of them. You can have all the Keys and anything else you want. Just leave me alone, okay? Leave me to spend the rest of my days in Meladyne, and don't bother me anymore. Please?"

Alyssa kicked her again, and gave her a few choice words that made everyone behind her gasp. They all watched with satisfaction as Marvalonna forced herself onto her knees with no lack of difficulty. She clawed at the ground, whimpering pathetically, attempting to stand up. She finally managed to climb to her feet, stumbling off in the opposite direction, clutching her head in her hands. "Hey!" Alyssa called after her. "I'll be taking that back, if you don't mind!" Marvalonna turned to face Alyssa, and Alyssa caught sight of her miserable face. Her normally neat black hair was in a tangled mess, and black makeup ran down her cheeks as pitiful tears spilled from her eyes. It was a hideous sight, one almost bad enough to make Alyssa feel guilty. But all it took was remembering one poor, innocent soul the Dark Queen had tortured and beaten to make that guilt disappear. Marvalonna threw the Silver Key at Alyssa, and the miniscule object landed at Alyssa's feet. "Now go. And don't you ever come back." And with that, Marvalonna, last remaining royal of Meladyne, turned and staggered out of sight.

CHAPTER 29

For a moment, all was silent, and then all at once a cheer broke out, and everyone hugged and kissed and rejoiced in their victory. Tears of joy and relief found their way down Alyssa's cheeks as she took her sister into her arms. "We did it, Bella!" she shouted over the commotion. "We can go home now. It's gonna be okay. I won't let anything like this ever happen to you again, I promise."

Bella beamed back up at her. "It was all you, Alyssa. You're the reason we're still here. We won because of you. You're a hero."

Alyssa shook her head. "You were what stopped me. If you hadn't, I would've killed her. You made me remember I'm light."

"Hey, guys, I hate to be Johnny Raincloud, but we still don't have the other three Keys. Everybody in the other three regions of Sunolia is still trapped there, including your parents," Sylvie pointed out.

The excitement died down the slightest bit. "Yeah, Alyssa, what was with that? Why couldn't you get the other Keys out?" Violet wondered, curiosity in her dark eyes.

"I don't know. It has to be some other kind of spell."

"Well, then how are we going to get the other Keys?"

"We can worry about that later," Alyssa suggested. "We'll get a team of people out here and figure out how to counter whatever spell is on them. But for right now, we won! Let's celebrate! We'll get all those prisoners out, clean everything up, and have a party tonight!"

There was another cheer, and everyone piled back into the car, laughing and joking and smiling. There was talk of seeing long-lost relatives and hope they were still all right. A five-hundred-pound weight seemed to have been raised from everyone's shoulders, and the tension that had always existed was gone. There were no barriers anymore, no danger, no fear. Everything was okay. That was how a car full of kids should look. Even Selena had a spark of hope in her eyes, and though she wasn't smiling, her face was no longer carved from stone.

As they approached the colony, doors were flung open and people tore out of the car.

Alyssa watched, beaming, as her friends ran sobbing into their family's arms, and the news was spread that the queen was gone and the people were free. Bella was dancing around with people, telling wild, exaggerated versions of the battle. Only Selena remained with Alyssa. She was standing on the tips of her toes and seemed to be looking for someone over the people.

"You don't see your family?" Alyssa asked gently. Selena stood back down on her feet and let her eyes drop to the ground. "Hey, there are thousands of people here. I'm sure they're here somewhere." Selena just shook her head slightly and turned to leave. It broke Alyssa's heart, seeing someone unhappy in the midst of so much joy, but she knew her friend wasn't comfortable with emotions, so she let her go.

Slowly, the crowd was led out of Meladyne and into Aquamarinia. Alyssa could only imagine what it looked like to the people in her mortal neighborhood, as thousands of rejoicing people bearing scars and weapons made their way across the street from Ricky's house into Alyssa's front yard and disappeared into the ground. But she was too ecstatic to care. People were reunited with their loved ones, and a party followed that night.

"Alyssa!" Sylvie called from across the lawn. They stood in the meadow a few miles from the fire pit, and everyone was laughing. Music played loudly, snack tables were set up everywhere, and people were scattered for miles. "You have to meet my family, come here."

Alyssa allowed herself to be dragged to Sylvie's little British family, and she shook hands with her uncle and father. "This is Alyssa McCaw. She's the one who saved us. And doesn't she look simply *stunning* in that dress? I picked it out myself . . ."

Alyssa had endured many of these introductions, and she had smiled and shaken hands and nodded through every one of them. But the person she was really looking for she hadn't been able to find all day throughout the chaos of spirits and Sunolians and released prisoners everywhere. *God, where could he be?*

And then, just when she'd given up hope on seeing him, he was there. She felt him take her hand, put an arm around her waist, and spin her around gently to face him.

"You were *incredible* today," he whispered.

"Malcolm," she breathed.

"Have you found any of your family?" he asked, leading her in a slow dance.

She shrugged. "Can't say that there's much family to find. My friend Hazel should be around here somewhere. My parents are still in Terralith, and supposedly I have a brother somewhere that I've never met, but I could hardly pick him out of a crowd. What about your family? You find your sister?"

"Yeah, she's right over there." He gestured to a small blonde girl playing with Bella at the snack table. A middle-aged woman stood a few feet away who must've been his mother.

"She's beautiful."

"She's so much older than I remember her. But I'm glad she's okay. I didn't think she had enough strength to survive all of that."

"Tell me about it. Bella amazes me every day. These little ones have so much more in them than we think they do."

Malcolm agreed. "So . . . what now? Are you going to go back to the Mortal World, or . . .?"

Alyssa shrugged. "I really have no idea. We still have to figure out how to get the other Keys so I can see my parents, but after that I don't know where we're going. And you? I assume you'll be going back to Switzerland?"

"Well, I—"

But Malcolm never did finish that sentence, because in that instant an earsplitting explosion rang through the air and the light was sucked from the world.

CHAPTER 30

The light was literally gone. Alyssa couldn't see a single thing. The place erupted in confusion as everyone began to panic.

Oh no. What is this? It was over! It's supposed to be over. I was going to go home and get my life back. This isn't fair! I wanna go home!

The sky above them was illuminated suddenly by a silvery light, and Alyssa could make out the silhouettes of people scrambling around, desperately calling out for their families. Alyssa's shirt was seized from behind, and she was spun around to see an enormous, bald man—a former prisoner, no doubt—demanding, "What is this? I thought you said it was over! You think this is a joke, little girl?"

Alyssa shook her head vigorously. "Please, please, I don't know, sir, I really don't, I have nothing to do with this . . ."

"ALYSSA MCCAW!" a voice boomed from above, so loudly everyone winced and covered their ears with their hands. The man released Alyssa and ran—to where, she didn't know, since the voice seemed to be coming from the sky. Probably just as far away from her as possible.

"You can't have Alyssa!" Malcolm shouted bravely. He placed himself in front of her body protectively, though Alyssa didn't know how much good that would do. "You'll have to go through us first!"

"Who are you and what do you want?" Violet demanded, eyes searching the sky for the source of the voice. "How dare you trespass on our own land and steal our light!"

"WHO AM I? I AM LUNTAI, THE GREATEST OF ALL DARK FORCES!"

"No, you're not!" Bella shouted defiantly. "Marvalonna and Karvokono are, and we defeated them!"

Luntai laughed, a cold, cruel, awful sound. "NO, CHILD, I *CREATED* MARVALONNA AND KARVOKONO. I CREATED MELADYNE AND ALL OF ITS CITIZENS. I AM THE MOON AND THE STARS AND THE NIGHT. I AM DARKNESS ITSELF. I THOUGHT MY SERVANTS COULD TAKE YOU OUT FOR ME, BUT I NOW SEE I WAS FOOLISH TO TRUST THEM WITH THE TASK. BUT NO MATTER. FROM THIS POINT FORWARD, I AM YOUR NEW MASTER. SURRENDER AT ONCE!"

"No way!" Alyssa yelled. "I am Alyssa McCaw. You want to fight me? Come at me, bro! Did you see what I did to your servants? Were you even watching? I tortured the king and queen to death, and all your servants disappeared with them. Do you think I am afraid of you?"

They were bold words, but her whole body trembled violently and all she could think was *I'm dead, I'm dead, I'm so dead.*

Again the sky boomed with thunderous laughter and the force replied, "THOSE SERVANTS WERE MERE SHADOWS OF THE POWER I POSSESS. YOU DARE TO CHALLENGE ME, YOU INSIGNIFICANT LITTLE MORTAL?"

"Yeah, she dares! And we're with her the whole time, too!" cried one of the prisoners they'd rescued. There were cries of agreement from everyone else around.

Alyssa thought about how she defeated Marvalonna. *Darkness,* she thought. *Darkness is the most powerful kind of magic. It worked once, it'll work again.* Once again, she reached inside herself and withdrew the magic, that part she was supposed to bury so as not to hurt people, that darkness. Once again she found the foreign words to the spell she had used before and spat them out at the sky, using all the strength she had left. But the spells weren't effective this time. They seemed to bounce off of the sky and did no damage anywhere. Alyssa could feel her energy draining as she spoke longer than she had before, and finally she collapsed to the ground, unable to use any more magic. Malcolm picked her up, his arms wrapped protectively around her body.

Luntai chuckled carelessly, obviously unscathed by the spells. "FOOLISH GIRL! YOU CANNOT DEFEAT DARKNESS WITH DARKNESS!"

Alyssa felt exhausted, barely able to move her arms, but she forced the fuzz out of her head, making herself think clearly. *You can't defeat darkness with darkness. Then what can . . .?*

"Light," she mumbled.

"What's that?" Malcolm leaned an ear down to her lips. "What did you say?"

"It's light, Malcolm," she said a little louder, sitting up in his arms. "The only thing that can defeat darkness is light! Of course! They're like positive and negative forces. The only way to balance them out is by making them equal."

He looked at her. "What?"

"Okay, so let's say without the Keys or Luntai or any power sources, the balance between light and dark is equal. It's at zero, neither positive nor negative, right? But they have three of the Keys and Luntai, so they offset the balance. The power is uneven. I've been trying to fight the darkness with darkness, but you can't get back to zero by adding more negative numbers. The only way to get back to zero is with a positive number: light. Does that make sense?"

Her friend nodded. "So we need light power. Sunlight."

"As much as we can get."

"NO MORE TALKING! I WILL TAKE OVER NOW WHERE MY SERVANTS HAVE FAILED ME. I HAVE CREATED A NEW ARMY, AN INVINCIBLE ONE! COME FORTH, MY CHILDREN!"

The sky opened up, and a vortex of soldiers appeared, falling to the ground like rain. Only these weren't Meladynians; they were men. Huge, bulky men with the ugliest weapons Alyssa had ever seen, ones she didn't even know the names of. Thousands upon thousands of them poured out, shouting battle cries and charging forward. It was chaos; people screamed and ran everywhere.

"SURRENDER THE KEY TO ME, ALYSSA! ALL I ASK IS FOR THE KEY AND YOUR LIFE. IF YOU REFUSE, MY SERVANTS WILL TEAR EVERY LAST ONE OF YOUR PEOPLE TO SHREDS!"

The terror ripping through Alyssa's body nearly immobilized her. *I must keep going,* she told herself. *I can't stop, come on, push . . .*

She tore through the people, sprinting as fast as she could across the meadow.

"Where are you going?" Malcolm called after her, struggling to keep up.

"To the Mortal World! There's still sunlight there! I have to get as close to it as I can so the magic is stronger!"

"You can't do this by yourself, Alyssa! What about the soldiers? We can't fight them; we're not even armed."

Alyssa bent over, stuck a hand into her boot, and pulled out a small, razor-sharp knife. "Seriously? I'm disappointed in you, Malcolm. After all we've been through, none of you have enough sense to carry a weapon?"

He threw his hands up. "Sorry."

"You need to find Caleb. He's got a buttload of weapons all stockpiled up somewhere. He can supply everyone. You'll have to fight; hide the children. I'll stop him as soon as I can."

"I'm coming with you, Alyssa. You can't do this on your own."

Alyssa stopped running and turned to face him. "Yes, I can, Malcolm. They need you here. I've gotten us this far. Do you trust me?"

He looked into her eyes a moment. "Yes. I just don't want to lose you."

"Hey, I'll be fine." She took his face in her hands and kissed him gently, savoring the moment. After all, it may be the last chance she would have. She wanted to remember this before she died. His soft lips, the way his body seemed to melt into hers, the way his arms wrapped around her waist and pulled her close, the sweet smell of him. This was how she wanted to remember the world: beautiful, perfect, romantic. But then it was over, and she was released back into the cold, cruel world. "I promise," she whispered, and took off in the other direction, eyes stinging with tears and lips still tingling with the force of the promise she couldn't possibly keep.

CHAPTER 31

 Alyssa ran into Caleb a few minutes later, dashing at top speed back to the fire pit. Actually, she literally ran into him, smashing into his chest as she turned her head.

"Ow," she muttered, rubbing her nose. "Caleb, I need your help."

"Already on it, kid." He and the people surrounding him were holding some kind of weapon-looking contraptions. They looked like pistols, only slightly longer. They were transparent, and instead of bullets contained tiny golden creatures squirming around inside. They weren't animals—more like little blobs of jelly—but they were definitely alive.

"Caleb," she breathed, intrigued. "What . . . what *is* that?"

"I call them solar pistols," he answered proudly. "I've been working on them for months."

Alyssa watched in awe as the girl next to him fired hers, and a little jelly blob exploded from the end. But before it could reach its target, she shouted the words "silver arrow." The blob turned into just that—a flawless, sleek, beautiful silver arrow—and found its mark in the soldier in front of her.

"The ammo is alive. It never runs out because it reproduces every time one is fired. They can turn into whatever you like. Just say what you need it to be after you fire and before it hits. They speak any language, too, mortal or magical."

She watched another boy fire a solar pistol, this one speaking Spanish. "*¡Bala de Oro!*" he commanded as the

279

blob transformed into a golden bullet and lodged itself in the soldier's heart. The soldier stumbled and fell.

"Can they kill?" she asked.

"No, but they'll knock you out cold for at least two hours. I also have these," he said, pulling a few bows and quivers off his shoulder. "Remember the Darkkeshade berries? The tips of these arrows are coated with the poison. One shot and they're dead."

"Oh my God, Caleb, you're a genius!" Alyssa cried, throwing her arms around his neck.

"Here, take one." He placed a pistol in her hand and closed her fingers around it. "What do you need?"

"Time, as much as you can get me. Watch out for Bella, okay? Thank you so much, you're awesome." She gave him one last quick hug and took off.

"ALYSSA MCCAW!" Luntai was calling. "WHERE ARE YOU? SURRENDER TO ME, ALYSSA. SURRENDER OR THEY ALL DIE!"

Alyssa winced but kept going. She needed to find someone who could get her to the portal faster; it would take hours running. She stopped people occasionally, but most were in too much of a panic to pay her any attention. "Please!" she wailed. "Can anyone wind travel? Can anyone help me?"

"Alyssa!" she heard someone calling out to her. At first she thought it was just Luntai demanding her surrender again, but this voice was higher, quieter, and feminine. "Alyssa, can you help me? Please!"

She rushed toward the sound to find a water spirit crouched over a Sunolian. She recognized the water spirit— she lived in the pond they often swam in. Her name was Neri, and she was a sweet little thing. Everyone had always loved her, and the boys had relentlessly flirted with her. Alyssa didn't know the Sunolian—at least, she thought she didn't, considering they all looked the same. But she had a silver Meladynian arrow protruding from her shoulder, and she was gasping desperately in pain, her eyes wide. Thick golden blood poured from the wound, soaking the grass beside her.

"Please, can you help me, Alyssa?" Neri begged as Alyssa neared. "She's hurt, and I don't know what to do."

Alyssa tried to think. "The Lake of Time," she remembered suddenly. "It can heal. Neri, do you know how to wind travel?"

The spirit shook her head, white hair settling around her blue shoulders. "No, but I can control water. I can travel between water sources."

"Okay, then do it." She shot her solar pistol into a soldier attacking from behind. "And please hurry."

They made their way backward, in the opposite direction of where Alyssa was trying to go. It felt painfully counterproductive, but she forced herself to keep going. Another ten minutes or so and they came upon a small creek running through the woods. It was only ankle deep, the water sparkling clear.

"This is deep enough?" Alyssa asked.

"It just has to be water," Neri replied, cradling the Sunolian in her arms. "Are you sure we shouldn't take the arrow out?"

Alyssa shook her head, stepping into the cool creek. "We don't have anything to wrap her arm in. She'll bleed out. We have to wait until we get there."

Neri nodded and chanted out a Sunolian water spell. The water around their ankles churned, then rose around their heads, swirling in a tornado of water until nothing around them was visible except the water. Tiny droplets splashed Alyssa's pink, sweaty face, the contact feeling amazing. Then it was over just as quickly as it had started, and they were treading water in the middle of the Lake of Time.

"That was pretty cool," Alyssa sputtered, trying to swim. The water in this lake was warm, like a bathtub, and just being in it made her drowsy.

"Get out of the water, Alyssa," Neri commanded. "It's too powerful for you in such a high dose."

Alyssa struggled to swim, but the water was making her sleepy, and Sylvie's heavy party dress was dragging too much. Sleeping wouldn't be so bad . . . Now that she thought about it, she hadn't slept in over twenty-four hours and had been casting much more powerful magic than usual. She was exhausted. She attempted to fight it but just couldn't hold on. She felt her eyes slowly drooping shut . . .

"Alyssa!" Neri shouted, slapping her across the face. "Wake up, we've got things to do."

Alyssa felt the water around her growing cooler, a magic-induced current pushing her toward the shore. She was dragged out of the water and slapped a few more times, and finally began to regain some strength. When she could sit up, she saw that the arrow had been removed from the Sunolian's arm and no sign of damage, not even a scratch, remained. Standing up was difficult in the waterlogged dress. She tore it from her body, popping several buttons off in the back, thankful she had the undershirt and shorts. It was too bad, since it really had been a beautiful dress—all blue and sparkles, gripping and flowing in all the right places . . . but never mind the dress now. She had far more important things to worry about.

"Are you two going to be all right?" she asked Neri and her friend, and at their nods, she prepared to take off.

Feeling the heel of her boot digging unpleasantly into her ankle, she bent to unstrap it. *Might as well go barefoot,* she thought. The soft Sunolian grass couldn't hurt her feet. But as she was bent over, she happened to glance at the water and saw the three pictures that told the past, present, and future. She'd seen them several times before and they had always been the same, but this time they were different, and it caught her attention.

In the first space, rather than the image of her sixth birthday party, it was a scene playing continuously in loops—a doctor handing a little blue-eyed baby to a woman she'd never seen before. The woman, lying in the hospital bed, took the baby into her arms and kissed the man standing beside her. Then she beckoned a child to her side from out of the room. He was a little boy bearing the same wavy blonde hair and blue eyes as Alyssa. They showed him the baby and he smiled, patting her head and saying something to his parents.

"It's me," Alyssa whispered. "And my parents and my brother."

The second was as it had been before—merely her reflection, as clearly as if it were in a mirror. She was instinctively appalled by her appearance, the curly bun she had worked so hard on sticking up in all kinds of directions, undergarments soaked through with water, eyeliner running down her face.

But the third was what worried her the most. Every time before she had seen a normal future, just as she had always wanted it—a husband and children standing happily together. But not this time. This time the third space was nothing but hazy blackness. There were no people, no family, nothing. Complete darkness.

"Neri," she whispered, her voice shaking. "What does that mean?"

The Sunolian beside her answered, looking grave. "It means it's impossible to tell. There's so much going on right now that even the Chronicles can't predict whether you'll live or die. But most likely, you're going to die."

Alyssa made herself stand back up. *That's not news, I already knew that,* she thought. *This has always been dangerous. I can't quit now or everybody will die.* But the thing about danger, Alyssa had found, is if she told herself it was going to be okay, she wasn't afraid, she'd do anything for the people she loved. She told herself this not because it was true, but because she had to keep going and it was the only way she could make herself. But the few times she had actually stared death right in the face, when she was actually about to die and finally realized there was no escaping it, that was when she would realize: She didn't want to die. She loved being alive and was absolutely terrified of what was going to happen to her after she died. She could be heroic all she wanted, but right before the end, there was this moment when all she could think about was herself and what was going to happen to her and how much she didn't want to die. And this was what Alyssa was feeling in that moment. That immobilizing shock of *I am really going to die.*

"Alyssa, come on!" Neri was shouting. "What are you doing?"

Alyssa snapped back into focus, though her heart was still racing and her stomach had begun a nervous churn.

"I'm going to save you, that's what I'm doing." She handed Neri her knife. "Here, defend yourself. I'll see you on the other side, okay?"

"Yeah, of course," the water spirit said confidently as Alyssa began to depart. "The other side of the portal. I'll be there." Alyssa nodded and gave her a small smile. Then she took off at a jog toward the portal.

The door to the Mortal World was only about a ten-minute jog from the lake. Alyssa went as fast as she could, striking down soldiers all the way with her solar pistol. But she really was fatigued, and the darkness pulsing through the air was taking a toll on her energy. At last she reached the portal, panting, feeling ready to pass out. The Silver Key still hung from a chain around her neck; she wasn't stupid enough to leave it behind. But she didn't need it to get out of Sunolia. The borders were weak enough from the lack of light magic to penetrate easily. All she had to do was grab the edges of the hole and hoist herself up, the way she would out of a swimming pool.

She stood back in the middle of her own street in Chicago. Just like before, the road was dark and quiet, but this time it was a different kind of quiet. A deadly silence rather than a peaceful quiet. All of the streetlights had gone out, and no stars dotted the sky. Despite the fact that it was late afternoon, maybe four or five, the sky was completely dark, lit only by the haunting full moon in the sky. The air was freezing from lack of heat from the sun, even though it was midsummer.

She would have to reach through, to dig deep in order to get through to the sun. It would take energy, a *lot* of energy, probably enough to kill her. But she had to do it. She had to give Bella and her friends a future, even if it meant sacrificing her own.

So Alyssa rooted her feet to the ground, closed her eyes, and took a deep breath through her nose, inhaling the polluted air from the city. The time for being afraid was over. She couldn't be frightened anymore. She had to push everything away and concentrate. Nothing else was allowed to matter anymore. She heard a voice, ringing through her head, clear as day. *Focus, Alyssa, focus.* She told herself, *No one is here to help you anymore. You're all on your own. The whole world is depending on you. You can do this.*

Taking another deep breath and closing her eyes once again, she pushed every emotion she had out of her system. She had been training to do this for months, but it was a whole different situation in real danger. It was harder. But still, she managed, imagining herself in her Neutral Zone. It was dark and empty. *Nothing exists,* she told herself over and over. *Only me and this power.*

She imagined a light, but not a small light as she had before, meant for nothing but illumination. This light was huge, overpowering. She was in outer space now, floating right before the sun. The star was blazing hot, so bright it should've been blinding. But rather than turn away, she faced it head on. She beckoned to it, urging it to follow her. Outside, she could feel her arms warming. It was working.

The girl put both hands out, palms toward the light, and moved them to her left. The sun followed suit, swerving left as well.

She could hear a voice from outside, muffled, as if spoken through a window. "ALYSSA, I HAVE FOUND YOU. YOU ARE WEAK AND YOUNG AND SMALL. YOU ARE POWERLESS TO STOP ME. SURRENDER AND IT WILL BE LESS PAINFUL FOR EVERYONE."

She forced herself to block out the voice, to direct all her power into the light. Very carefully, she opened her eyes to see a light blazing above her head, lighting up the dark sky. As she widened her arms, the light spread out across the sky, giving the whole street a golden glow, the way one might envision heaven.

The mortals were starting to creep outside, sensing something odd happening. Many pointed at her and whispered her name. Others stared, amazed at the sky, and still others retreated back into their houses, throwing their arms protectively over their wives and children. Alyssa could hear their murmurs, theories about being dead or dreaming or carried away by unicorns. Old Mrs. Azalea was running around frantically, announcing that the Lord had come and they all ought to repent while they still could. Alyssa silently urged them to go back inside their homes; she didn't want to hurt them. But, cruel as it was, she couldn't think about them. She had the whole world to think about.

Alyssa didn't know what to do at this point. She seemed to have formed a barrier—a shield for the darkness, and Luntai seemed to be struggling to penetrate it. She was holding him back, but didn't know how to actually stop him. She knew she couldn't hold out much longer— the energy was draining rapidly from her. Her arms shook with the weight of the sun, her legs trembling as she fought to hold herself upright.

As her knees buckled and she fell to the ground, she desperately grasped for any possible way to strengthen the barrier and drown Luntai out. Black spots appeared in her vision, and it was becoming impossible to focus. *I have to reverse the way I beat Marvalonna. What was I doing differently then?*

And then she realized. Alyssa wasn't supposed to block out her emotions; she was supposed to let them in. She had overpowered Marvalonna with dark emotions:

hatred, anger, fear, pain, sadness, danger, misery. But now she had to do the opposite. She had to let the light emotions in: joy, love, exhilaration, hope, comfort, safety. So with the last of her strength, she forced away the darkness and imagined everything light she could. She remembered her sister, beaming after being accepted into the top ballet class at her studio. She remembered squealing with delight as Hazel made her run through the freezing cold sprinklers at the golf course. She remembered Ricky, doing a dance to imitate Hazel as she bent over with laughter. She remembered her mother embracing her when she'd had a bad day at school, and her father spinning her around in the air. She remembered swimming and joking and dancing with her new friends in Sunolia. She remembered Malcolm's warm lips against hers as he pressed her against his body. And she remembered happiness and life and light.

She imagined all of that light being channeled into one power, and with the moan of one last spell, the world lit up with a golden light, so bright and warm and powerful Alyssa couldn't see anymore. It filled her with energy, and she stood as all the power ran through her. The black spots crowded in on the edges of her vision, and she could hardly hold on anymore, but she heard a voice ringing out, strong and powerful. Not the voice of Luntai, but a different voice, a woman's.

"YOU HAVE SET ME FREE, ALYSSA. YOU HAVE SAVED ME. YOU HAVE SAVED US ALL."

Just as she was ready to collapse, Alyssa spotted a figure in the shape of a beautiful woman, thirty feet tall at least. No features were distinguishable on her face—she was made of nothing but pure light. Alyssa could feel all of the energy drain out of her and watched as the light in her and all around traveled to the woman until she was the only source of light in the dark world. *Solaris,* Alyssa thought. *The sun in human form. I saved her.*

Solaris produced a luminescent bow and arrow from thin air and drew the arrow back. Letting it go into the sky, it seemed to puncture the darkness. Then the light spread across the heavens, illuminating the street and turning the sky a brilliant blue. Solaris turned toward Alyssa, and though she couldn't see any eyes, Alyssa knew the sun was looking straight at her. Then Solaris got on one knee as if proposing and bowed her head. It took Alyssa a moment to realize what was happening. *The sun was bowing to her.* Then Solaris rose once again, and with an enormous, graceful leap, disappeared into the air. In another second the sun was shining down on them, and the world was peaceful. And then Alyssa collapsed.

CHAPTER 32

Alyssa opened her eyes in the infirmary. Light was filtering in through the translucent walls of the tent. She struggled to sit up and found only a few bandages wrapped around various injured body parts. Once she'd managed to prop herself up against the soft pillows behind her, everything that had happened rushed back to her in a flood.

"I'm alive," she whispered. "Oh my God! I'm alive! I won!"

Alyssa sprang out of bed, no longer drowsy. She felt great, better than she had in years. She felt *alive*. Glancing down at her bedside table, she found a neat pile of folded clothes along with a glass of water, hairbrush, and a note written in loopy, girly handwriting.

Hey girl,

Congrats, we won! You were spectacular. I'm so proud of you. We're going to get the rest of the Keys as soon as you wake up, and then we'll be able to find your parents! Your brother's here; he's super cute and he can't wait to meet you. Bella's doing great. There were a lot of casualties, but not nearly as many as there could've been, thanks to those awesome guns Caleb made. We'll have a funeral tomorrow. All the injured people should be okay. Get out here as soon as you're awake; Malcolm keeps asking for you. I left you some clothes and shoes.

Luv ya,
Sylvie

Alyssa changed her clothes quickly, anxious to see her friends. After running the brush through her hair, she burst outside into the bright morning light.

People were everywhere, talking and joking and laughing. Many ate breakfast around the fire pit. It took everyone about two seconds to notice she was there, and then she was instantly swarmed by people, congratulating and hugging and kissing her. She picked up her little sister, swinging her around, relieved she was all right.

"You saved us, Lyssie! I can't believe it! You saved us."

"Did you ever doubt I would?"

The smile on Bella's face was worth fighting a thousand wars for. "Not for a minute." Then her eyes lit up, as if remembering something. "Oh, hey, guess what? We have a *brother*! Isn't that great? He should be around here somewhere. Come on, he's so nice, you've got to meet him!"

Alyssa fought her way through the crowd with her sister, shaking hands and smiling as needed. It took a long time to find him through the thousands of people surrounding her, but Bella spotted her target after a half hour or so and took off at a sprint to get to him.

He was leaning against a tree, chatting away with another boy and grinning. He looked so much like Alyssa there was no mistaking that they were related. He had the same wavy blonde hair, the same light-blue eyes, the same light freckles across his nose. He wasn't too tall, but a few inches taller than Alyssa. Doing the math in her head, she guessed he'd be about twenty-one, twenty-two. The phrase *able to pick you out in a crowd of a million people* came to mind. And when he turned to look at her, his smile reminded her of Bella's mischievous grin.

"Alyssa!" he greeted, his voice smooth and charming. "Oh my gosh. You have grown so much! You look great!"

He picked her up in a bear hug and Alyssa realized he must remember her from when they were little. By the expression on her face, he seemed to realize she didn't remember him, and his face fell, just a bit.

"Oh, that's right, they had your memory wiped. Well, um, sorry, that was awkward then. It's just, I missed you so much. Okay, let's start over." He extended his hand. "My name's Nick. I'm twenty-two years old, I spent most of my life in Mcladyne, and I'm your brother."

Alyssa smiled and took his hand. "Well, I'm Alyssa. I'm fifteen years old, I live in Chicago and also Sunolia, and I just defeated the darkest force of all time."

"Cool. But did you say fifteen?"

"Yeah, why?"

"I just can't believe how old you two are now. How old are you, Bella?"

"I'm ten."

"That's insane. Last time I saw you, you were wearing a diaper."

"Alyssa!" Alyssa turned around to be tackled in a hug by Sylvie and Violet. "You were amazing! I can't believe you survived!"

"Hey guys," Alyssa laughed. "Good to see you, too. Hey, do you guys know what happened to Hazel? Is she all right?"

"Yeah, she and her family are fine," Violet replied. "We stopped over to check on them earlier." Alyssa breathed a sigh of relief, thankful her friend was okay. "Oh, Malcolm's waiting by the Lake of Time. He's been dying to see you," Sylvie said, a teasing look on her face.

"If I didn't know better, Sylvie, I'd say you were in a hurry to be alone with Nick here," Alyssa teased back.

Alyssa had never seen Violet so happy. Sylvie, sure, but Violet was usually more held back. But when you've just saved the world, there's no such thing as holding back.

Alyssa jogged anxiously toward the lake, excited to see Malcolm again. She spotted him talking to Matthew, who was leaning on a crutch with what looked like a broken leg. She tried hard to stroll over casually, but when he turned to look at her, everything inside her broke and she sprinted toward him, tackling and kissing him with everything she had.

"Whoa, whoa, we got PDA up in here!" Matthew announced.

But Alyssa ignored him, no longer caring what the world thought of her. She'd just saved its butt, after all. So she only pressed her lips harder against his, moaning dramatically just for effect on Matthew. Matthew, in turn, made gagging noises and left.

Once he was gone, Alyssa released Malcolm, smiling at him. "You were amazing, Miss McCaw," he said.

"Not so bad yourself, Malcolm," she smirked.

"So," Malcolm asked, picking himself off the ground, "have you figured out how to get the other Keys yet?"

Alyssa nodded. "Yeah, I have. It's light. The only thing powerful enough to destroy darkness is light. I didn't understand before, but now I do."

"So, all these thousands of years of conflict, and all you have to do is think happy thoughts?"

Alyssa laughed. "Pretty much. Faith, trust, and pixie dust. But I have a question, too. Why did Luntai wait so long? Why didn't he just fight me himself first?"

Malcolm shrugged. "I guess he didn't think he'd have to. He could sit back and watch his servants destroy the sun without getting his hands dirty. But when they all failed, he had to do it himself. Same thing with Solaris. Though I think she wanted to keep peace rather than destroy Luntai."

"But what . . . what happened? To the moon, I mean? Is it, like, gone?" Alyssa wondered.

"No, it's still there. But it can't fight back anymore. It's what it should be—a giant rock."

Alyssa nodded. "So what happened during the battle? What did you guys do?"

Malcolm shrugged. "We fought. What do you want me to say? The soldiers were strong—*very* strong. They had armor made out of some crazy metal; we couldn't penetrate it with anything. But there were gaps in it, and their faces were uncovered, so Caleb's solar pistols and Darkkeshade arrows did the trick. You just had to have good aim. You should've seen Selena. She was incredible. But then all of a sudden, out of nowhere, there was this flash of light, so bright nobody could see anything. Then it disappeared, and all the dark soldiers were gone. Dead or alive, they just weren't there. The sky was blue and Luntai was gone. Just like that. Nobody knew what happened. Bella found you in the street unconscious."

Alyssa quickly recounted her tale, telling him about her magic and Solaris and collapsing on the street. Malcolm was staring at her incredulously by the time she had finished. "Solaris. The actual sun herself. She bowed to you?" Alyssa nodded, and Malcolm let out a delighted cry. "My girlfriend is awesome!" he cried, and Alyssa rolled her eyes, turning to look for other people.

But as she turned around, she found herself once again looking down at those three shimmering images in the Lake of Time. The first two were the same as always, but the last showed a strange picture of light, shifting around and glittering.

"Hey, Malcolm, what does that mean?" she asked, pointing at the third picture.

"It means your future is light. No matter what happens, you'll always return to the light." Alyssa smiled at this. *No more darkness,* she thought.

"Well, what exactly is it we're waiting for, then? Let's go get your parents back!"

"Wait a second, Alyssa!" a little voice called out. Alyssa turned and beamed when she saw little Seraphina running toward her. "Alyssa, we did it! We can go home now! My brother is taking me back to Tennessee to find my dad. We're going to be a family! We're going to be safe!"

"That's great, Phina. I'm so happy for you!" Alyssa picked up the little girl, twirling her around.

"Oh, and your heart! It's completely light, just like the Sunolians. The shadow disappeared. You conquered the darkness, Alyssa. You won!"

"*We* won," Alyssa corrected, smiling.

"Come on, Alyssa. Phina, I'm taking Alyssa to get the other Keys. I'll see you later, okay?" Malcolm said.

Seraphina nodded and skipped off with a smile and a wave.

Alyssa heartily followed him toward the portal, chatting lightly with people along the way. By the time they reached the Mortal World, it was midmorning. The street was in a state of confusion: ambulances lined up, people being interviewed by Channel 6 News while neighbors stood in huddles.

"Oh, no," Alyssa muttered. "Get back down there, right now."

"What? Why?"

"Just do it!" she hissed, shoving him back down the hole and dropping down herself immediately after. "Those people will recognize me in a second; I lived next door to them my whole life. After my parents, Hazel's family, Ricky, and I went missing, and considering what happened last night, we are gonna need to keep a low profile."

"Right, a low profile. How are you planning on doing that? Can't we just run?"

"No, that'll look too suspicious. Like the door in our front yard. Why hasn't anybody noticed that yet?"

He shrugged. "Most mortals are oblivious. They see what they want to see. Except us, of course! We're special!"

"Yeah, yeah, whatever. Everybody knows you're special. We need to get over there."

"Girl, you think too much," Malcolm accused. He pulled his sweatshirt off his shoulders and wrapped it around her head, concealing her face and hair.

"Hey! What are you doing?" Alyssa cried, clawing at the thing to try to get it off. "Let me go!"

"Just shut up and do what I say, will you?"

Once again they traveled into the Mortal World, but this time, Malcolm ran down the street, his hand over Alyssa's shoulders. "Hey, everybody move, I've got a contaminated child! Yeah, that's right, she's contagious, we've got to lock her up in this house before it spreads!"

She allowed herself to be shoved through the gaping hole in the side of Ricky's house, disregarding the caution tape and the bewildered expressions of the neighbors, and shoved into the corner away from the view of the street. Then she pulled the jacket off her head and glared at him. "Contaminated child? What does that even mean?"

He shrugged. "Hey, it worked, didn't it? And, uh, what did you guys do to this place?"

"Oh, Violet drove a car through it. Can we move on?"

He shook his head. "You are the strangest army general I've ever seen."

"Hey, it worked, didn't it?" she mocked.

The duo sauntered down the stairs, following the path of destruction to the basement. The door had been completely thrown off its hinges by the car, so getting in was no problem. The place was completely deserted, free of Meladynians and evil monarchs and all. That's when a thought dawned on Alyssa. "Malcolm," she started, "you remember Ricky? Where do you think he is now? Him and the other Meladynians. Luntai created them. Do they have, like, souls?"

He raised an eyebrow. "Do *we* have souls?"

Alyssa shook her head. "I don't know."

"I don't know either. But what I do know is that he had a heart, dying for you like that. And I also know that you have a heart, risking your life for us the way you did. I will always respect you for that."

"Hey, we all risked our lives in that fight. We should all be respected."

"Yeah, that's true. Well, don't worry about Ricky. I'm sure he's up there with your parents and Maegan and all those other good people we lost."

Alyssa slipped her hand into his and rested her head on his shoulder. They walked in silence for a while, and by the time they reached the Twilight Hollow, both were babbling small talk. The tree once again loomed over them, but somehow it didn't seem quite so intimidating anymore. It was no longer ringed with fire, and she stepped effortlessly within the perimeter. Once again she pinched the Golden Key between her thumb and forefinger, but this time she ran her happy-thought string through her head, the one she'd used to defeat Luntai. The Key slipped easily from the tree. Beaming at Malcolm, she made her way around the tree, releasing the other two from their slots.

"All right, now we've gotta get them back to the Garden of the Dawn. Then the world will be light, and we'll be safe."

"Okay. Let's go home."

* * *

Alyssa's feet ached miserably by the time they got back to the fire pit; they'd been walking for nearly eight hours. Malcolm suggested they sit down and rest a while, and Alyssa cordially agreed. She sat by herself in a chair, watching the happenings around her. The people had settled down a little, but some were still desperately seeking loved ones. Alyssa sighed contently, fingering the other three Keys of Power. It was amazing, the feeling of holding that much power in one's hands. But Alyssa had long since grown sick of it and couldn't wait to finally have the burden off her shoulders.

"Hey, Selena," she greeted her friend as she came to sit down. "Have you found your family yet?"

As if on cue, the girl suddenly jumped off the bench, her eyes nearly popping out of her head. Alyssa had never seen that clear of an expression on Selena's face before, but it was evident she was no longer trying to hide it. Following her gaze, Alyssa could see an older man, along with a young boy and a young man on top of the dining hill. They all had the same Pacific Islander dark skin as Selena and most of the same features. Selena fell to her knees, clapping both hands over her mouth in disbelief.

Alyssa heard a sound from the girl crumpled at her feet then. At first it was just a small sound—a whimper, nothing more. But it was repeated, a little more audible each time, until it finally formed a word. "Dakota . . ." It was a faint whisper, barely audible, but definitely there.

"What . . . what did you say?" Alyssa breathed, flummoxed.

"Dakota!" Selena's face broke into a smile, tears brimming in her eyes. She leapt off the ground and threw herself at the trio, laughing and crying at the same time. As Alyssa stared, her mouth hanging open like an idiot, she felt a body beside her and turned to see Caleb grinning, his arm in a sling.

"I don't believe it," he said.

They hurried after Selena, watching as she embraced the old man.

"Papa!" she cried. "Oh my God, Papa, I thought you were dead! Oh, and Dakota!" She picked up the little boy and twirled him around in the air, kissing his face all over. "You're so big, Dakota, I never thought I'd see you again! Oh, my baby, I love you so much, I'll never let you go again, okay? It was my fault, I'm so sorry, I'm so sorry, I love you. I promise." And when the young man touched her arm, she set Dakota on her hip and used her free hand to take the man's face, kissing him passionately.

Once they had calmed down a little bit, Alyssa managed to stutter, "You . . . you can *talk*?"

Selena nodded, still clutching Dakota to her body. "Yes, I can. This is my father, Tapu, my boyfriend, Anoki, and my son, Dakota."

If it was possible for Alyssa to be more amazed, she was. "Your . . . your *son*?" She glanced at the boy, who was probably five or six years old. "How old are *you*?"

"I'm twenty-two. I know, I'm older than I look. So when everyone here said I was nineteen, I went with it."

Her voice was slightly accented, and a little deep for a girl. Alyssa imagined she'd have a nice singing voice.

"So . . . you wanna tell us anything else? Like, oh, I don't know, why you haven't spoken for the past five years?"

Selena's eyes dropped to the ground in embarrassment. "Right after Dakota was born, I got in a huge fight with Anoki and my dad over who got to raise him. The night following, I was furious, and told them that my son was mine, and they could never have him. So I ran away with him, out of the little tiny town we lived in in Hawaii, to find my own place. We spent that night at a hotel, but the morning I woke up, Dakota was gone. I thought Anoki had taken him, and I was outraged about it. When I went back home to find him, the people there were gone. Not just my family. *Every person in the entire town.* Not that it was a big town, there were probably only a thousand people in it, but still, that's a lot of people to suddenly go missing. I was terrified, alone, and scared, and I wanted my son back. I was going to the police station, to find out what had happened, and I tripped over this door in the ground, like the portal you came in through, only this one was meant for me. I assume you've heard about the Haven Portals, the special ones that don't require a Key that are only meant for one person? Yeah, that's the deal—if Meladyne takes your family, a Haven Portal appears for you and takes you to Sunolia. So I found one of these on the way to my car, and I was desperate for any chance of finding my son, so I went through it.

"I talked to Cressidalaina once I got here, and explained to her what had happened to all the people. She told me about Meladyne, but was stunned that they would take an entire village of people like that; they'd never done anything like it before. It made her worry they were getting more serious about their search for the final Key. She told me I couldn't go back to the Mortal World because it wasn't safe. She didn't know why I had been spared, and she wasn't going to take any chances of them getting me, too. So, naturally, I freaked out and told her I had to save my kid. But she deactivated my portal, forcing me to stay for my own good. She told me the best thing I could do for my family was learn to fight.

"And so from that point forward, I devoted my whole life to fighting. I didn't communicate with the people here, and I didn't let any of my emotions show. I thought I could keep myself from being hurt that way. They couldn't take anything away from me if I didn't have anything, right? But that wasn't how it worked out. I fell in love with people even though I wouldn't show it, and then you and your sister came along and there was a war and I lost people I love anyway. So I'm sorry I blocked you out, I really am. It was selfish and cowardly, and I know all of you lost people too, and I really should've helped more than I did. So I'm sorry."

Alyssa didn't know what to say. "Selena . . . I . . ." She couldn't even imagine something like that happening to her.

"My name's not Selena. It's Winta. Silent Selena is just what they called me because I never told them my name."

"That's a beautiful name. But what happened to the rest of the people?"

Winta pointed to the other side of the hill, and Alyssa looked down to see hundreds of Hawaiians mixed in with the spirits and Sunolians and everyone else. The most intelligent thing Alyssa could say was, "Wow."

"I know, right? It's incredible." She turned back to her boyfriend. "And you . . . you raised him? All by yourself?"

"Well," Anoki blushed. "The others helped me a lot."

"I'm so sorry. Both of you. All those things I said before . . ."

"None of that matters anymore, Winta," her father said in a low voice. "We're together now, and that's all that matters."

"Thank you, Alyssa. For everything." Winta wrapped her muscular arms around Alyssa in an awkward hug.

"Hey, you were amazing. You're by far the greatest fighter we have."

Winta laughed. "Well, I don't know about *that*, but thanks anyway."

By this time, Malcolm was beside her again, asking if she was ready to go.

"Yeah, Malcolm, just a minute." Alyssa moved to the little boy wrapped in Winta's arms. "Dakota, you've got the best mommy in the world. You listen to her, okay?"

The adorable kid nodded, his huge brown eyes warming her heart. "Good boy. Bye, Winta!"

"Goodbye, Alyssa."

* * *

"Are you ready?"

"I think so."

Alyssa stood with Malcolm just outside of the Garden of the Dawn, all four Keys clutched so tightly in her hand they dug into her palm. "Malcolm, are you even sure this is a good thing?"

"What do you mean? It's light. Of course it's a good thing."

"Yeah, but Malcolm, we don't even know what kind of power this is going to unleash. This could turn out really badly."

"How could this turn out badly?"

"I . . . I don't know. It's just a lot of power in one place." He took her hand. "We've made it this far. We can't go back now."

Alyssa swallowed, took a deep breath, and squeezed his hand. Then she stepped forward.

An amazing feeling surged through her, the same as when she'd defeated Luntai. Only this one was much more powerful. She had more energy than she'd ever had in her life, as if she'd drunk eight hundred glasses of coffee. She felt spectacular and could feel all the cuts and wounds on her body closing up. When she looked down at her feet, she found that she was actually hovering three feet above the ground. "Uh, Malcolm? What exactly is happening?"

He shrugged. "I don't know. Just hold on."

"This doesn't require, like, a sacrifice or anything?" She panicked as a light began to surround her.

"Don't worry. Light magic would never need anything like that," Malcolm tried to reassure her, but she could see sweat glistening on his forehead.

The sunlight surrounded her, and she tried not to be afraid. There was obviously no way she could get out, so she might as well just suck it up and take it. Alyssa squeezed her eyes shut, clenching her hands into fists, fingernails cutting crescent shapes into her palms. Her tank top and black pants molded together in a dress sort of form, and she had a strange itch on her back that she couldn't quite reach. Her shoes slipped off and disappeared into the light, and she noticed gold nail polish she didn't remember putting on. Another minute of this, and the light faded. Her body collapsed to the ground, and she lay unable to move for a moment. When she could finally lift her head, Malcolm gasped.

"That's incredible," he breathed.

Alyssa picked herself off the ground and caught a reflection of herself in a shiny, polished rock in the corner near the blood-red roses. She now wore a gold, sleeveless dress that glittered in the light and fell just past her knees. Her tennis shoes had been replaced with golden flats, and her eyes had turned the hazel-gold color of the Sunolians. Her skin was pale and completely flawless, not a cut or bump or blemish. But the thing that astonished her more than anything were the pair of sparkling, beautiful wings that sprung from her back. She looked at Malcolm incredulously.

"Sunolia needs a new leader," he told her. "You are the king's daughter."

Alyssa's eyes traveled up to the reflection of the gleaming jeweled crown resting elegantly atop her blonde hair. "You don't mean . . .?"

Malcolm grinned. "That's right. All hail Princess Alyssa Claudia McCaw, the rightful ruler of the land of Sunolia, the radiant human form of the sun itself." He dropped to a knee, half-joking, half-serious.

"But . . . but that's not right. My mom should be the queen if my dad's the king. I'm not the queen."

"Your father refused the job the minute he ran off with your mother. Your mother cannot hold the position because she is not Sunolian. Your brother has already said he doesn't want the throne. That leaves you next in line."

The muscles in Alyssa's back twitched, and her wings fluttered a bit, raising her feet off the ground. Malcolm stood up, pulled her back down, and kissed her, whispering, "You are the most stunning woman I have ever seen." Then he pointed toward the far right corner of the garden. "Right through there is Pyrocladia, birthplace of the fire. And there is Whisperia, land of winds. And just through those branches there is Terralith, world of the earth. And that is where your birth parents are right now, waiting for you. How would you like to meet them?"

"Right now?"

"Absolutely. Right now."

"All right. We'll go meet my parents. We'll travel the four realms. And then I've got a kingdom to rule."

ABOUT THE AUTHOR

Elena Schauwecker is fourteen years old and lives in Memphis, Tennessee, with her little brother and sister. She has always loved reading, and her books inspired her to write. When she is not writing, she is in her school's color guard and loves to act in musicals. Getting this book published was a dream come true, and she hopes to continue writing in the future. She encourages kids everywhere to follow your dreams, whatever they may be. You can achieve anything if you're willing to work for it.